Liz Coley's short fiction has appeared in *Cosmos* magazine and speculative fiction anthologies. Her passions beyond reading and writing include singing, photography, and baking. She plays competitive tennis locally in Ohio to keep herself fit and humble. With a background in science, Liz follows her interest in understanding 'the way we work' down many interesting roads. *Pretty Girl 13*'s journey into the perilous world of dissociative identity disorder is one of them.

PRETTY GIRL THIRTEEN

Angie Chapman was thirteen years old when she went missing. Three years later, she reappears, and she doesn't remember a thing. But some people do — people who could tell Angie every terrifying detail, if they weren't locked inside her mind. With help, Angie slowly begins to unravel the darkest secrets of her own past. But does she really want to know the truth?

LIZ COLEY

PRETTY GIRL THIRTEEN

Complete and Unabridged

CHARNWOOD
Leicester

First published in Great Britain in 2013 by
Harper
An imprint of HarperCollins*Publishers*
London

First Charnwood Edition
published 2013
by arrangement with
HarperCollins*Publishers*
London

A catalogue record for this book is available
from the British Library.

ISBN 978–1–4448–1766–9

Published by
F. A. Thorpe (Publishing)
Anstey, Leicestershire

Set by Words & Graphics Ltd.
Anstey, Leicestershire
Printed and bound in Great Britain by
T. J. International Ltd., Padstow, Cornwall

This book is printed on acid-free paper

For J, who survived.

Acknowledgements

Many thanks are due — to my supportive community of writers, including NaNoWriMo, SCBWI, the SF&F Online Writing Workshop, and Context; to my first readers, Rachel Lentz, Gio Clairval, Jodi Meadows, and Erin Stocks; to my middle readers, Deborah Yeager, Kate Coley, and Gemma Cooper; to all the friends and family who watched and encouraged my growth as an author; to my agents, Joanna Volpe and Nancy Coffey, who believed in the promise; and to my editor, Katherine Tegen, who made it happen.

PART I

You

PROLOGUE

LOST TIME

You had forgotten how early the sun rises on summer campouts — and how loud the birds sing in the morning. You scrunched down in your warm sleeping bag to block out the green light that seeped through the nylon tent, but there was no way you were going back to sleep until you took care of something. As you shrugged off the sleeping bag, you sighed.

"Sup, Angie?' Livvie's whisper emerged from the folds of her sleeping bag.

Katie rustled lower into her plaid cocoon and pulled it closed over her head.

'I just have to go to the tree,' you answered, Girl Scout code for taking care of business.

'Anyone else up yet?' Liv cracked one eye and squinted at you.

'I don't think so.' You sniffed. 'No one's started the breakfast fire.'

Liv's one eye widened. 'It's not our turn, is it?'

'Nope. Go back to sleep.'

You unzipped the tent and slipped out into the fresh, pink morning. Rosy clouds lofted high above the trees. Pine needles underfoot muffled the sound of your flip-flops as you snuck away from the collection of tents. No one else was stirring. The sun hadn't warmed the air yet, and the T-shirt you wore left your

3

arms bare and goosebumpy.

A few thousand pine trees surrounded the clearing where the troop had pitched camp yesterday afternoon — lodge-pole, ponderosa, Jeffrey, sugar pines. Mrs. Wells had made you memorize their bark and needles to earn your tree-ID badge. You found the trail you'd tromped along yesterday to walk into the campsite and headed down it a little way, looking for a thicker stand of trees. That was about as much privacy as you could get in the great outdoors. Tiny ripe August thimbleberries lined the path, and you munched a few as an early breakfast, the tart red juice staining your lips and fingers. A fallen tree with a saucer-shaped fungus lay across the path, and you filed it away in your brain as a landmark. Then you left the path and headed twenty feet or more into the woods to a good squatting place.

You spun in a slow circle to shake off the feeling you always had out here that someone was watching, before you hitched down your sweatpants and crouched. It was an art, peeing in the woods without splashing your feet or clothes, at least for girls.

A twig snapped sudden as a rifle shot. Your heart bumped in shock. Your eyes swiveled toward the direction of the sound, expecting a squirrel. A rabbit. A deer. Anything but a man, who blended invisibly into the undergrowth except for his narrow, dark eyes — eyes that stared at you with an almost familiar hunger.

'Shhh.' He put a finger to his lips, walking toward you.

4

You struggled with your sweats, humiliation and shock making your hands clumsy. You couldn't break your gaze from his eyes, couldn't see his face for the intensity of the unblinking stare that held you. You opened your mouth to talk, to scream, to plead, but nothing came out — your throat tight, as if a noose looped it and he held the knot. A moment later, he reached for you. His right hand covered your mouth and his left held your arm behind your back in an unbreakable grip. You still hadn't breathed.

'Don't fight me, pretty girl,' he whispered, pressed against your body, his moist lips touching your ear.

Fight him? Your limbs were soft, weak. Your knees on the edge of collapse. You couldn't even take a step, to run, to flee. How could you fight him? Your stomach clenched, and the sound of wind rushed through your ears, a hurricane in your head.

Above the roar, you heard a little girl's high-pitched voice call, 'Quick. Hide!'

I opened the rusted gate for you to slip inside.

Stabbing pain pierced between your temples. Still you stayed, frozen in his grip. We tugged, pulled at you until something broke loose. For just a moment, you contracted to a tiny, hard point of light, felt yourself cut away from your body.

You hid. We kept you hidden till it was safe.

It was a long, long time.

1

INTERROGATION

'Go back now,' A voice said. Angie felt a poke between her shoulder blades. She tripped forward a step, arms out to catch her balance.

'Don't,' she protested, whirling to look behind, but no one else was there.

She shivered and shook her head to clear it. When the wave of dizziness passed, she opened her eyes again. She blinked hard at her street. Her cul-de-sac. Her neighborhood. The sun was halfway up the cloudless azure sky. Hot Santa Ana winds tousled the sweet gum trees. A hint of red tinged the edges of the falling leaves. Sharp-pointy seed-pods scattered across the sidewalk. In August?

An unexpected weight tugged at her left hand — just a plastic grocery bag. Where was her camping gear? She hefted the bag to look inside, and that was when the strangeness hit her. She dropped it in surprise and studied her left hand. Something was really wrong here. This wasn't her hand. Those weren't her fingers. These fingers were longer, thinner than they were supposed to be. And a strange silver ring circled the middle finger. The skin was dry and rough. Dark scars circled the wrists like bracelets. She turned over her right hand, studying unfamiliar cracks and calluses on her palm. She clenched it experimentally. It felt . . . wrong.

Angie frowned and spun to look again behind her. How had she gotten here? She didn't remember walking this way. She was just . . . in the woods?

Her stomach growled, and her right hand flew to her waist — taut, thin. And where had this hideous shirt come from? Flowers and ruffles? Not her style at all. And no way would Liv or Katie have bought it. She wouldn't have borrowed it even if they had.

She picked up the bag and peeked at a collection of completely strange clothes. A sick feeling replaced the emptiness in her belly. Her head felt floaty, disoriented, disconnected.

Angie's eyes traced the houses around the cul-de-sac. Everything there was familiar, thank God. The cars in the driveways looked right, which was reassuring, until she caught sight of Mrs. Harris, pushing a stroller, just entering her garage. Mrs. Harris didn't have kids.

She broke into a run, feeling for the first time the blisters on her feet, the ache in her legs. Home, she had to get home. Of course. She'd been lost, in the woods. Now she was home.

She felt under the woven grass mat for a key and opened the red front door. 'Mom!' she yelled. 'Hey, Mom, I'm home!' She stepped through.

Tumbling down the front stairs, feet sliding, face a screaming mask of disbelief, her mom burst into tears. She engulfed Angie in her arms, speechless, gulping.

'Mom!' Angie said into her hair. 'Mom, I can't

breathe.' She dropped the bag of clothes with a small thump. She brushed a wisp of hair from her lips. Silver threads mingled with Mom's loose brown curls.

'Can't breathe . . . can't breathe?' Mom let go enough to hold Angie at arm's length and devour her face with her eyes. 'Can't . . . ' She laughed, a tight, hysterical bark. 'Oh my God. Oh my God. A miracle! Thank you, God. Thank you.' She raised her eyes to the ceiling. 'Thank you,' she said again.

Upstairs, a toilet flushed, and Dad's voice called down the stairs. 'Margie, what's all the commotion?'

Mom whispered to Angie, 'Oh, your father . . . He'll just . . . ' She couldn't speak. Her face was white. Too round and white.

Dad's tread on the landing filled the pause. For a moment, he stood there, his hands plastered to his cheeks. His eyes met Angie's and filled with tears. 'Angela? Are you really . . . ' His voice choked off.

Angie looked back and forth between the two of them. 'Um, yeah. I'm really . . . What's going on?' It wasn't just her. Something was wrong with her parents, too. A shiver passed across her shoulder blades.

'Angel?' Dad whispered the word. He stood on the landing, frozen in weirdness. His black hair was completely gray. His damp eyes looked a hundred years old.

Angie's heart began to race, and her feet tingled like they wanted to take off running. 'You guys are totally freaking me out.'

'We're freaking you . . . ?' Mom's hysterical laugh broke out again. 'Angie, where . . . where have you been?'

'You know.' Angie's stomach squirmed. 'Camping?'

The way they stared and stared at her made it hard to breathe. 'Camping,' she said again, firmly.

Dad started down the stairs. 'Camping,' he repeated. 'Camping?' His voice rose in pitch. 'For three years?'

★　★　★

Angie locked the bathroom door and pressed her back against it. Her familiar towel set, cream with roses, hung on the rack, just where she'd left it. It smelled like Tide. She'd never been so happy to see a towel before. It was perfect. It was right. Unlike her parents.

Were they kidding? Were they crazy? She couldn't have been missing for three years. That wasn't the kind of thing a person would . . . just forget.

She turned on the sink first, then glanced up at a face that looked back at her with clear gray eyes. In that moment of utter surprise, she forgot how to breathe.

The girl in the mirror could have been her older sister, taller, thinner. Her cheekbones were sculpted, where Angie's were soft and round. Her face was pale, where Angie's was tan from a summer at the pool. The girl had long, dirty-blonde hair, where Angie's was highlighted and bobbed. The girl had serious arm muscles, gray skin, healed-up scars, and another thing that made the girl in the mirror a stranger. She had a curvy shape — breasts. Angie dropped her eyes to her chest. What the hell. Boobs? Where had those come from?

She fingered the top button on her shirt, scared to look.

A wooden pounding startled her. 'Angela! Angela, for God's sake, don't do anything.' Her father's voice sounded panicked. 'Don't . . . don't . . . '

Angie turned the lock and opened the door. 'I . . . I wasn't,' she said. Her face flushed with guilt. For what?

Dad's face was drawn with tension. A bead of sweat stood out on his forehead. Angie was mesmerized by it. She realized only half his chin was shaved.

His gaze slipped to the right, avoiding her. His voice was low and hoarse. 'Detective Brogan will be here in fifteen minutes. He said not to touch anything that might be considered evidence.'

'Evidence of what?' Angie asked. The sound of running water filled the heavy silence while Dad hesitated over his answer. His attention darted to the sink.

'Oh God, Angela. You didn't wash anything yet. Right?'

She held up her filthy arms, dirt so embedded in her creases and pores that she had turned gray. 'Evidence?' she repeated. 'Of what, Dad?'

Dad's mouth twisted around for a few moments. The sweat rolled lower. 'Evidence of whatever, wherever, or whoever.'

Angie looked at him in confusion.

His forehead creased with lines. Dark hollows circled his eyes. 'You really don't know what I'm talking about, do you?'

Angie felt stupid. He expected something from her. She didn't know what, but she could feel his anger simmering. Something stirred inside, and she walked to him and wrapped her arms around his waist. Her head came up to his chin. 'I love you so much,' she said. She felt him stiffen and pull back. She must have done the wrong thing. Her arms dropped. She turned cold, inside and out.

'I — I have to finish shaving,' he said randomly, his head turned away from her. 'Shut off the water. Go wait downstairs with your mother.' He walked down the hall and closed the bedroom door behind him.

Angie had this vague idea that it might be a good idea to cry. But everything was tangled and frozen inside, seized up like the giant breath before pain arrives. She thought about chewing a fingernail, but it was dirty. And 'evidence.' Her stomach clenched again. Evidence of what?

The unusual ring on her left hand caught her eye. Why couldn't she remember where she'd bought it? The question made her strangely nervous, and the single warning throb of a headache coming on poked her temple. She twisted the silver band loose and placed it in the soap dish. The pain passed. It was probably Livvie's, or Katie's. Better not to think about it too hard.

The sound of Dad's razor hummed as Angie hurried down the top flight of stairs. She stopped halfway, her feet pinned to the landing. She hovered like a lost child, halfway between Dad upstairs and Mom downstairs. Her pulse beat the passing seconds. Someone was coming. A detective, Dad said. She watched the front door until the frosted glass darkened with shadow.

Mom flew from the kitchen to answer the double knock.

A tall, ginger-haired man stood framed in the doorway. Mom threw herself into his arms with a muffled sob. He patted Mom's back with one hand and looked over her head to the landing, where Angie still hesitated.

The man's eyes went wide. 'Angela,' he whispered. 'Welcome home.'

He separated himself from Mom and held out his right hand, palm up, half an invitation, half a handshake. 'Please,' he said. 'Will you come down?'

Dad had called him a detective, but he was wearing blue jeans with a tear starting in one knee. The sleeves of his dark plaid shirt were rolled to the elbow. He looked casual, comfortable. He looked — amazed.

Angie took the four steps to the bottom and reached for his outstretched hand. It was huge, and hers disappeared as he pressed it between both of his.

'L.A. County Sheriff's Department. Detective Phil Brogan,' he said. 'Sorry to appear like this. I was gardening, and I didn't waste a moment when Mitch called.' His hand was rough and

12

calloused, but he held hers like a newborn kitten, with care and tenderness. He tilted his head and studied her face with a tiny smile.

Angie's tension began melting away, her chill warming, until the moment he ruined it.

'This is incredible,' he said. 'I feel like I know you already.'

She instantly felt stripped, exposed. A complete stranger who knew her. Her breath caught in a gasp. She caged the sob before it could escape. If she let it start, she might never stop.

'Lord, I'm sorry, Angela,' he said immediately. He let her hand slither away. 'Mitch told me on the phone there might be memory issues. That you aren't sure how long you were gone or where exactly you were. Disorientation. That's not unusual.'

Was that true? Angie tried to decipher his eyes. Blue, kind, honest. She didn't read a threat there. Okay. So maybe what was happening to her wasn't unusual. She felt a flicker of hope. Maybe he could actually help her figure this out.

She nodded, and he smiled gently. 'Come.' He gestured to the family room with his head. 'We don't have to stand here like bowling pins.'

A clunk sounded upstairs, and Angie imagined a giant ball rolling down the stairs, knocking them all off their unsteady feet, but it was only Dad. The corner of her mouth twitched. The detective caught it and smiled back with his eyes. Fascinating eyes. Orange specks dotted the dark blue irises. She'd never seen anything like them.

Dad walked ahead without sparing her a

glance and clicked on the fire with the remote. 'She looks cold,' he offered as explanation. Of course, the heat from the gas fire, locked safely behind glass doors, was too weak to reach her.

Angie made a full sweep of the room, finding everything familiar and in its place. Soft green cushions on the beige leather sofas. Floor-length drapes with leaf patterns, pulled back to let in the daylight. Old cabinet-style TV with the remote and printed guide on top. Piles of jumbled books in the bookcase on the side wall. There was no way three years had passed in this room. No way. Nothing had moved.

The detective settled into the chair closest to Angie's corner of the sofa. His expression softened, and he rubbed the palm of his hand across his stubbly chin. 'Angela, I'm so sorry. I know this is difficult for you. Very confusing.'

Did he? Angie wondered. Had his reality ever changed in the blink of an eye? She studied her shabby knees. They turned blurry as she squeezed away dangerous tears. Stop.

Brogan placed a featherlight hand on her bowed head. 'I imagine all you want to do right now is reunite with your family and be left in peace.'

She nodded a fraction of an inch, grateful for his sympathy. She could tell he meant it — he understood how unstable she was. At least, it didn't feel like just a police technique to warm her up for questioning.

Beside her, Mom squeezed her hand, and Angie looked up into the detective's steady gaze. Unexpected freckles dusted his cheekbones. 'But

. . . ,' she offered, sensing he was leading up to 'but.'

'But my job is to figure out whether we have a criminal case to pursue here. Especially if we have a fresh trail. Do you understand?'

Her throat suddenly got the 'I'm about to throw up' feeling. She swallowed it down, 'Criminal? Did I . . . Did I do something wrong?'

'Not you, Angie,' Mom burst out, her fingers accidentally digging into Angie's palm. Angie flinched.

'Margie.' Brogan raised his eyebrows at Mom. 'Sorry, Angela. There are just a few questions I need to ask you right now. Then we'll move on to other procedures.'

'There are a few things I want to know too,' Dad interrupted. 'How on earth did you find your way home, Angela? Did anyone help you? Did you walk the whole way?'

'Yes.' The single word escaped her lips, but it didn't make any sense. From where? Angie had no idea.

'Don't be ridiculous, Mitch,' Mom said, shushing him. 'It's more than thirty miles to where she disappeared.'

'Downhill,' Angie whispered. No one heard her. Where had that thought come from?

'Besides,' Mom continued, 'she could have been anywhere. Out of California entirely.'

Brogan stood up and began a slow pace across the room. Angie followed him with her eyes. He'd changed — not a comfortable guy in torn jeans anymore. The soft sympathy face was gone.

15

He was a panther, hunting. A cop, patrolling. She put herself on guard.

His voice changed too — it was flatter, clipped. 'Angela. Any idea how long you were gone? Any hint of location? Anything at all?'

'No! I . . . uh, no. No idea.' Angie gestured to her parents. 'They say it was three years. But . . . I don't know. That doesn't seem right. It was just a couple of days.'

'Did you run away on purpose?'

Angie's forehead wrinkled. 'Run away? No. Of course not.'

'No trouble at home? At school? At church? You didn't need a break? From something? Or someone?' His gaze was probing, encouraging, and scary, all at the same time. He paced and watched and listened.

'No. What are you talking about? Everything's fine. Was. Fine.'

Mom slid an arm around her. Angie leaned into the hug to prove her point.

Brogan nodded. He spoke slowly and carefully. 'Did you arrange to meet someone? Did you visit an internet site and become close to an interesting person?'

'I'm not an idiot! No and no.' What stupid questions. Exhaustion gripped her. What did she have to say to end all of this?

The detective shrugged. 'Okay. We didn't find a trace of that kind of history on the computers you use at home or at school. Still worth asking, though.'

Dad finally quit standing watch and dropped into the other armchair with a loud sigh of relief.

16

What was he thinking? That she would actually sneak off with someone?

Brogan caught Dad's eye and gave him a 'watch yourself here' look. It was easy to read the detective's face. 'Angela, have you ever experimented with alcohol or drugs? A lot of kids your age have. Answer honestly — we won't be angry or shocked, and we can get you help.'

'You can tell us, hon,' Mom said. 'We won't judge. I swear.'

Dad looked like he might, though, his elbows grinding a hole in his knees.

Mom patted his arm and said in an obvious aside, 'That could explain her fuzziness on the details.'

Angie groaned. 'No, I haven't. I've never drunk anything but Communion wine. I've never tried drugs. Just a cigarette. Which was completely gross, by the way.'

'May I see your hands?' Brogan asked. It wasn't a request. It was an order.

She rolled her eyes and wordlessly stuck her arms out. They were too long, too thin, too pale, and she imagined they were someone else's arms stuck on her body. Brogan traced the unfamiliar scars on her wrists with a finger, flipped the hands over to examine the short, ragged nails, then back over to the dirty, rough palms. His finger explored the groove left by the ring on her middle finger, the cleaner, paler skin revealed.

He met her eyes with a question. 'Know anything about this?'

A knifelike pain hit her behind the ear. She winced and shook her head, which he took to

17

mean no. The ache drifted away. Her head cleared. It felt like fog lifting.

He pursed his lips. 'Humor me a sec. Arm wrestle me.' He dropped into the chair again and set his elbow on the coffee table, thumb up.

'You'll win. Your hands are huge,' Angie predicted. 'Plus your arm is much longer than mine.'

One side of his mouth smiled. 'Humor me. Please?'

Angie snorted. 'Right.' She grasped his hand and pushed. Her smaller fingers disappeared in his grip, but his arm wavered. He pressed back. She met him with resistance, startled at the strength of her skinny arm. Lean muscle bulged. Without warning, his arm gave way and she flattened him. 'You let me win,' she accused.

'Maybe a little. You've obviously been doing manual labor. For a long time. You're very strong for your size.'

'Oh my God.' Mom erupted from her seat, hands twisting. 'Manual labor? White slavery, do you think?'

How lame, Angie thought. But Brogan seemed to take the question seriously. 'No, Margie. Not likely. She's been relatively local.'

'Local? All this time?' Dad's voice trembled oddly. 'What makes you say that?'

'Her clothes smell of pine sap and wood smoke.'

Angie sniffed her sleeve. He was right. Well, of course, that made sense. Didn't she make s'mores around the campfire only last night? Smells don't linger for three years.

'Of course,' she said simply. 'I was camping.'

'You remember nothing else?' Brogan asked.

This was getting exasperating. 'Look,' she said. 'I told you. All of you. I don't remember anything else. I was camping. Then I was here. I don't remember being driven home or dropped off or walking. Nothing. I was just here.'

'Angela, how tall are you?' The detective held his palms to her parents to keep them from jumping in.

'Five-one,' she answered without hesitation. In her side vision, Mom's head shook slightly.

'And how much do you weigh?'

'That's kind of personal, isn't it?' she asked.

Brogan gave a full-faced smile for the first time. 'Sorry. Yes. And I'm terrible at guessing. A hundred and ten?'

'Wow. You are terrible.'

'Told you.' He was honest, anyway, and his grin was contagious. 'Sorry. More?'

Angie laughed, for the first time. 'Ninety-five, last time I checked.' Her laugh sounded creaky, hoarse, unused.

'And how old are you?'

'Thirteen,' she said.

Mom started to open her mouth. A hissed 'Si — ' escaped before Brogan cut her off.

Dad missed the gesture. 'She's sixteen,' he insisted. 'You're sixteen now, Angela. Don't you understand what we've been telling you?'

Angie's head buzzed. What was wrong with everybody? Dad was so stiff and angry — he only ever called her Angela when she was in trouble. She was supposed to be his little Angel.

19

But she hadn't done anything wrong, except maybe get lost. And that wasn't her fault. And besides . . . she was home now.

Anger bubbled up from nowhere. 'Will you stop this stupid game? I'm thirteen.' Her voice caught in her throat. 'I'm thirteen.'

Tears blurred her view of the detective's face, but she spoke straight to him in tight, furious words. 'I'm Angela Gracie Chapman. In three weeks, I'm starting eighth grade at La Canada High School. I'm thirteen years old. And I think I've been lost. But I don't know for sure. I want to take a shower and eat and go to bed.' She crossed her arms tightly across her chest, trying to ignore the soft bumps that weren't supposed to be there.

Mom stood. She placed an arm around Angie's shoulder, like a magic cloak of protection. 'Detective. She's right. We all need a little adjustment time here. Can't this be finished later?'

Angie felt such a rush of relief. Mom would get rid of everyone and tuck her into bed, and when she woke up, everything would be normal again.

'I'm sorry, Margie. I wish we could.' Brogan focused on Angie. 'As far as the question of your memory, Angela, I think we're dealing with some retrograde amnesia and post-traumatic stress here. You know what that is?'

'I can't remember anything because I'm too freaked out,' she snapped.

'Something like that. I'd like you to meet with our best forensic psychologist as soon as

20

possible. Mitch, Margie, I'll set up the appointment and call you.'

'So are we done?' Angie asked, just about on her last blip of energy.

'Right after the medical exam,' Brogan said. 'I'll call ahead and expedite it.'

Dad turned his attention to something beyond the window. His expression was absolutely flat, like a stone statue. His shoulders hunched up to his ears.

'Oh, come on, Phil,' Mom protested. 'Is that necessary? Now? She's exhausted. Look at her,'

Brogan caught the desperate, pathetic look Angie threw him. His mouth turned down, and he switched back into the guy with a hole in his knee. 'Yeah. I know. But we have to. I'm so, so sorry.'

Why did he keep apologizing? It didn't change anything.

Brogan lowered his voice, even though there was no one else to overhear. He spoke to Dad's back, not to her. 'Angela has obviously been living with someone. She hasn't been on the street. She hasn't been starved. She's been taken care of. There may be important DNA evidence. We don't want to let any more time elapse before collecting it.'

'From her clothes?' Mom asked. 'We can just give them to you.'

The detective gave Mom a pointed look and, finally, swiveled his attention to Angie. 'Angela, without being able to rely on your memory, we need to see whether you've been sexually assaulted.'

Angie's temper flared again. 'Just say it, Detective. Don't spare my feelings. Raped. You want to know if I've been raped. Don't you think I'd know? Don't you think I'd remember something like that?' Her chest heaved, as if she'd just finished a mile run.

'Do you remember, Angie?' he asked gently.

The image of narrow, dark eyes flashed through her mind and vanished in a spasm of pain. Then her mind was empty, clear — her anger evaporated as if the storm in her head had just died. She was calm. Blank. Relieved. Safe. 'No. Nothing. I don't remember anything.'

'My point exactly,' he said.

'Can I please shower after?'

'Absolutely. Margie, please bring her a change of clothes, since we'll need to keep these.'

In the front hallway, he snapped on a pair of rubber gloves and picked up the grocery bag. 'Do you know what's in here, Angela?'

She shrugged. 'Just some clothes, I think.'

'Recognize this?' He pulled out a checkered blouse.

She shook her head. A queasy feeling started up again in her stomach.

He probed lower and removed a yellow apron. Angie wrinkled her nose. 'Nope.'

He reached in again and retrieved a tiny, black lace cami.

'Good God,' Dad said, turning pale. His hands combed roughly through his hair and locked behind his head.

Angie felt her own hands tremble. 'Not . . . not my style,' she said lightly. A lump formed in her throat. Where had she gotten these things?

Brogan reached into the bag again. 'Ah. No wonder it's so heavy. Recognize this?'

She squinted at *The Joy of Cooking* in his hand. 'Mom has that one. I don't really cook.'

At the bottom of the bag was the strangest thing — a slim metal bar, pointed on one end, flat on the other. Brogan balanced it across his gloved palm. 'Recognize it?' he asked, in a tone that was supposed to be casual but immediately put Angie on guard again.

'No. What is it?' Angie asked.

'Looks like a shiv. An improvised knife.'

'Why would that be in there?' Angie asked.

Brogan watched her with his orange-flecked panther eyes. 'My guess is that you packed the things most precious to you. This might have been used for self-defense or — '

'I've never, ever seen that before,' Angie said quickly. The edge of the metal looked wicked sharp. Dangerous. 'How much damage could you do with a little knife like that?' she asked.

'Oh, no doubt it could kill someone,' Brogan said calmly. 'If you knew how to use it.' The way he lingered on 'you' gave her shivers.

2

EXAMINATION

'Are you okay with this, Angie?' Mom asked for the third time in three minutes. Her cheeks were flushed red, like she was embarrassed by the flurry of activity their arrival had caused at the emergency room.

'I just want to get it over with,' Angie said. A dull throb sat between her ears. She was too tired to feel anything stronger. Mom was anxious enough for both of them anyway. 'Not like I have any choice, do I?'

Detective Brogan turned at the sound of her voice. 'Technically, you do. They'll need your consent. But I can't emphasize enough how important this is to the investigation.'

On soft, white-sneakered feet, a nurse approached with a clipboard. She glanced between her paperwork and Angie, a wave of pity crossing her face. 'Let's head back to an exam room and go over this.'

Dad looked like he wanted to say something, but instead he picked at his thumbnails. 'I'll just, uh, I'll wait here with the detective.'

The room was shockingly white, except for the cloud-scape painted on the pale blue ceiling. The exam table was much too short to stretch out on, and Angie wondered how she wouldn't fall off. She listened with a numb, detached feeling while the nurse explained the rape kit procedure. This couldn't be happening.

The nurse held out a pen. 'Sweetie, here's where you sign. Okay?'

Very slowly, in perfect handwriting, she wrote Angela Gracie Chapman, wishing she had a few more middle names to make it take even longer. The blank line next to it asked a question she couldn't possibly answer. 'Mom, what's the date?'

'September eighteenth,' Mom answered.

Angie blinked hard and wrote it in. Then she handed the pen to Mom to sign as the 'parent/guardian of minor.'

Without a word, Mom drew a single line through the year and corrected it.

Angie swallowed the acid in her throat. Three years. Gone with the slip of a ballpoint pen. How could things like that happen?

Mom's hand still hovered over the page. 'She's never even had a pelvic.'

'Do you want to be in the room with her?' the nurse asked.

Angie met her mom's flustered look. She shook her head. 'That would be too weird,' she said. 'Mom should wait out there. With Dad.'

The nurse touched Mom's shoulder. 'Mrs. Chapman, I'll be present for the entire procedure. I'm very experienced with this sort of case. Why don't you give me her change of clothes?'

Mom's face was stuck between guilt and relief. She signed the form and kissed Angie on the cheek. 'I'll be right nearby, hon. Just right by. Out here.'

As the door clicked closed, Angie felt much less than sixteen, less than thirteen, even. Maybe seven. She wanted to call Mom back to hold her hand, to tell her it would be okay soon. She wanted Mom to remind her to get a sticker on the way out or to ask her where she wanted to get a double scoop when they were done. That's how she always got through checkups, the embarrassment of taking off her clothes, the chill of the room, the dreadful anticipation of the needle.

'Okay, Angela. Hang in there.' The nurse spread a tarp on the floor. 'Please stand in the middle of the pad and place all your clothes on it, not touching the floor.'

'Why?' Angie asked as she unbuttoned the flowered top. She fumbled with clumsy, quivering fingers.

'There may be evidentiary hairs or fibers on your clothes. Shoes, too.'

'Oh.' Self-consciously, she unzipped the pants she was wearing. She couldn't call them hers — she'd never seen them before. She slid them to the ground, pushing off her shoes. Her skin glowed white in the sterile light. It shrank against her muscles as she broke out in goosebumps. Next, she peeled off her socks.

'What are these scars from, sweetie?' the nurse asked, pointing to Angie's feet.

She followed the nurse's finger. Her stomach flipped over. Sour liquid burned a path up into her throat. Around each ankle ran a two-inch band, a thick, lumpy welt of scar tissue. She clamped a hand over her mouth to avoid throwing up. 'I don't know,' she whispered between her fingers. Tears collected at the corners of her eyes.

Oh my God. What had happened? Her legs were gross! Disgusting! She would never, ever wear sandals again.

She crossed her arms over her bare chest, hands tucked into her armpits, and trembled in her panties. They were small and faded, but familiar in all the strangeness. They were actually hers. Pale butterflies chased across her hips. She focused on them, trying to draw comfort from the only thing that made sense.

The nurse glanced up from her clipboard. 'Everything off, sweetie, and hop up on the exam table. There's a paper gown on it.' She touched the wall-mounted intercom to call for the doctor.

Angie dropped her butterflies and dove for the table. The stiff, disposable gown scratched, but at least she was covered again. Her knees were blue and knobby as her legs hung loosely over the edge. She watched all the clothes gathered into a plastic bag and tagged.

'Quick manicure now,' the nurse said. She scraped under Angie's nails and saved the gunk in a small vial. 'Excuse me.' She peeked under Angie's paper gown, 'Not enough hair to comb,' she commented mysteriously, and dropped the paper back over Angie's lap. Angie crossed her ankles tighter together.

'Open, please.' Mechanically, Angie opened her mouth for a huge swab. Her gag reflex kicked in, and she breathed hard through her nose so she wouldn't vomit. Her cheeks and tongue were

27

thoroughly scrubbed and the swab dropped into a long glass vial.

The nurse picked up her pen and clipboard. 'Date of your last period?'

Angie flushed. 'I haven't started yet. I'm sort of a late bloomer.'

A sharp knock, and the doctor entered. Angie's breath caught. The doctor was a man. Oh God. She'd never been examined by a man.

Knees pressed together, Angie shivered and watched him closely. He looked old, with white hairs mixed into his beard and a wrinkled, friendly face. At least that was less humiliating than a cute, young doctor. She loosened her laced fingers and shook the hand he offered. Hers was sweaty, his warm and dry.

'Hi, Angela. I'm Dr. Cranleigh. Is there anything you'd like to ask me before the examination?'

She thought. 'Will it hurt?'

'There may be about thirty seconds of discomfort or cramping. That's all. Okay?'

Angela nodded. No false promises. She liked that. 'Even though I'm a virgin?' she asked.

'Even if you're a virgin,' he replied. 'I understand that you may be suffering from traumatic amnesia, yes?'

She nodded again.

'I'm very sorry about your ordeal.' He turned to the sink to wash his hands.

What was the correct response to that? 'Um. Thanks.'

The nurse hovered in the background, now a silent observer. Angie wondered what she was thinking, how many other young girls or women she had seen through this. Maybe it was different if you actually had been raped, if you were filled with fury, if you were aching for vengeance.

But she wasn't.

Dr. Cranleigh snapped on a pair of latex gloves. 'So. A mystery. We're looking for clues then, to explain anything about what has happened to you, where you have been. Think of us as a team. I promise to be as quick and gentle as possible. You promise to tell me if anything hurts. If we need to stop and take a break, we can do that. Also, very important, Angie, tell me if anything in the examination triggers a memory — a memory of any kind. Okay?'

Angie wasn't so sure she wanted to trigger any memories. Something truly awful had happened to her feet. She couldn't bear to look at them, dangling down from the edge of the examining table. And there were those dark ridges on her wrists as well. There must be a really good reason she couldn't remember.

A bubble of resentment rose to the surface of her mind. She didn't have to be here. She could have refused all this. Maybe she still could. Why was it so important to find everything out, anyway? Couldn't everyone just be glad she was home and leave her alone? She was safe. She was alive. Let it go.

'Okay, now, Angela,' Dr. Cranleigh said. 'I am going to check you for bruises and scars on the outside.' With impersonal and quick hands, he lifted the gown and examined every inch of her skin while Angie focused on the light above her,

29

which flickered slightly. One fluorescent bulb was yellower than the one beside it, and she concentrated on the pattern of blinks.

Dr. Cranleigh spent a considerable time on her feet and wrists before he paused to jot a few notes and take photos. She watched the hands of the clock creep around and breathed in time with the ticks, trying to ignore the nauseating, dull, rubbery sensation when he touched her scars.

Angie forced herself to ask. 'What do you think . . . I mean, what could have done that to me?'

The doctor met her question square on. 'Healed wounds like these are typical of repeated chafing from restraints, most likely metal, not leather. The wrists suggest something more like rope or twine. The appearance is not consistent with self-injury. Any thoughts?'

'No,' she answered numbly. She'd been restrained? Shackled? She chased the word around in her mind, trying to find a wisp of memory. Her mind resisted, pressing back with dark blankness. 'I just don't know.'

'Thank you, Angela. Now lie down please, with your feet in these stirrups, knees up and apart, so we can look for any internal injuries.'

Angie's chest suddenly squeezed too tight to breathe. *Hide!* a tiny voice screamed. A blinding pain shot through her skull, and she covered her eyes with her hands.

In the distance, she heard the doctor's voice. 'You may feel a slight pressure . . . '

But she didn't. The headache lifted as quickly

as it had come, and her eyes fluttered open with surprise. The nurse extended a hand to help her sit. 'All done, sweetie,' she said. 'Thank you for being so cooperative. You can get dressed.'

All done? That was the exam? Where was the doctor? He couldn't have snuck out in the two seconds her eyes were closed, could he?

Her heart skipped a beat. It was only two seconds, wasn't it? She hadn't blacked out, had she?

Angie's eyes flicked from the nurse to the clock. Only a few minutes since she last looked, and they'd been talking for part of that. Relief eased the tightness in her chest. Guess the doctor was just quick on his feet.

Anyway, thank God it was all over. Time to go home and forget all of this. She smiled briefly at her unconscious choice of words. Could you forget about forgetting? Maybe so.

In spite of all the evidence, proof even, she didn't feel like three years were missing. If she could just convince her parents to chill, she could get on with her life as usual — call her friends, go back to school, pick up where she left off. Why not? She pulled on the soft sweater Mom had brought and hugged her arms around herself. Trust Mom to remember her favorite oversized fuzzy blue sweater.

Angie slid her slender legs into the pair of tan cords, feeling almost normal again, until she stood straight and realized the pants were a couple of inches too short. And there it was. Proof again. Who was she kidding? She couldn't just continue with her life as usual. Her life didn't fit her anymore.

The nurse walked Angie down the corridor, to a room marked PRIVATE. 'Doctor's talking to your parents. Go on in, sweetie. Good luck with everything.'

Yeah. Good luck. How was she supposed to be a size-thirteen girl in a size-sixteen life?

Angie put a hand on the knob and began a slow twist. The doctor's voice penetrated the door, and she paused to listen to what he was telling Mom and Dad. She caught, 'Severe lacerations . . . unusual internal scarring . . . no doubt of repeated assault . . . ankles . . . not typical of self-mutilation . . . wrists . . . suicide . . . good health . . . not pregnant . . . psychiatric . . . '

Angie retreated to the hall bathroom, cranked the bolt, and sank against the locked door, weak at the knees. *Repeated assaults. Internal scarring.* The words whirled in her brain. Oh God. This wasn't the kind of thing that happened to real people! This was TV stuff.

She'd left for camp as a normal kid, someone who belonged in a sitcom or family drama. Now she was the unwilling star of her own special crimes unit episode. Someone was rewriting the script of her life. Without her permission.

Angie didn't realize she was crying until a tear rolled off her chin and splashed the cold tile floor. What was she doing here? What happened? According to Mom and Dad, more than a thousand days had been stolen from her. And no matter what the calendar in her head said, the flow of time and some cruel experience were written all over her. Right there. On her arms and legs and face.

Salty teardrops burned tracks down her cheeks. She smeared them off with the heels of her hands.

Angie stepped to the sink to splash cold water on her face, and there she was again. That stranger in the mirror. With the eyes that looked old and tired, full of knowledge they refused to share. Regretful, concerned.

Angie hurled a handful of water at the image. 'I want my life back, you bitch,' she hissed at her reflection.

Oh, Angie, you were so angry at us. You didn't know how we saved your life — how I worked with the girls and the gate to keep you pure and hidden and untouched, our Pretty Girl-Thirteen. That's what we called you. We're sorry there was nothing we could do about the scars.

★ ★ ★

'She can't start school yet,' Dad said. 'Not until we get a thorough psychological evaluation. We don't even know which grade to put her into, after all.'

He and Mom were 'discussing' her life in the front seat as if Angie weren't there inches behind them and hadn't just been strip-searched in the hospital. She felt sore and sticky, though she couldn't remember any part of the short exam to account for it.

Dad hadn't made eye contact with her the whole way through the hospital and out to the car. When Angie tried to slip her hand into his, he fake sneezed and moved his hand away to get a handkerchief. Was sixteen too old for public displays of affection? The rejection hurt, all the same.

'Eighth,' Angie said, leaning between their seats. 'I'm supposed to be in eighth grade. And I've already missed almost three weeks of school. I have to get started.' Her double scoop of mint-chip ice cream sat melting and untasted in its cardboard cup on her lap. At least Mom had remembered.

Mom's face ran through three tries before she found an expression she liked — polite disagreement. 'It's only three weeks. And the school will help us with tutoring to catch you up — I'll insist on it. But hon, you need to be with your peers right now. You need their emotional support.'

'My peers are in eighth grade,' Angie insisted.

'Angie, your friends are all in eleventh grade now — : Livvie, Kate, Greg.'

'Greg?'

Oh my God. She hadn't thought of him in . . . well, whether it was three years ago or two days, the recollection of Greg was a ray of light that pierced this strange, dark day.

A whole bunch of them had gone to Soak City Water Park together at the end of July for the last great adventure of summer. It didn't start out as a date for Angie and Greg, but then everyone else in the group ditched them at the lazy river.

34

The joke was, they didn't even notice.

They floated along on their stomachs like seals, sharing one raft. Their feet trailed out behind them in the swift, warm water, the sun blazing down on their backs. And pretty soon, their legs were sliding against each other, and Angie was really glad she'd just shaved. Around the river again, and their feet were twined together and when Greg put his hot, tanned arm across her back, it was the most natural thing in the world to turn her head and look into his shining eyes and meet his kiss halfway. Chlorine and cola flavored.

They crashed into a wall, bumped teeth, cracked themselves up, and kissed some more until the teenage lifeguard blew a whistle and screamed, 'Watch where you're going or I'll kick you out!'

'Ooh, attitude,' Greg said. 'Give them a whistle and they're boss of the world.'

Angie giggled. 'So do what he says and keep your eyes open this time!'

They floated around one more lap, lips and eyes locked on each other but blind to everyone else in the water, in a personal bubble the size of one raft and two people. By the end of the day, they were officially going out. But then they hadn't actually *gone* out again before the campout.

Greg. Wow. He was a junior now — how incredibly awkward. How could a junior go with an eighth grader? Wait. She wasn't, really. But what if he was going with someone else now? That was totally possible — likely, even.

Her heart raced at the idea of seeing him again, but which track was it speeding down — anticipation or fear? Like it was yesterday, she could still taste his kisses.

'Mom, there's no way I'm skipping to eleventh grade. No way. Think about it. I'm totally unprepared. I can't catch up that fast.'

Dad jumped in. 'Which is why I suggested we give the psychologist a chance to weigh in on the decision. Especially since she has this temporary mental block. Who knows what else it might have affected — spelling, algebra — who knows?'

'She needs a normal routine,' Mom said. 'And her best friends.'

A dreadful thought socked her in the stomach. The air punched out of her in a moan. They might not be her best friends anymore. They might have nothing in common. The in-jokes would all be stale. She wouldn't know the songs and shows and websites they were talking about. And she'd be an oddity, a celebrity, the girl who disappeared for three years.

'Dad's right,' she blurted. 'And I might want to go to a new school anyway.'

'Well, we'll just have to see,' Mom said, admitting defeat in her own way. 'Detective Brogan very kindly arranged for the psychologist to see you tomorrow afternoon. All you have to do for the next twenty-four hours is eat and rest and put everything else out of your mind.'

'It already is,' Angie said with a hint of bitterness.

Dad pulled the car into the garage and killed the engine. His shoulders hardened into a wall.

'Angela, I'm not so sure you want to remember anything based on what Dr. Cranleigh told us. Repression is a natural defense. If even half of what he suspects is true . . . well, never mind.' He turned his head away, but not before Angie caught the sickened look on his face and the swimmy film of tears in his eyes.

'Don't get me started,' Mom hissed at him, pinching the bridge of her nose. 'Right now we're celebrating our Angie's miraculous return, however it happened.' She slammed the car door. 'I'll start dinner while you clean up,' she said. 'Your favorite? Macaroni and cheese?'

They were acting so weird. So emotional. Angie's stomach hurt. She could only nod and pretend it sounded good.

'Welcome home, Angie,' Mom said. 'Remember we love you with all our hearts, no matter what.' She gave Angie an uncomfortably tight hug.

No matter what? What was that supposed to mean? Angie stood in the circle of Mom's arms for a minute before breaking loose.

She ran upstairs and opened the door to her bedroom, like the door to a time machine. Everything was picked up and in place, the way she'd left it before the campout. Her cozy blanket was folded in a square on the rocking chair. Her guitar was put away in its niche by the window.

The dresser top displayed a set of four colorfully beaded cream cheese tubs for her jewelry — rings, necklaces, bracelets, and earrings sorted out from one another. A plastic

37

palomino horse, saved from a storage bin, galloped toward a photo of Angie, Livvie, and Katie squished cheek-to-cheek-to-cheek in a Disneyland giant teacup. She dragged her finger through the thick layer of dust over everything.

Her finger came to rest at the foot of the angel statuette Grandma had given her for confirmation a few months ago — or what felt like a few months ago. She picked it up, and stroked the pure white ceramic wings, dusting off a small cobweb that had been spun between them. An unusual choice, she thought again. Not a sissy-sweet Hallmark angel, but a strong, sexless boy-girl with narrow lips and bright eyes. It looked purposeful, even fierce, like Old Testament angels who frightened mortals with their flaming swords. She replaced it carefully, back on the dust-free spot.

In one of the jewelry tubs, the thick silver ring caught her attention. Oh. She'd left it in the bathroom, but somehow it had migrated back to her room. She picked it up for a closer look.

The ring was engraved all the way around with six tiny leaves branching off a single stem, familiar and unfamiliar at the same time. She probably should have turned it in as evidence. A beam of sunlight from the window sparkled off an irregular pattern on the inside curve. What was that? An inscription? She squinted to read it: DEAREST ANGELA, MY LITTLE WIFE. The words bounced off a brick wall in her memory, leaving the reflection of one panicked thought. *No one should see this.*

The ring leaped onto her third finger and

nestled into its groove, like it belonged. She must have worn it a long time to reshape her finger like that. She twisted and tugged until the ring pulled free of her knuckle, reluctant to leave its proper place. Her hand looked pale and naked.

She slipped it back on, forgotten already.

The bed was neatly made, with Grandma's summertime patchwork quilt. On the bedside table was a bookmarked paperback — *Animal Farm* — which she'd been reading before the trip. Beneath it was her journal. The lock was broken, and it flopped open, somewhere in the middle of seventh grade. The familiar handwriting looped across the pages, day after faithful day until the last entry. August 2. She had written this in the tent by flashlight. Last night. No, not last night. More than three years ago.

She tried to imagine her innocent excitement as she read her own words. 'Ouch. Long hike in. Everything hurts but camp stew was amazing and s'mores even better. Tomorrow we hike along the crest trail. Cool. Can't wait.'

Before that, every page was filled. After that, every page was blank. It gave her the shivers.

Mom's voice came from the doorway. 'When they brought that back from the campout, it was all I had left of you.'

Angie kept her eyes down. She whispered, 'You broke the lock. You read it, didn't you? My private journal.' Not that she had any great secrets, but there were a lot of very personal comments about Greg. About his body, his arms, his lips. The blood rushed to her cheeks.

Mom crept up behind and slipped her arms

around Angie's waist. Mom's chin nestled on Angie's shoulder. 'I'm sorry, Angie. We had to for the investigation. Any clue . . . '

'Oh God. He read it too.'

'Dad? No, no. I told him there wasn't anything he needed to know. Just girl stuff.'

'I meant Detective Brogan.' Angie shrank with embarrassment. Of course he'd read it. That was his job.

She felt Mom's nod against the side of her head. 'Anyway.' Mom's voice brightened into forced cheerfulness, trying to sound normal. 'I didn't change anything in here. I wanted it to be just right when you were found.'

Angie turned and hugged her hard, a life preserver in this crazy, wind-tossed sea. In her arms, she felt Mom sob and shudder once. 'I never gave up,' Mom said. 'Believe me.'

Angie rubbed her face into Mom's shoulder. 'Do you think I'll ever remember?'

For a long moment, Mom was silent. Angie pulled back and caught the tortured expression on her face, the mourning in her eyes, a split second before she fixed her expression.

Finally, Mom answered. 'For three long years, all I've wanted was to know what happened to you. Now . . . I don't honestly know if I want you to remember.'

On that point, we had to agree.

3

EVALUATION

Dawn light filtered through the curtains a little after six thirty. Angie had the strangest urge to leap out of bed and start cooking, but that was ridiculous. She didn't know how to cook. She stretched like a cat, working the stiffness out of her legs. Her feet touched the carpet with a jolt. The blisters and rubbed spots clearly hadn't healed overnight. She forced herself to look away from the scar bands around her ankles.

'If I can't see them, they aren't there,' she lied to herself.

Angie listened for her parents moving around in the house. Water was running — probably Dad's shower. She padded over to the dresser to find some clothes. She picked out one of her favorite tops, a long-sleeve tee with a dark blue silhouette of a rock climber on a pale blue background and sparkles spelling out ROCK ON. Katie had given it to her to celebrate their rock climbing badges last May . . . last . . . May. Oh no. She held it up to her chest and realized it was at least two sizes too small now.

Well, great. Wonderful. What would she wear? She crushed the shirt into a ball and hurled it across the room. It landed on the carpet dents where her rocking chair usually sat. The chair had moved three feet closer to the window.

41

Carpet skids showed where it had been dragged since yesterday. Angie frowned and dragged it back.

With a heavy sigh, she went back to the dresser for the too-big gray sweatshirt she liked to wear when she needed to feel cozy. Without rolling up, the sleeves were just the right length now to cover her wrists. She glanced into her dusty jewelry dishes for inspiration and realized with a start — they weren't dusty. In fact, the entire dresser top was clean. And so was her desk, and her nightstand, and the windowsill.

Had Mom snuck in at midnight to clean? How totally stupid, but how totally nice of her.

'Knock, knock.' Mom's voice on the other side of the door startled her.

She jumped back into bed, not to be caught standing there in her underwear. 'Come in, Mom,' she called.

Mom pushed the door with her foot, her hands filled with a bed tray and a plate of steaming pancakes. Pancakes in bed! It didn't get any better than this. And she was starving, even after eating half the macaroni and cheese last night.

'Don't think I'm going to do this every day,' Mom said with a little smile. 'Just days that end in Y.' She couldn't tear her eyes away from Angie's face. Maybe she expected her to disappear again overnight.

'Thanks, Mom. This is great, really, but you don't need to make such a fuss.'

'Of course I do,' Mom said. She perched on the edge of the bed and set the tray across the

42

bump of Angie's legs. She fluffed the pillows behind Angie's back.

'The novelty will wear off, and then I'll just be spoiled.'

'No, it won't. Never.' Mom laughed and stroked her hair. 'Can I brush this for you? It's grown so long.'

'I'll probably get it cut soon,' Angie said. 'Feel more like me.'

Avoiding mirrors was possible, but ignoring the strange sweep of silky hair over her shoulder wasn't. It made her wonder about all the things she couldn't remember — washing it, brushing it smooth every morning. And that led to where had she slept? What had she eaten? Who had cooked for her? Was someone missing her now that she was gone? Ugh. All too weird to think about. Better not to think at all.

She squeezed a huge glob of fake maple syrup over the four-high stack of buttermilk pancakes, watching it waterfall over the cliff into an amber pool on the plate.

Mom was silent until Angie looked up again, wondering why she was so quiet. Mom's face had that smoothed-over sad look again. 'I'm sorry you don't feel like you. Maybe once you're back in school, or taking guitar again — I'm sure Ms. Manda would be thrilled to . . . ' She trailed off.

Angie shrugged.

'I'm sorry,' Mom said again. 'I'm not helping, am I? Who do you feel like?'

'That's the weird thing.' Angie cut a wedge with the side of her fork. 'I'm the same person on the inside as when I packed for camping. But my clothes don't fit right, my hair is all wrong, and when I walk by a mirror it's like I'm seeing the ghost of Angie-yet-to-come. It's creepy.' She stuffed the whole wedge of dripping pancakes into her mouth. The sweetness stayed on her lips after she swallowed. She sighed. 'I don't know. Who do you see?'

Mom took her left hand. 'Just my daughter. A lovely girl on the verge of becoming a young woman.' She rubbed Angie's knuckles, her fingers stopping on the strange silver ring. 'Pretty,' she commented. 'I don't remember this ring from . . . from before.'

Angie didn't either, but something stopped her from admitting that. 'Sure. I've had it for a long time.' A half-truth.

'Oh. Okay. Guess I'm getting old. So, what would you like to do today?' Mom asked. 'Shop for a few clothes that fit? And school supplies? Your appointment isn't till three, but I took the whole day off.'

'Wait. You work? Since when?' Mom was a stay-at-home full-time volunteer.

'The library finally got a budget increase about two years ago, and since we needed . . . well, since I'd been such a faithful volunteer, they hired me.'

Angie didn't miss the slip. 'You needed the money? Did Dad lose his job?'

Mom's silver-brown curls jostled as she shook her head in quick denial. 'No, no. Everything's fine there. He even got promoted to district sales manager. No. We just . . . it was expensive

44

looking for you. Private detectives, advertising. And for God's sake get that look off your face. Don't think either of us regrets a single penny.'

Angie shrugged off the sudden feeling of guilt. It wasn't her fault. She wasn't a runaway or a juvenile delinquent. As far as she knew.

'It's okay, hon. We'll all be fine.' Mom gave Angie an extra-hard squeeze as if to convince herself. A drop of syrup spilled onto the quilt.

Angie dabbed at it and licked her finger. 'Have you told anyone else yet? I mean, there aren't a bunch of reporters on the lawn waiting for me to finish my breakfast and shower, are there?'

Mom made a show of going to the window and pulling back the curtains to check. 'Nope. Not even one camera crew. Phil, Detective Brogan, is doing his best to keep any leaks out of the department until you're ready. That'll be hard. You, my dearest, were a very high-profile case.' She gazed out the window into the far distance. 'So speaking of telling people, are you going to call Livvie today?'

Oh God. What would she say? *Hi, Livvie, I'm back from the presumed dead? I didn't get ravaged by cougars. What's new with you?* Definitely not a conversation she wanted to face right now. 'Uh, no. I think I'll wait till after the psychologist.'

Mom's eyebrows pressed closer. 'But maybe your friends . . . ' She stopped, readjusted. 'No, sorry. Of course. You need time to absorb the idea yourself before you deal with other people. That's sensible. But I did call Grandma, of course. Last night after you fell asleep. Uncle Bill is driving her down on Saturday.' Mom let the curtain drop.

'Yuncle Bill?' Dad's much younger brother was only eight years older than Angie, hence the nickname she gave him when she was six and he was only fourteen — young uncle was 'yuncle.' She hadn't seen him for ages. 'What about Grampy? Isn't he coming?'

Mom's face froze. The silence lasted a beat too long. Angie bit her lower lip. Oh no. Please don't say it, she prayed.

But Mom did. 'Oh, Ange, hon. Of course you wouldn't, couldn't know. We lost Grampy six months ago.'

The bottom fell out of her stomach. Her cheeks went numb. Silent tears splashed onto her pancakes. What else had she missed?

She choked out the words. 'What else, Mom? Anything else I need to know? Anything else I missed?'

Mom's left hand darted to her stomach, her right to her mouth. Her eyes searched the room. 'I . . . no,' Mom said.

A blind person could have told she was lying. 'What, Mom? Spill it. Could anything possibly be more heart-breaking than never seeing Grampy again?' And then an awful possibility crossed her mind, watching Mom clutch herself like that. 'Cancer? Oh God. Please, please don't tell me you have cancer.'

'Oh, honey, no! It's not . . . it's . . . it's good news, at least.' Mom bit her lip. 'We're expecting.'

Angie's mind blanked. 'Expecting what?'

46

'Angie, hon, I'm pregnant.'

A swooshing sound drowned out her mother's next words. She saw the lips moving, but she couldn't hear for the raging storm in her mind. Oh God. It was true. A new baby. They *had* given up on her. They really had.

And even worse was the thought that while she lay lost and shackled, maybe hungry and cold, maybe tortured and scared, Mom and Dad were kissing and planning and baby-making and moving on without her.

Without warning, she heaved up all over the plate, all over Grandmas beautiful hand-stitched quilt. Mom slammed both hands over her own mouth and ran from the room.

You helped our mom clean up your vomit in embarrassed, tense silence. Girl Scout wanted to help restore order, but we had agreed to give you this chance. It was too soon to bring you back inside. It was too soon to give up hope that you could manage on the outside.

While the laundry ran, our mom suggested shopping again. And since your old clothes didn't fit our body, you agreed. You knew you would need them for school soon, anyway.

Mom tried to resurrect the old ritual at the mall, stopping first for cinnamon pretzels the way you always did before, wanting to re-create the closeness, the innocent times. You forced yourself to eat the whole thing, while your stomach

47

cramped. *At least it made her smile.*

The salesgirl at Abercrombie looked at you funny when you said you didn't know our size. You took an armload into the dressing room alone and stripped down to try everything on. It was the first time we had seen our whole body in front of a mirror, and I let each of the girls borrow the eyes, just to peek, until our mom knocked. 'Everything okay? Need any different sizes?'

I suppose I let them take longer than I should have. You startled as we retreated and you found yourself with a roomful of untouched clothes and your hands cupped over your breasts, weighing their unexpected fullness.

'Hang on,' you snapped at her. 'I haven't even started. I'll let you know.' You finally tried on all the clothes, but alarmed at the price tags — thirty-five dollars for a T-shirt? — picked only three shirts and one pair of jeans.

'That's all you're getting?' our mom asked. 'I thought this was your favorite store.'

'That's all I wanted from here,' you said. 'Let's go somewhere less designer.'

Mom let a little relief show on her face. Money must be even tighter than she'd let on.

When you left the mall, there was a little surprise waiting for you in the shopping bag for later. One of us had very expensive taste and very light fingers.

Detective Brogan came by at two o'clock to explain a few things before Angie's appointment with his psychologist. Dad had gone to work, as if it were an ordinary Monday, back to the usual routine. Mom and Angie sat on the sofa with the empty cushion dividing them. Brogan glanced between them, and one eyebrow lowered slightly.

'Everything okay here?' he asked. He was wearing a dark suit instead of weekend clothes, his chin was shaved smooth, and the faint scent of citrus wafted from his aftershave.

'Of course, Phil,' Mom answered cheerfully, while Angie thought, *This guy doesn't miss a thing*.

Studying Angie's face, he said, 'We're going forward on a presumption of kidnapping, based on the physical evidence and statements. So Angela, recovering your memory is going to be critical if we're going to find and prosecute the kidnapper — more importantly, prevent him from finding a new victim, if we're not too late.'

Words flew out of her mouth. They weren't her own. 'Why are you so sure he's still alive?'

'A good question.' The detective flattened his expression to open curiosity. 'Is he?' Angie saw the flecks in his eyes take on that hunting gleam.

She shifted on the couch, slightly flustered. What had she asked exactly? 'What do you mean? Is he what?'

'Is he alive?' He asked it so casually, Angie could have missed the implication that she knew more than she was saying.

But she didn't. 'How should I know?'

'The tone of your voice suggested you just

might.' He didn't go further. She read it in his face, though. The sharpened shiv he'd held so carefully yesterday might be a murder weapon.

'I don't know,' she said.

'You used the word 'he.' We're talking about a man? One person?'

She searched her brain, trying to force it to cooperate. It remained stubbornly blank. 'I don't know. It just came out that way.'

'Okay.' He levered himself up with his hands on his knees. 'Let's hope Dr. Grant can help us find some answers. I wanted to make sure you understand that the usual doctor-patient confidentiality laws apply. Even though we have an investigation, Dr. Grant can't reveal any information that you don't give her explicit permission to reveal to me or to your parents.'

'Not to us?' Mom gasped.

Though his answer was for Mom, Brogan's reassurance was really aimed straight at Angie. 'Angela needs to feel completely safe and comfortable with the doctor's discretion. Believe me, at this point, I'm truly more concerned about her recovery than the investigation.'

'Don't worry, Mom. I'll probably tell you.' The hurt expression on Mom's face was small payback for the load she had dumped on Angie this morning.

'Good luck, then,' Brogan said as he reached for the front doorknob. 'I think you'll like Dr. Grant.'

Angie's lips moved. The words came from her mouth, but again they weren't her own thoughts — they came out of left field. 'Besides, if he isn't alive, that would be self-defense, wouldn't it?' It was like someone else was having a conversation with the detective.

His eyebrows flew up. 'Most likely. Any more questions?'

'Definitely not.' Angie clamped her jaw shut.

★   ★   ★

She didn't expect Dr. Lynn Grant to be beautiful. A doctor with a plain name like that should be narrow-nosed, gray-haired, and pointy-chinned. Dr. Grant looked like a Gwendolyn Foxworthy or a Meredith Johanssen, with tons of white-blonde hair softly curling against round cheeks. Instead of a white lab coat, or something stiffly professional, she wore a shell-pink cashmere sweater set and white wool trousers. All she needed was a pearl choker to complete the glamour ensemble. Oh wait. She had one.

It would have been easier to spill her guts to someone less perfect, if she had any guts to spill. Of course that's why they brought her here in the first place, to dig into the guts and see what they could find inside.

In the car, Mom had tried to warm her up to the idea. 'Keep an open mind,' she began. 'A counselor can really be helpful.'

'Right. Like you've ever gone to one.' The words came out hard and bitter instead of teasing, like Angie intended.

'Your father and I saw a grief counselor for more than a year. She was helpful.'

'Is she the one who told you a replacement child would make it all better?'

The steering wheel jerked slightly as Mom flinched. 'I never, ever, ever, ever gave up on finding you.' A surge on the accelerator punctuated each 'ever.'

Seems like Dad did. Angie bit back her automatic response. She knew it wasn't entirely fair, and if she threw out an accusation that sharp, it would cut Mom to the bone.

Wow. Maybe she really did need a counselor.

Mom sat in the waiting room, her hands strangling an old magazine. Angie knew she wouldn't read any of it in the next hour.

Angie tried to calm her own jitters as she followed the psychologist into her private office. The walls were paneled in pale wood with lots of knots. They felt like a hundred eyes.

'Sit anywhere you like,' Dr. Grant said, and Angie knew that was like the first test. Open mind, she reminded herself.

The room wasn't overly large, but aside from a tidy desk, there was space for a stiff vertical armchair facing a blue velour couch, a beanbag in a corner, and a plushy leather recliner. What would a sane person choose? She had no idea, so she decided to throw the test back at the doctor. Angie sat on the desk, careful not to knock over the vase holding a single white rose.

Dr. Grant didn't crack a frown or a smile, just wheeled her desk chair around. She folded her hands in her lap, comfortably. Angie realized her own arms were crossed like a shield and casually let them slide down to rest on her knees.

'So, Angela Gracie Chapman. What do you prefer to be called?'

Oh God. Another test, she thought, and hesitated too long over the answer.

'Your mother called you Angie,' Dr. Grant said. 'Is it okay if I do the same?'

Angie shrugged. 'Whatever. Dad calls me Angel. Strangers call me Angela.'

Dr. Grant smiled a little. 'Okay, Angela. I hear you. But I don't anticipate being strangers for long. You can call me Lynn or Doctor or Dr. Grant. Whatever you like.'

The silence stretched, and finally Angie said, 'So what am I supposed to do?'

Dr. Grant nodded. 'That's the question of the moment, isn't it? What are you supposed to do?' She waited.

The confusion and frustration of the last twenty-four hours tumbled out. 'I have absolutely no idea.' Angie flung her hands up dramatically. 'They totally don't get it. I mean, look at it from their perspective. They say I was missing. They searched for three years. They spent a ton of money. They eventually got over me and moved on. And then I came back.'

'They moved on?' Dr. Grant asked.

'Did you know my mom is pregnant?'

'No, Angela. I didn't know that. Pregnant.' She let the word hang in the silence.

Angie picked the rosebud out of its vase and stared into the heart of the white petals. So pure, so clean. 'So I guess that was their backup plan. Replace me.'

'I understand your feelings,' she said. 'That's a

very natural reaction. Do you want to talk about it?'

Angie shook her head.

'Okay.' The doctor moved on without pushing. That was surprising. 'What else don't they get?'

The outermost petals were browning just at the curled edges. Angie picked one and slid the silken texture between her fingers. 'They think I'm sixteen.'

'But you're not sixteen.'

She felt a glimmer of hope. Finally. Someone believed her. 'I'm thirteen. Three years passed for them? No time at all passed for me. Like . . . ' How could she explain? She snapped her fingers. 'Like that.'

'Hmm.' Dr. Grant snapped her own fingers, with a puzzled expression. She gestured to a large filing cabinet. 'The case notes the department gave me are very sketchy. Why don't you tell me about the last three days you remember, in as much detail as you can recall.'

So Angie told her about packing for camp, about almost forgetting her toothbrush. She did remember details, like taking her journal, like needing new flashlight batteries, like looking up the weather online and seeing that it might be colder than usual, especially at that altitude, and deciding to take sweatpants. That couldn't have been three years ago — it was all so clear. She remembered the early morning meet-up in the parking lot at school. She remembered sitting next to Livvie in the Suburban and talking about Greg and how excited she was to have a for-sure date for homecoming. Everything was crystal clear in her head — the first day of hiking in, the campfire songs that first night, ghost stories in the leaders' tent, then s'mores and off to bed without brushing teeth anyway. Angie told Dr. Grant about waking up early and wondering whether anyone had started the breakfast fire. She remembered eating thimbleberries and looking for a private place.

The doctor listened intently as Angie's narration came to a sudden stop. She raised her brows with encouragement. 'Go on.'

But there was nothing else, like a door had slammed. The hollow silence echoed. Angie glanced around the office in dismay.

Over the doctor's shoulders, she noticed a pair of pine knots in the paneling. They watched her, like dark, staring, narrow eyes peering out of the wood. She tried to look away, but they nailed her with a rising sense of panic. Strange and familiar. The breath froze in her lungs. Trapped. The roar of storm winds filled her ears. Through the swirling gale, someone screamed, *'Quick. Hide!'*

And then the room was perfectly quiet.

'Angela . . . Angela?' the doctor asked. 'Hide from what, Angela? What was in the woods?'

Angie stared at Dr. Grant. 'Hmmm?'

Dr. Grant leaned forward. 'You said, 'Quick, hide.' Hide from what?'

'No, I didn't,' Angie said. 'I said, 'Thimbleberries.' That's what was growing in the woods.'

The doctor's blonde eyebrows pulled so tight they nearly touched. 'After thimbleberries. It was quite clear. You became frightened and you yelled, 'Quick. Hide.' Who were you talking to? I thought you were alone.'

Angie plucked another petal and dropped it on the carpet. 'I really don't know what you're talking about.'

'Hmm. Okay. Maybe I misheard,' Dr. Grant said. 'So you gathered and ate the berries. Then . . . ?'

'Then I was walking home.'

'All the way from the campsite to home? You knew the way?'

Angie shrugged. It was hard to care. 'I guess. I don't remember.' Three more petals hit the floor. 'No, I don't know the way. But I realized I was nearly home, just at the end of our street. My feet hurt a lot — I must have walked a long, long time.'

'Did you notice anything else unusual?'

Angie picked at the only thorn on the smooth-stemmed rose. 'You mean besides it was September instead of August? Besides it was three years later? Besides I was taller and thinner? Besides I was wearing strange clothes instead of my pj's? Anything unusual?' Her voice climbed the scale with each *besides*. 'Nah. Not a thing.'

'So everything had changed. Instantly.'

A rising sob squeezed the back of her throat. 'Everything except me. I'm still me when I close my eyes. I don't know who's been living in my body for the last three years, but I assure you it wasn't me.' She waited for the doctor to say how silly and unreasonable that sounded.

Dr. Grant didn't even blink. 'So where do you think *you* were?'

'A rocking chair,' she answered reflexively. Then, 'I don't know why I said that. I have no idea.'

Steepling her fingers under her chin, the doctor pursed her lips. 'Curious. Angela, I think I would like to get your mother's permission to try hypnosis. We may be able to push past the thimbleberries. How would you feel about that?'

She felt — well, she wouldn't call it hopeful. She was just being open-minded, that was all. 'If you think it'll help, go for it. I don't see why you need Mom's permission, though. I'm the one who needs help here.'

'I'm glad you see it that way, Angela. I'm glad you understand that you need help. Still, I am going to pop out and advise your mother.'

While she was out, Angie moved to the couch. Not knowing what to expect, she figured that if she fell over when she went under, it might as well be soft.

Dr. Grant smiled without comment at Angie's relocation. 'Mom's on board. Are you ready?'

Angie nodded, wondering about the device in Dr. Grant's hands. The doctor touched a switch, and Angie watched the light travel back and forth. It was vaguely annoying. Back and forth. Back and forth.

'Am I supposed to feel different yet?' Angie asked.

'Patience. Relax. Just breathe in and out,' Dr. Grant said in a swaying voice. 'In and out. Imagine a pine tree, a perfect pine tree.'

Angie let an image creep into her head, a perfectly symmetric dark green tree, like the kind a little kid draws. Like a Christmas-card tree.

'There's another one beside it,' the doctor said. Angie imagined another tree, taller.

'Now there's a woodsy smell,' she added. 'Can you smell it? Breathe in and out, very slowly. In and out. In and out.'

Angie did. She breathed slowly, and caught a hint of pine and wood smoke. 'Yeah, I think I can smell something.'

'Now add five more trees.'

She saw them. Unreal.

'Can you take a step toward them?'

In her mind, Angie stepped closer to the trees. She stood and turned around in a circle, slowly. The knots in the paneling watched her relentlessly.

'What are you looking for, Angela?' the doctor asked. 'What do you see in the trees?'

'No. Stop,' a loud voice said.

'Angela, Angela.' The doctor had a hand on her arm.

Angie blinked. The light was gone, and she was sitting in the beanbag chair. 'How . . . when?'

The doctor had an extremely serious expression on her face. 'I think we have an unexpected complication,' she said.

That's when she told you about us. That's when the doctor said, 'I think we've found the explanation for your amnesia.'

Of course, you wanted to know more.

Dr. Grant had a textbook open on her desk. In large, bold type, the section was

58

headed with the words DISSOCIATIVE IDENTITY DISORDER (DID). 'I strongly suspect that your mind is carrying several alternate personalities — multiple personalities you developed to help you cope with the trauma of being kidnapped. We call them 'alters' for short.'

'That's crazy!' you said. 'You're telling me I'm insane? Schizo? Delusional?'

'No, no. Not at all. The word is 'dissociated' — pulled apart.' She hurried to reassure you. 'Alters experience things that are too hurtful or frightening for you. They form a protective barrier between you and what's happening. That way you don't have to remember. They're the brain's ultimate survival mechanism.'

She was so right. We gave ourselves a pat on the shoulders.

But you laughed. 'That's ridiculous. Why do you think I have multiple personalities?'

'Well, for one thing, there's the long time period of lost memory.' Dr. Grant leaned over to collect the fallen petals from the floor. 'For another, I've just spent half an hour talking to one of them. She calls herself Girl Scout. She's worried about you.'

PART II

We

4

REUNION

When they left Dr. Grant's office, Mom gripped a photocopy of the textbook article and a page of web references. Angie trailed her unhappily back to the car. She didn't believe any of it. There must be more rational ways to explain her lost time, her blank memory. And jeez, they were just talking about camping. Of course Angie would have mentioned she was a Girl Scout. The doctor just got confused, is all — must have misunderstood something she said. Angie would straighten it out next time. She had been starting to like Dr. Grant, to tell the truth, and she didn't want to argue with her.

'Do you think . . . ,' Mom began awkwardly as she started the engine.

'Come on, Mom. Isn't that a bit out there? I thought we already decided that I have temporary amnesia from post-traumatic stress. That, I can believe. This multiple-personalities thing? Not.'

'Yes, well, Dr. Grant did say it wasn't exactly typical, right?'

'Sure. The book she showed me said blah-dee-blah a pattern of abuse and blah-dee-blah in infancy or early childhood. I mean, I don't have that. I had a perfectly normal childhood, right? I mean, you and Dad didn't tie me up or stuff me in a closet and torture me, right?' She laughed.

Mom tried to match her light tone and failed. Her voice squeaked. 'Of course we didn't. What a ridiculous notion. No one could love a child more than we loved — love you.'

She corrected herself quickly, but the slip was another stab in the heart. Measuring Mom's waistline, Angie wondered how long she had to get her feet back on the ground, to fix her life before the baby came and messed everything up again. She didn't ask.

★   ★   ★

Angie put her guitar away, fingertips throbbing. Aside from mirrors, nothing else reminded her so much of the obvious time gap. Chords didn't fit under her hands the same way — her longer fingers kept overshooting. And then, in spite of all the unexplained calluses on her palms, she'd lost the useful ones four years of guitar lessons had built up.

Mom's call to supper echoed up the stairs. Angie hurried down, but her feet stuck fast on the landing at the sound of raised voices. Dad's voice — no, his words — glued her in place.

'Just not the same,' he was saying. 'Look in her eyes. Something's missing. She's angry, then she's, I don't know . . . brain-dead. Flat. For God's sake, I haven't seen her cry even once.'

What did he expect? That she would sob all over him? He'd never been that kind of teddy-bear dad, and now he was so uncomfortable and distant. She'd seen more of his back than his front.

Mom's hushed reaction was too soft to hear, but Dad's response sounded loud as a megaphone. 'I don't know. Just damaged. There's no spark, no bounce in her.'

This time a few of Mom's words came through. ' . . . time to readjust . . . more if she remembers. And you know what Dr. Grant thinks . . . '

'That's bullshit, and you know it!' Angie had never heard Dad yell like that, or use that kind of language with Mom.

She thumped deliberately all the way down. Bounced hard so they had to notice. The voices stopped. She glared between her parents, who now had this strained silence to explain.

Mom whacked a spoonful of mashed potatoes onto Angie's plate. 'We were starting to discuss school again,' she said with deceptive calm. The spoon clanged on the edge of the pot.

An obvious evasion. Plus, what was left to say? They'd already had a discussion about private school, a fresh start in a new place. Sadly, out of the question. Dad crushed that hope with the excuse that with Mom working, it was too far to drive. The crease between his eyes told Angie that the truth was, after the search for her, there wasn't enough money. Sacred Heart was out for the same reason, plus they weren't Catholic. That left La Canada High School, the place where everyone knew her as the girl who disappeared. Sure, the grades seven and eight teachers and classrooms were separate from nine through twelve, but it was still a small world. Same campus. Too small.

The only remaining question was what grade. Thank God Dr. Grant backed up Angie. With everything else going on, she said, and now this possible weird diagnosis, she ought to go back to school at the level where she felt most comfortable. Also, as soon as possible before she missed any more.

'I've already decided.' Angie striped the pile of potatoes with her fork. 'I'm going to start in ninth.'

'But — ' Mom began.

Angie cut her off. 'Look, my old friends will be around, but they're juniors. I can't take classes with them. You can't expect me to, even with tutors.' Since she had been a year ahead in math, ready for Algebra I, that would put her in the regular stream for ninth. She'd always been an A student in language arts, so she wasn't afraid of skipping one year. But that was where she drew the line. Skipping more than one grade was too stressful to think about.

'I still think you'd want to be with your friends,' Mom said, a slight whine in her tone.

Dad chewed his baked pork chop and kept his opinion to himself.

Mom couldn't let it go. 'I really think being with kids your own age will help . . . will help you feel like yourself again. Your words.'

'Two days, Mom. I've been getting used to this supposedly sixteen thing for two whole days.'

Mom sighed and rested her forehead on her

hands, elbows on the table. 'Sorry. Okay. It's just strange to think you've been aging in my mind but not your own.' She gave a tight, sad laugh. 'I even lit candles on all your missed birthdays.'

'So, where are all my presents?' Angie met Mom's startled glance with the hint of a teasing smile. 'Where's that red convertible I always wanted?'

'That sounds more like my Angel,' Dad said. The worry lines on his forehead smoothed down a bit. He leaned back and loosened his tie.

Angie's newborn smile stretched into a grin. Peace restored.

She didn't entirely know why the idea of contacting her old friends filled her with terror, why she couldn't even pick up a phone. It was just so hard to jump into the middle — much easier to start over. Blending in with three hundred ninth graders who didn't know her, who had no expectations of her, sounded safer. If she caught up, she could move up.

'So we're agreed,' Angie said. 'Ninth.'

Mom nodded. Dad shrugged.

'Anyway,' Angie added, 'are you in such a hurry for me to graduate and get out of the house?'

'Absolutely not.' Mom served the green beans, and not another word was mentioned about skipping ahead.

⋆ ⋆ ⋆

Wednesday morning, she walked through the doors of La Canada High School with a backpack full of school supplies. Angie still hadn't called her old friends to tell them, to warn them. Only the school administration knew that the missing girl had been found and had re-enrolled. They were just as anxious as the Chapmans to avoid turning the school grounds into a media circus. Detective Brogan had performed a miracle, keeping the press off the scene so far.

According to Mom, the teachers had been instructed not to make a fuss of any kind. Since none of them knew her personally — she hadn't had any of them in seventh — her mysterious return wouldn't affect them anyway. She was just a curiosity, no more. So she hoped.

Somehow, she'd had this crazy notion that she could slip into school unnoticed and disappear in a sea of ninth graders. But Stacey Tompkin's punky little sister, Maggie, who was apparently in ninth grade now, recognized Angie as she squeezed into the back of first-period English. Her round green eyes kept swiveling from the whiteboard up front to gawk at Angie, as if making sure. Stacey had been on the campout, and her tagalong sister knew all the 'big girls' Stacey hung out with.

Five minutes into school and she'd already been recognized.

After class, Maggie dashed to the desk next to Angie's before she could gather up her stuff. 'You're Angie Chapman, right?' she asked breathlessly. 'You disappeared.'

Angie kept her voice low. 'Well, I'm back,'

'Yeah. I can see that,' Maggie said. 'But why

68

are you in my class?'

What was she going to say, anyway? She knew the question would come up over and over. 'I didn't go to school for three years,' she answered.

'Lucky,' Maggie said. 'I mean . . . ' She stopped with an embarrassed, stricken look on her face.

Angie took pity on her. 'Not really. Now I have to catch up. A lot.'

Maggie's face lit up. 'I know what. I'll make you copies of all my notes so far.' She grabbed Angie's arm. 'And I can come over and, like, tutor you, but just for English and history. Maybe Jessica should do math, and Alan can do science.'

She peered at the departing line of kids and yelled, 'Hey, Jess, Alan, come here. Guess what?'

Angie slipped her arm away. 'That's okay,' she began. 'I don't need . . . '

But it was too late. The two who had to be Jessica and Alan headed in their direction. Another kid behind them yelled, 'Oh my God. Is that Angie Chapman? The Gone Girl?'

Oh Lord. Angie stood helplessly as the kids who hadn't left already surrounded her. She felt an arm on her shoulder, a hand on her waist.

'I'll carry these,' a boy said, and snatched her backpack from her. 'Where are you headed next? I mean what class?'

The clump shepherded her through the hall six doors down to math. Angie disentangled herself from the two girls who'd linked her arms on either side, like Scarecrow and Tin Man

69

dragging her off to meet the Wizard. 'I think I can handle it from here, guys,' Angie said. 'Um. Thanks.'

Half the group dispersed and half stayed for math, waiting till Angie picked a desk before they surrounded her like bodyguards. Trying to plot her getaway, she didn't hear a word the teacher said, but since she had two folded notes in her hand offering to study for next Friday's test together, maybe that didn't matter.

The classroom door opened onto a mob scene. Kids were holding their phones, supposedly off-limits during school, reading the screens. They looked up as the math class spilled out. She heard her name cut through the hubbub, spoken high and low. Everyone must know by now. The buzz of the excited mob was deafening.

She grabbed Maggie. 'Get me to the bathroom,' she hissed in her ear.

Maggie raised her voice. 'Make way. Coming through.' She elbowed their way through to the girls' room door.

Oh God, Angie prayed. Please don't let every day be like this.

At the end of the day, all she wanted to do was get home and shower off all the handprints, throw her clothes in the wash, and listen to silence for a while. She was hurrying for the bus with an armload of books in front and her backpack bouncing against her spine when she heard Livvie's unmistakable voice closing in on her from behind.

'Hey, you. New girl. Slow down.'

She walked faster, a nervous feeling in the pit

of her stomach. She'd only had to deal with ninth graders so far. What would her old friends think?

'Hey, wait up,' a deeper voice called. Heavy footsteps followed her at a run. A hand stopped her at the shoulder. 'Hey, you dropped — holy crap,' he said, catching sight of her face. 'Oh my God, you look so much like someone I used to know. Whoa.'

Angie grabbed the ninth-grade vocabulary workbook in Greg's outstretched hand. She would have recognized him anywhere, anytime. His black-lashed eyes hadn't changed, nor his thick wavy Italian hair. But he'd sure grown up from his thirteen-year-old self. In the most amazing . . .

He'd already turned to yell back to Livvie. 'Hey, Liv. Check it out. Who does she remind you of?' Back to Angie. 'What's your name, anyway?'

Angie's mouth opened, but nothing came out. Livvie jerked to a halt, staring at her. All the color drained from her cheeks. She reached a hand forward and lifted Angie's long hair back from her face. Angie stood frozen in place as Liv traced the pale scar line under her chin from the time they'd been practicing spin jumps into the pool. Liv whispered. 'Oh my freaking . . . no way. Are you for real?'

Angie bit her lip and nodded. She couldn't breathe.

Livvie squealed. 'Oh my God, oh my God. Gregory, you idiot. It is Angie. Back from the dead, or what?' She wrapped her arms around

71

Angie and threatened to break a rib with her python-strength hug. 'You didn't call . . . How long . . . ? Where . . . ? Oh, shit, there's too much I want to know all at once. Tell me, now. Now! Now! I insist!'

Breath exploded out of Angie, breath she didn't know she'd been holding. 'Livvie!' She squeezed back. Her cheeks burst with grinning, the first completely happy moment she'd had. Mom was right. She should have called.

Greg gaped and gulped like an air-drowning fish. 'You . . . but . . . holy crap.'

His arms joined the group hug, long enough to wrap them both. 'Un-freakin-believable.'

Angie leaned against him, immersed in his warmth. Wow, he'd grown. His heart was racing right under her ear — almost as fast as hers. As a thirteen-year-old mini-stud, he'd been hot, no doubt. As a sixteen-year-old dark-eyed hunk, he was scorching.

His hand rested on her waist now, but she didn't mind. Not at all. His eyes took all of her in. 'We thought you were for sure dead. Everyone thought so. You vanished!'

'Well. I'm back.' Angie found it hard to catch her breath, impossible to explain.

'I . . . we all lit candles for you.' His forehead creased.

'It was so beautiful,' Livvie said. 'You would have loved it. I mean, if you could've been there.'

Greg broke up in hoots of laughter. 'If she'd been there? Liv, think about it.' He shook his head, smiled wide, and wagged his finger at Angie. 'You know, you stood me up for homecoming, which I knew you would never, never do unless you were really dead. I believe you owe me an apology.' He moved his finger to lift her chin. 'Care to apologize and explain?'

A happy giggle escaped her lips. 'I'm sorry. And yes, I'll explain as much as I can.' She noticed a couple of heads turned their way, studying her with curiosity. They began to move — her gravity field was drawing them in again. 'Not here. Somewhere private.'

'Chah,' Liv agreed. 'Greg's house. It's walking distance from here. We can be private and you can tell all!'

Greg put an arm around each of their shoulders. Angie's heart raced through the roof. It was like no time had passed for them either. All still friends. And the way Greg's fingers casually twisted through her hair, maybe he still felt the way she did. A low, laughing voice in her head said, *Don't worry, honey. We know how to find out, don't we?*

She snorted in surprise.

'What?' Greg asked. 'Share the joke.'

'Sorry, a fly flew up my nose,' she lied. 'Hey, where's Katie? What's up with her?'

Liv's answer was completely unexpected. 'Kate? Yuck. We don't hang with her anymore. She's, like, so immature, such a prude. We were having this bonfire last fall, and Kurt's older brother got us a keg and she told.'

'Told who?'

'Her parents, the cops, the school. It was grievous. Kurt got three days' suspension since he was hosting.'

An immediate sense of panic flooded her. 'What? You can't tell on your friends! That's so completely wrong. She'll burn in hell.' Angie was startled by the urgency and fear in her own voice. Hell? She didn't even believe in Hell. Where had that come from?

Greg laughed. 'Well, she got burned, all right. No one talks to her anymore. She's lower than the outcasts.'

A fate worse than death in high school. Poor Kate, Angie thought. But she did it to herself. Telling. Didn't she realize?

The sky hung overcast above them, and the breeze picked up — not a hot Santa Ana wind, but a preview of cooler weather. Angie shivered in her thin brown sweater — she hadn't thought to buy a new jacket during her shopping spree. Greg pulled her closer under his arm, which totally made it worth freezing all the way to his house. He kept turning his head to look at her. She could feel his glance on her cheek, which was most certainly blushing.

Greg unlocked the front door and sent the girls into the kitchen. 'Grab whatever you want to eat,' he said. 'I have to make sure the coast is clear.' He disappeared.

'He's shoving his dirty clothes under the bed,' Livvie explained. 'He's a total slob at home.' She stuck her head in the fridge and held out a can. 'Want a Diet Coke?'

Angie accepted. 'Thanks. It is so great to be with you guys again. You have no idea what kind of day I've had. Mobbed, flocked all day. Totally crazy.'

'I hear ya. Want some rum in it?' Liv asked. 'I know where they keep it.' She grabbed two more cans and closed the door with her knee.

Angie was shocked. That was a change — the Liv she knew was a responsible straight-A student. But she said only, 'No thanks. I've got a ton of homework. First day back, you know.'

'I know!' Livvie squealed. She rested her Coke-filled hands on Angie's shoulders. Liv used to peer down at her from five-four. Now they were eye to eye. 'But back from where, my mystery girl?'

'Still a mystery.' In a dramatic, confiding voice, Angie added, 'Total amnesia.'

'You're kidding me. No, really. Where were you? Follow me.' Liv headed to what had to be Greg's room. 'Was this, like, a reality-TV-stunt thing? Do you have a hidden camera on you? Because my butt's not my best side.' She turned and grinned over her shoulder at Angie. Okay, that was more like Liv.

Greg's room had that hastily cleaned-up look. The chair teetered with books and papers. The floor sported a couple of candy bar wrappers next to the trash can. The hunter-green plaid comforter hung crookedly on the low queen-sized bed. Greg sprawled up against the black bolster pillows along the wall, shoes off. Livvie handed him the two cans, slipped out of her flats, stepped into the middle of the bed, and sat pretzel-style. Angie copied her, careful not to spill her drink.

Greg took a large gulp and burped. He frowned. 'But why is the rum gone?' he said in a slurry British accent.

Liv cackled. Angie didn't get it.

'Pirates,' Liv explained at Angie's blank look. 'Jack Sparrow?'

Angie shook her head helplessly. 'What?'

'The mo-vie,' Livvie said as to a four-year-old. '*Pirates of the Caribbean.*'

'Oh. I've never seen it,' Angie said. 'Is it good?'

'Never seen it?' Greg exclaimed. 'Have you been living under a rock?'

Livvie glared and smacked him. 'Greg, you total jerk.' She wrapped a possessive arm around Angie. 'A little sensitivity, please?'

'Probably,' Angie replied to him. 'Total amnesia.' She'd decided the two-word answer would cover a lot of ground.

'No way,' Greg said, his dark eyes big and round. 'That's totally cool. I mean, you could have been anything, anywhere.'

'Abducted by aliens,' Livvie said.

'Living in a tree house, or a castle!' Greg suggested.

Livvie squeezed her arm. 'When you never came back to the tent that morning, I was the one who had to go wake up the grown-ups and tell them. I was completely freaked out. You know?'

Livvie was freaked. How long had she waited to tell? Could they have found her faster? That was a terrible, terrible thought. Angie pushed it far from her mind.

Greg had a mischievous sparkle in his eyes. He bonked her gently on the head with his palm. 'Did that help? Maybe we can cure you. Hey, what's the last thing you remember?'

Angie wracked her brains. 'Saying 'total amnesia.''

Greg punched her lightly in the arm. 'Before that.'

'Nothing,' Angie said.

'That is not an acceptable answer,' Liv chided. 'You remembered us.'

Angie sighed. 'Here's the whole story, as much as I know. Girl Scout camp. Woke up early. Talked to Liv. Remember? Snuck out to use the tree. Got lost in the woods. Three years go by. Presumed dead. Showed up in the neighborhood. Here I am . . . Not terribly dramatic, is it?'

'I, for one, am disappointed,' Liv said with a pout. 'I expected a juicier tale of abduction and debauchery.'

'What's debauchery?' Angie asked.

'No, seriously,' Liv said. 'Do you think it was something awful? Like you were a slave or a harem girl?'

Angie's thoughts flew to the scars hiding under her socks. 'I . . . no. I don't remember.' Too serious. Change up. 'Sure. Like this could be the body of a harem girl.' She drew exaggerated swells with her hands where she had these new curves and slim hips.

Greg's eyes followed her hands. His smile wasn't mocking, though. Something else. 'Hang on,' he said. 'Maybe you *are* dead. I mean, maybe you're a ghost. Let's check.' He reached over and tickled her.

Well, one thing hadn't changed. She was still

incredibly ticklish. She collapsed in giggles, nerves on fire all up and down her sides.

Greg was relentless, his fingertips everywhere. 'We're the only ones who can see you, and you came back to haunt us because you have unfinished business on earth.'

Liv grabbed his hands away. 'Let the poor ghost breathe,' she said tartly. 'Anyway, she looks solid to me.'

'Then a zombie!' Greg announced. His hand slowly traced the writing stitched across the chest level of Angie's sweater, and she pinged deep inside. 'An Aberzombie!' He rolled over with his head in her lap. 'Don't eat me, Angie. Don't eat my brain,' he pleaded. His curls tickled her arms. She suddenly wanted to lean over and kiss him, but not with Liv looking on.

Liv pursed her lips. 'Don't be ridiculous, Greg. You're being ridiculous.'

A phone rang, and Livvie grabbed it out of her pocket. 'What, Mom?' she snapped. 'Shi — ooot. Be right there.' She scowled. 'Forgot I'm babysitting. Hey, Angie, I'll give you a ride home. The school bus is way gone.'

Angie met Greg's eyes. His face said what she was thinking. Unfinished business. 'That's okay. I can wa — '

'I'll drive her,' Greg jumped in. 'No big. You're already late.'

Liv snatched up her book bag and jammed it on her shoulder. She hesitated at the doorway. 'So, bye then,' she said. 'Call me, Ange. As soon as you're home.' She waved her phone in the air. 'Same number. Remember it?'

Of course. She'd only called it a million times. 'Forever,' she said.

'Then maybe the rest will come back. So yeah. Call.' Liv lingered another moment, glowering at Greg, before she whirled and left. A moment later, the front door slammed.

The air felt thinner as soon as she was gone. Angie took a deep breath.

Greg relaxed back against the pillows, his fingers woven behind his head. His legs stretched out in front of him, his feet huge and hairy. In a good way.

'Is it true?' he asked. 'What you said? Or did you just not want to tell Livvie? I wouldn't blame you. She's such a loose lips.'

Angie felt like she should defend Livvie — she never spilled other people's secrets — but then again, Liv might have changed there, too. 'No. It's really true. I have this giant mental block. But I have a psychologist helping me with it.' The whole medical evidence thing, the words and phrases she'd overheard, she didn't want to think about. Definitely didn't want to share.

'Well, you look great,' he said. 'It can't have been too awful.'

Look great? It wasn't the first compliment on her new appearance, but it was the most meaningful, coming from him. Maybe she could learn to like her big eyes and narrow cheeks.

'I love your hair this way,' he said, stroking it all the way down the back of her head and halfway down her back. 'It's like honey pouring.'

She'd never cut it!

His fingers pressed against her back, bringing

her just an inch closer to him. 'C'mere,' he said. 'I missed you. I missed you so much. God, we were all so sad. It was awful wondering . . . and wondering. At eighth grade graduation, you know, they rang the bell for you, thirteen times. I felt like they were ringing you out of existence.'

His eyes were sad and faraway. 'I didn't want to believe it.' He twisted a strand of her hair between his fingers. 'And now, here you are.'

Angie ached to hold him, comfort him, close the distance. She wasn't sure what to do.

But someone knew. You just needed a little help, Angie, and I knew who to send. The ache ran down from your heart, through your belly, and lower. It shivered you. With a little push from us, you shifted and straddled his thighs, put your arms around Greg's neck, and opened his mouth with your tongue. He devoured you, like a sweet candy, kisses and more kisses. Closer and closer you pressed while the hot shivering took you out of your mind. She moved your hands for you, knowing the way to show how much you loved him.

Then he broke the slow spell. 'Angie.' He said your name, first as a sigh. Then, 'Angie.' It was louder, harsher. And you popped up, scared and embarrassed. Your eyes opened, and the face you saw wasn't the sweet boy in the lazy river you remembered. Cheeks flushed, pupils huge, sweaty brow. 'Angie, I can't,' he said. 'I'm sorry. But it's like, me and Liv? We're — '

You leaped off the bed, stared at your hands like they didn't belong to you. Which was true, in a way. They had a mind of their own. So to speak.

5

INVITATION

'They're trying to take over my life, Dr. Grant,' Angie complained. She had moved to the sofa, figuring that sitting on the desk again would look like an act of defiance. And she didn't want to be defiant. She wanted help.

The doctor was wearing a pale blue sweater set today. It set off her eyes, a matching robin's-egg blue. Carefully tweezed eyebrows rose at Angie's outburst.

'Your parents? The other kids at school?'

'Well, yes, them too. No, the . . . the personalities. The alters?'

Only a tiny twitch of her head betrayed the doctor's emotional reaction. 'So now you are aware of their presence? At our first meeting, you weren't so sure.'

The power of those brilliant eyes compelled honest gut-spilling — a good feature for a psychologist, Angie thought. 'Well, yes. At our first meeting I was in denial. Right? I thought I was just spacing out during the fuzzy dropped time. You know, when it was just seconds here and there — I could make excuses to other people, and to myself.' She forced herself not to break the eye contact. 'I mean, everyone tunes out occasionally. Right?'

'Of course.' Dr. Grant slow-blinked, a subtle nod. Go on.

'But now much weirder things are happening. Things that make me think you . . . you may be right.'

'Such as what?' the doctor asked in a level voice. Calm, interested.

Obviously, Dr. Grant didn't find any of this strange. Multiple personalities. Dissociated identities. Splintered consciousness.

If it weren't happening to her personally and screwing up her life, Angie would have found it fascinating. However, under the circumstances, the idea that her body was saying and doing things she couldn't control — things she didn't even know about — terrified her. Humiliating herself with Greg was the worst so far. She still didn't know what exactly had happened, and she wasn't about to ask. It was worse than humiliating. Whatever she'd done was so off-base, he told her to leave. Ugh. It made her blush all over again to think about it.

She'd dodged Greg and Liv for two days now, hiding deep in the ninth-grade pack for camouflage. And that wasn't too hard. They stuck to her like Velcro from the beginning to the end of the day. Which was getting incredibly tiresome. When would her novelty wear off?

'Angela?' The doctor broke into her thoughts. 'Are you still with me? Or am I in the presence of another?'

'Oh, sorry. Yeah. It's just me.' She offered a halfhearted smile. 'No one more exciting.'

The doctor gave her an encouraging pat on

the arm. 'You were going to tell me of the weird things that led you to believe you may be experiencing DID.'

Angie rolled her eyes. 'Yeah. Example One: Someone dusted my room and folded my clothes while I was asleep.'

'Your mother?' the doctor suggested.

'Nope. I asked her.'

'Hmm.'

'Example Two: Someone keeps moving my rocking chair. Not me. Not Mom.'

'And that's disturbing because . . . '

'She sits in it and rocks for hours. There are new lines and footprints in the carpet every morning.' Angie raised three fingers and continued. 'Example Three: I went to bed early the other night because I was exhausted, probably from all the stupid rocking, and when I woke up in the morning, someone had done my math homework.'

'How . . . industrious,' Dr. Grant commented.

'Her handwriting sucked, and she got half the questions wrong. Not helpful.'

'Ahh.' The doctor tugged the sleeves of her cardigan and smoothed them. 'Perhaps the alter believed he or she was being helpful. After all, your mind created them as protectors. The instinct to protect is still in there' — she pointed to Angie's temple — 'though we believe you are out of physical danger.'

'Hold up a second. He?' Angie blinked hard. 'I thought you said she was a Girl Scout. You think there's a guy in my head?'

The faintest hint of a smile lifted Dr. Grant's

lips. 'It's okay, Angie. We don't know one way or the other yet. But generally speaking, alternate personalities can take on either sex and any age,' she explained. 'Whatever is appropriate to their role. Suppose you needed a big, tough guy to stand up to heavy beatings?' She flexed her arm muscles to demonstrate. In the blue fuzzy sweater, the effect was lost. 'It would be possible even for a small girl like you to have a big, tough guy alter.'

'In-ter-est-ing,' Angie said. 'He'd feel kind of lame in my clothes, though.'

That earned her an honest laugh. 'Sometimes people discover alternate wardrobes in their belongings, representing the tastes of their alters.'

A lightbulb went off. 'So that explains it!'

'Yes?'

Angie blushed. 'When I changed for gym yesterday, I nearly died. I was wearing ho underwear. I don't own that kind of thing.'

The doctor's eyebrows twitched only slightly as she asked, 'How do you define 'ho underwear'?'

'It was all black and lacy and slutty,' she whispered. 'Like a thong. I sure didn't buy it, and I know Mom didn't buy it for me.'

'So, you worry that these alters are choosing clothes for you and taking on some of your chores and homework, perhaps rocking in the night when you would rather be in bed. Would it help if you understood their motivations?'

'It would help if they would cut it out. How do I make it stop?'

Dr. Grant rested her chin in her hands, leaning close to Angie. 'That will require communication and negotiation. You're reclaiming your position as dominant and they're naturally resisting.'

'Oh my God. You make them sound like real people.'

The doctor nodded. She rolled her pearl choker absent-mindedly with her left hand. 'Angie. This is something you absolutely must realize. They *are* people, sharing your brain space, mapped into different neurons in your brain. They have a physical reality. They aren't figments of your imagination. You share some things, like a body, a pair of parents, et cetera. But your traits and desires might be worlds apart.'

Angie was silent, thinking about the word 'desires.'

Dr. Grant waited patiently. 'What are you thinking?' she asked after a long minute.

Angie concentrated on the pattern of light filtering through the loose woven curtains. 'I'm afraid they're going to get me into trouble. I had . . . an incident. You won't tell my mom any of this, right?'

The doctor made the gesture of locking her lips and throwing away the key. 'You, Angie, are my patient. Not your parents.'

She took a deep breath. Confession was good for the soul. Souls. Right? 'Okay. Besides suspecting that the ho-wear is probably shoplifted, which is bad enough, I have a problem with a guy.'

'Oh dear. Unwelcome advances?' Dr. Grant asked.

'You could say that.' This was so embarrassing. 'But not by him. By me. Part of me, like, attacked him. I, um, got physical in a way that's completely NOT ME.' She couldn't help raising her voice. Then she whispered, 'Can they hear me? The alters?'

'Can you hear them?' the doctor reflected back.

Angie sighed. 'Only a couple of times, I thought maybe I heard a voice and no one was around, but I figured it was just my imagination. How does that work?'

'It's absolutely fascinating,' Dr. Grant replied, her blue eyes shining with the enthusiasm of an expert. 'In the memory centers of your brain, different sets of neurons hold the separate memory patterns of the alters, however many there are.'

'However many?' Angie gasped under her breath, but the doctor went on.

'The connections between them are few or nonexistent, which is how the alters can keep their secrets from you, the dominant Angie, and from one another. When you hear their voices, the speech centers of your brain are activated just as though you were hearing them from outside yourself. We've seen all this with functional MRI studies and PET scans.'

Angie felt the dismay on her own face.

Dr. Grant frowned. 'Does it help you to understand this? The science, I mean?'

'I suppose so.' Not really. She'd read a bunch

87

of websites, a bunch of threads. It all seemed so weird and unlikely when other people talked about their own experiences. But it was real. It was her reality. Her life. And currently she was time-sharing it with someone who liked to shoplift sexy underwear.

'Do you have questions?'

'Only a million,' Angie said. 'But the most important one is how to fix it. I don't want to blank out. I don't want to find strange clothes in my drawers or on my body. I don't want to do humiliating things. I want my life back. I want to be in charge.'

'I understand. Of course you do. You want to control the gate, and that's only natural.'

'What gate?'

'It's typical to have a personality who stands aside, stays inside, observing and recording and deciding who needs to come out in different situations — a gatekeeper. Like a boss who stays in the home office and decides who gets to go out on the road.'

'Great. How do I get that job?' Angie asked. 'So I can lock the damn gate.'

'Therapy, my dear.' Dr. Grant put down her notepad and folded her hands in her lap.

'So talk to her. Tell her it's time to retire. Time for a new boss.'

'I wish it worked that way, Angie. But gatekeepers are recluses. She'll never interact with us directly, but she's listening and remembering and directing traffic all the same.'

'She's watching? Listening?'

'I believe so,' Dr. Grant said with a tight smile.

'That's insanely creepy.'

'I can see why you'd feel that way. But remember, she pushed you out here again, to face the world. She has only your best interests at heart, and she thinks you're ready.'

'Fabulous.' All of a sudden she wasn't so sure. 'Am I?'

'That's why we're here, my dear. We're working on it, together.'

'All of us?' Angie muttered. She framed her words with finger quotes.

Dr. Grant's smile loosened, and she picked up her pen. 'Angie, how old are you now?'

'Thir — Four — Shoot, I don't know. Technically sixteen.'

'What do you imagine happened to you during the three years you can't remember? What do you . . . guess?'

Angie's eyes moved to the silver ring with its weird inscription. What did it say again? Something important. She felt a thick fog descend in her mind the more she concentrated on remembering. She rolled it around her finger to ease it over her knuckle, but her left hand pulled away. She tried again, and her left hand dodged her attempts. 'Did you see that? Doctor, did you see that?' she said with rising panic. 'It's like I'm possessed! You have to help me. Please.'

Dr. Grant caught her left arm by the wrist. 'We are not going to take the ring,' she said clearly.

Angie's hands settled on her lap, but her heart still pounded.

'Someone is very frightened of the story

coming out,' Dr. Grant said softly. She stared deep into Angie's eyes, to the inside of her head. 'But someone needs to know that you want to communicate. That it hurts you to be outside of the group.'

She swayed toward and away from Angie, holding her gaze. Keeping the eyes in focus made Angie dizzy, and she began to sway in unison.

The doctor spoke so quietly, murmuring soft words. Angie's ears rang with straining to hear. 'Someone needs to speak for the others, to let me help you help Angie. I invite someone to step out again, please. We need to talk. Angie can wait nearby.'

Angie rocked forward and backward, her eyes trained on the brilliant blue light of the doctor's irises, which got farther and farther away, until they merged into a single dot in the black sky. Still, her eyes stayed fixed on that pinprick of light. Beneath her, the rocking chair creaked slightly on the loose slats of the porch. Porch? Yes, there was a porch. She couldn't see it, just knew that's where she sat, on a wooden front porch. Déjà vu grabbed her — she'd been here before. For a long, long time. Behind her was an old gray cabin, cobwebs in the windows, rust on the nails. She rocked, looking forward. She couldn't see the cabin, but she knew it was behind her. She felt the weather-beaten, loose boards of the cabin invisible behind her.

And the tiny blue dot blinked once, and Angie knew that the porch rocker beside her was empty. Someone had been there, rocking like she was. But the chair was empty now, just finishing the last of its back-and-forth motion. A khaki Girl Scout sash hung over the arm. Angie couldn't see it in the night, but she knew it was there, a khaki sash, a needle and thread, left behind by the person who had left the porch. In her peripheral vision, there were still blacker places in the dark, silhouettes of more rockers and more girls rocking. A busy, quiet place, this old porch.

Behind her, a hole in the cabin. No, a doorway. Someone stood in the doorway, the door closed tight behind her, and watched and listened. A hand reached forward and pushed the back of Angie's seat. 'Go back,' a strong voice said. Angie tipped forward and fell into the blue gleam; it tugged with unworldly gravity until azure light shone everywhere. She blinked hard against the glare. Dr. Grant's face came into focus, the rest of the office dropping into place behind her. The light shrank down to the size of two blue irises watching her with a soft, compassionate expression.

At last, Angie found her voice. 'Did — did I pass out?'

The doctor shook her head. 'No. You do hypnotize quite readily. That will be a great help in our work.'

Angie spun with dizziness. 'So what happened? What did I say?'

Dr. Grant tilted her head. The effect was birdlike. 'Not you, my dear. Girl Scout spoke with me again. I know this will sound odd, Angie, but she asked me not to share our

91

discussion. She wants to tell you herself, but you won't let her. Apparently the wall between you is too thick for her to break through yet. I invited her to find a way. She wants you to hear her story first before the others.'

'Oh God,' Angie said. 'Others? That's so, so weird. How many? Did she say?'

'She named several.'

Angie's stomach hurt. 'How many is several?'

'She mentioned three, besides herself.'

'Four! Oh God. I'm a complete mess.' Her head sank into her hands, and the backs of her eyes prickled, but tears wouldn't come. 'What do I do? How do I get better?' She felt Dr. Grant's arm move to rest across her shoulders, offering warmth and acceptance.

'Watch and listen for messages. Be open. That's all you can do for right now. We need to move much further along the road of discovery before we can talk about recovery.'

'But I can? Recover?' Angie grasped at the word like an under-seat flotation device.

'Oh, certainly,' the doctor said. 'You'll have several options, but not yet. For now, listen to your inner voices. They may be trying to reach you directly, Angela.'

★ ★ ★

'How'd it go today?' Mom asked as she tucked Angie in and kissed her good night. It was a new ritual she was probably too old for, but she liked it all the same. Mom smoothed her hair. 'Any breakthroughs?'

92

Great. Mom wanted an instant cure, and Angie had just discovered her issues were even more incredible than they imagined. She shook her head. 'More like digging the hole deeper. And I'm at the bottom.' She raised her hands theatrically. 'Someone, throw me a rope! Please!' Maybe someone would hear and take pity on her.

Mom kissed the tip of her nose. 'I'll go to the hardware store. Get a good long one.'

'Ha. Pick up a ladder while you're at it.' Angie rolled on her side and stared at the slash of moonlight where her curtains didn't entirely meet. Mom clicked off the bedside lamp and tiptoed out.

⋆　⋆　⋆

Angie woke early and stiff, curled up in her rocking chair. The reading light was on, and the fuzzy blanket was tucked around her shoulders. Had she fallen asleep reading? Wait, she'd fallen asleep in bed, watching the moon cross a sliver of sky. That much she remembered.

Her journal lay under the rocker tread. Very strange. She hadn't touched it since her return — it belonged to the past. The twisted metal of the lock left it open to curious eyes, anyway. As she bent to retrieve it, her neck was one giant cramp.

The open page was covered with tiny, neat handwriting — not her curly, flowing style. She squinted at — it was a letter, addressed to her.

Breath caught in her throat. Her stomach

rolled in nervous anticipation. She stretched her neck side to side and started reading.

Dear Angie,

My name is Girl Scout. I wish we could talk. There's so much good stuff I could tell you about if you'd let me. You wouldn't believe how much I learned how to do while you were out.

First of all, I'm the reason our arms are so strong. You can thank me for that. Carrying water, splitting firewood — they build a lot of muscle.

See, when the man first took you to his home (well, you were actually already gone into hiding by then, so I guess he was taking me), he was very calm and reasonable. Sure, he did attach my legs with those heavy cuffs, because he didn't trust me not to run away. I would have back then, you know, before I realized how much I depended on him and he depended on me. It took me a long time to win his trust about unlocking me. That wasn't till he knew I wasn't going to leave him.

Anyway, when he first took me, I was shaking. I didn't know how to get back to camp if I could get away, and we'd walked for a long, long time in the woods. I lost my sense of direction, even looking at the mossy side of the trees. Plus, they were so thick and close, I didn't see our cabin till we were right there.

So he sat me down at an old, chipped Formica table with a brown ceramic pitcher in the middle and explained about how he was never very good at courting, and what he really needed was a wife, and how lucky I was he picked me out of all the other girl Scouts. He knew he wanted a girl Scout wife, he said, because we know all sorts of skills, like fire-building, and cooking, and sewing, that sort of thing. That's what he wanted, he said. A Girl Scout who could build the fire in the cabin stove (because there was no electricity) and cook for him.

I explained very politely that he had picked the wrong girl. I couldn't cook anything that didn't come in a box with 'just add water' instructions on the back. I really thought he would realize his mistake and let me go. Like I said, he seemed very calm and reasonable, apart from the shackles with chains that ran from my feet to the legs of the cast-iron stove. He said I had a week to learn, and he handed me an old cookbook, which he said was his mother's.

'You know how to light an oil lamp?' he asked me, and he showed me how to trim the wick and light it. 'Now be real careful,' he told me. 'You knock over a burning lamp and you'll burn up with my house.' He had a smile that nailed me to my chair.

You know how scared we all are of fire. Oh. Maybe you don't, but that's something all the girls have in common. It only makes sense when you live in a wood cabin that you can't ever leave.

I asked about a fire extinguisher, and he patted me on the head and said something about 'Always be prepared,' which is the Boy Scout motto, as you well know, not ours. Anyway, he didn't have one and he didn't plan to get one. 'Just be careful,' he warned me.

If you'd been there, well, you would have been as confused as I was. No running water, no refrigerator, no electricity, and he wanted a housekeeper? He told me then he was going to work, and I was to be a good girl and have dinner ready when he came back.

'When will that be?' I asked. I had to know how long I had to escape. Yeah, I actually thought that first day that I could escape. Can you believe it?

He pointed to an old windup clock on the wall with two heavy weights hanging from it and a key sticking out of the winder. 'Seven. There's some salt pork in the barrel in the pantry. You should be able to reach it okay. I measured the chains.'

'What's your name?' he finally asked.

At first, I didn't know whether to tell him your name. But then I thought, it would be good if he accidentally mentioned it to someone, because they should be looking for you already. So I told him Angela.

Then he pocketed the key to my leg shackles, kissed me on the cheek, said, 'Don't let the fire go out. Have a nice day, Angela,' and left.

I never heard an engine start. I didn't know how he came and went.

His kiss was drying on my cheek, and I thought, 'Wow, I'm in the hands of a madman.' So I started looking for a way out. The body of the cast-iron stove was already hot, but I grabbed at the feet and tried to lift one to slide off the restraints. I might as well have tried to lift an elephant. Not a hint of budging. I was hot and sweaty by the time I gave up on that; my hands were burn-blistered from trying to get a better grip on the stove. You can imagine.

So I thought, with all that sweat, maybe I could slide my feet out at the other end. They were pretty bloody by the time I gave up on that. I thought about smashing them flatter with the iron skillet (Girl Scouts are always resourceful), but I knew even if I didn't pass out from the pain, I'd never get far on my knees in the woods. I'd bet anything he was a good tracker, and he'd have me back here in no time.

So I sat at that cracked table and cried for a long while. Then I screamed for help till my throat felt bloody inside. Sorry to depress you with the details, but I wanted you to know that right at the start, I tried everything I could think of to get myself loose. I don't want you to blame me for not trying.

I had about ten feet of length in every direction from the stove, and that was enough for me to either walk through or see the whole two-room cabin. Gray wood walls. Two rooms. No bathroom, just a chamber pot with pink roses on it. No running water. Next to the stove on one side was a cradle full of split wood that I was supposed to use to keep the fire alive. On the other side was a narrow door, which opened into the pantry. I found the salted pork in a barrel. Sure enough — it was full of salt. Ceramic crocks on the shelves were filled with oats and rice and different beans. The few spice jars had faded labels. I smelled them, but not being a cook back then, I had no clue what they were. And besides that meager collection of ingredients, all I had to work with was a huge bag of flour and another bag of sugar.

I hefted the iron pan, wondering if I could swing it fast enough to be a weapon. I worked that scene out in my head over and over, but it always ended up with me lying in a pool of blood with my head smashed, so I gave it up. No knives in sight, not even in the jar of silverware. I didn't think I could fork him to death, not fast enough, anyway.

Not to depress or worry you, but I did consider breaking one of the ceramic crocks and using the sharp edge to off myself quickly before he could get home. I kind of liked the idea of cheating him that way, but I couldn't do that to you, Angie. I would protect you, but not that way. So I cried while the shadows got longer. Then I lit the oil lamps, opened the cookbook, and started reading. The clock hands were moving faster and faster toward seven.

Through the back door, I saw a well pump handle. I shuffled toward it and stopped short, wrenched back by the metal cuffs scraping the fresh scabs off my ankles. What was I supposed to do for water?

Lucky for me that first day, the pitcher on the kitchen table was filled to the top with water, otherwise I never could have made a small pork and bean stew and a pile of rice. I didn't dare waste any water rinsing the salt pork like the recipe book said I was supposed to.

When the man came in, he looked happy and excited. He rubbed his hands, kissed my cheek again. He pulled out a chair for me and sat me down. 'How was your day, dear Angela?' he asked me.

'Busy,' I said carefully, and he chuckled.

His face turned soft and round. 'Mine too. Crazy day at the office.'

It was completely surreal, like we were a couple on an old TV show.

He tried to pour water into the two tin cups I had put on the table, but of course, the pitcher was empty. He thumped it with a loud clatter and hurled my cup across the room. A fury possessed him, and I saw my first hint of the demon inside. He pushed back from the table, his face dark and thundery. 'Angela, I'm terribly disappointed. This table is not properly set.' He smacked his fist on the table, and his spoon flew off the edge. He walked toward me, his fist still clenched.

'I'm so sorry,' I said quickly, dropping my eyes to my lap. 'I couldn't get to the well. It's too far.' I gestured helplessly at the chains.

His face changed in less than a second. An entirely new mood. 'Oh, my poor dear. All my fault. I wasn't thinking.' He dropped to his knees next to my chair and tilted my chin back up. I held as still as a rabbit. He watched my eyes and I let nothing out, nothing at all.

Then he noticed the scabs on my ankles. He brushed them with his fingertips, and I held my frozen position. 'Your poor, poor legs. You must have tried so hard to reach the water. What a good girl you are. I'll bandage them for you after supper.'

While I sat and shook, he went out to the well and pumped another cold pitcher of water. He filled my cup and presented it to me with a gracious smile, watched me drain every precious drop, and refilled it. He dipped a spoon into the salty stew and tasted it, his eyes growing round with pleasure. He raised his cup. 'To you, my dear little wife,' he said.

I don't know what would have happened to me that first night if I didn't have two bowls filled with a delicious dinner. I'm fairly sure it saved my life, so that's good.

I knew perfectly well I wasn't his wife. You don't marry someone by stealing them and locking them in, and if he wanted a little wife, she wasn't going *to be me. Someone else could take that job.*

Someone else did. She can tell you about it. I wasn't there. I refused.

Anyway, the next morning, after the man was gone, I started making a knife out of an old spoon handle. There were nine spoons, one mismatched, and I hoped he wouldn't miss it. I thought maybe the new girl, the Little wife, could use it at night while he was asleep. But by the time it was sharp enough, she wouldn't take it, and I couldn't use it either. Not on myself. Not on him. So I concentrated on staying alive instead.

Yours truly,
Girl Scout

Angie let the journal slide from her fingers. So that was the alter Dr. Grant had met the first time, the one who worried about her. So cheerful, so can-do, at least the way she showed herself here to Angie. Smash her feet with a pan? Fork him to death?

If she was the one rocking in the night, well, it was hard to be mad at her. She was trying to reach Angie the only way she knew how. Her letter — what a great idea! — there was a lot of information . . . and a lot that was left out. Angie wondered whether to show the journal to her parents, to Dr. Grant, to Detective Brogan. There wasn't much in the way of specifics that would help the investigation — no name of 'the man,' only a loose description of place — a two-room cabin without electricity or water, a hint that maybe he worked in an office, which seemed unlikely. Crazed kidnappers didn't work in offices, did they?

But what it did tell her was how she might have lived for the last three years. She was confined inside except for heavy chores; she was cast in this weird role of thirteen-year-old housewife and had to play it to perfection; she had to please this man teetering on the edge of sanity. Except, that wasn't how *she* had lived — it was how this Girl Scout had lived for her. Reading the letter sparked nothing in the way of her own memory or emotion. The story was like hearing about something that happened to the friend of a friend of a friend. Would she ever remember it for herself? Did she actually want to?

6

REPRESSION

Angie sat on the bed and tried to straighten the twisted metal of the broken lock. She sure couldn't show Girl Scout's journal to Dad. He'd go ballistic or comatose, hard to know which. But maybe Mom. It seemed like she wanted to help, more than just by driving Angie to appointments. And Angie knew how much Mom loved her, even if things were really awkward. Would she love Girl Scout? Or the others when Angie made contact with them? Maybe she should give Mom the chance to understand.

'Hey, Mom?' she called. No answer. She scooted downstairs to the kitchen. The lights were off, and it didn't smell like breakfast cooking. 'Mom?' she called as she entered. No one was there. She dashed back up the stairs to Mom and Dad's room. She tapped the unlatched door. 'Mom? Are you in there?' The bedroom door swung inward.

'She's at the grocery store,' Dad yelled from his den. 'Getting ready for Ma and Bill.'

'Okay. Thanks,' Angie hollered back. She was reaching for the knob to relatch the door when she noticed an oversized brown leather notebook on the bedside table. Mom's side. Interesting.

Peeking back over her shoulder, she slipped

into the room and picked up the notebook — actually a scrapbook, she realized. Mom loved scrapbooking. Maybe this would give Angie an idea of what they'd been up to for three years — the vacations she'd missed, whatever.

She grasped the cover and hesitated. What if this was actually Mom's diary? A guilty feeling snuck down her spine. She shook it off. Mom had broken into *her* journal, after all. Fair's fair. She eased the door closed in total silence, took a deep breath, and lifted the cover. Her glance fell on . . .

Page one. A newspaper article for August 3, headline: GIRL SCOUT WANDERS AWAY FROM ANGELES NATIONAL FOREST CAMP, FEARED LOST. Her seventh-grade class photo was blown up huge next to it, zits and all.

Page two. August 6 headline: FORESTRY SERVICE EXPANDS SEARCH RANGE IN HUNT FOR MISSING TEEN. COUGARS SPOTTED IN LOCAL AREA. A map of the campsite was pasted in, with circles drawn like a bull's-eye.

Angie touched the crisp, yellowed page. Goosebumps peppered her pale arms. Mom had saved all these newspaper articles about her. Angie's feet fizzed, and the pit of her stomach swirled, but she turned the page over to . . .

Page three. August 17: SCOUT TROOP HOLDS VIGIL FOR MISSING GIRL. The color photo in the newspaper clipping showed Livvie's and Katie's and Mrs. Wells's sober faces lit from below by candles. A hundred points of light blurred behind them. That was a nice turnout. Very supportive, she supposed.

Page four. September 15: SAN DIMAS MOUNTAIN RESCUE TEAM MOVES TO HIGHER ALTITUDES IN FULL-SCALE SEARCH FOR MISSING TEEN. REWARD OFFERED FOR ANY INFORMATION.

Page five. November 22: TRAIL GROWS COLD, LITERALLY, AS SAN GABRIEL MOUNTAINS SEE RECORD EARLY SNOWFALL. FORESTRY SERVICE HALTS SEARCH FOR LOST GIRL. Wow. Three months and a bit. Then they called off the search. Her stomach dropped. About a hundred days and that was it.

Page six. December 4: LA CANADA HIGH SCHOOL HOLDS MEMORIAL FOR LOST STUDENT. Angie read the article about the speeches and songs with the disconnected feeling that this had to be about someone else. She spent a few moments picking out the familiar faces of teachers and parents and friends in the photographs.

Page seventeen. August 3: ONE-YEAR ANNIVERSARY OF ANGELA CHAPMAN'S DISAPPEARANCE OBSERVED AS A DAY OF MOURNING BY LA CANADA COMMUNITY.

Angie flipped the rest of the leaves with shaking hands, reading every yellowed, faded page until . . .

Page twenty-two. No newspaper. Just a beautiful photo. Brilliant orange- and red-leaved trees arched across a lawn. In the distance, gray-and-white rectangles gave it a surreal touch. A pot of white chrysanthemums in the foreground provided focus. What was it doing in this scrapbook?

Angie squinted. *What is this, Mom? A field? A . . .* The spot between her shoulder blades tingled. A cemetery? For sure, it was. The last scrapbook entry was a photo of a cemetery plot. Oh God. For her.

Oh my God. Her throat tightened with almost tears. They had given up on her, no matter what Mom said. They had called off the search and pronounced her dead. And wow. How inconvenient of her to come back just when they had their new life without her all planned out!

Angie's hands shook as she replaced the scrapbook, opened the door, and walked like a zombie to her room. Like the living dead. Yeah. That was her.

She thought about Girl Scout's note and how close she'd come to showing it to Mom. Crap. She really was all alone with this.

★ ★ ★

There was this lullaby Grandma used to sing to Angie when she was tiny: 'All the pretty little horses. Black and bays, dapples and grays.' Angie had been too small to understand all the words — what were dapples? Were they like apples? — but the tune stuck with her down the years.

It sang itself through her head as she waited for Grandma to arrive, circling around to the chorus over and over. 'Hush-a-bye. Don't you cry. Go to sleep, my little baby.' Strange words. The haunting melody deepened her sad mood, but tears wouldn't come.

The heavy feeling lifted as a chorus of happy

greeting sounds came through the floor. Grandma's voice! Angie's name floated up with them.

'Coming!' She combed her fingers through her hair but avoided checking the mirror. It was still too startling.

'Well, get down here, darlin'!' Grandma waited at the foot of the stairs, arms on her hips. 'Gimme a hug, will you?'

Angie flew into her arms, grateful that she still smelled of lavender and Ivory soap.

After a good, long squeeze, Grandma held her back at arm's length and measured her with her eyes. 'Well, guess I've shrunk a couple inches since you saw me last,' she said. 'A few more wrinkles, a few more white hairs. You're just as pretty as ever.'

'I'll say,' a male voice added. 'Pretty as ever. Got one of those hugs for your favorite Yuncle?'

Angie raised her eyes to the speaker. A tight buzz cut on top. A square jaw below. The unfamiliar face dodged in and out of focus. She blinked. How long had it been since she'd seen Yuncle Bill? He must have been just barely eighteen when he enlisted, which meant she'd been ten. Three years ago in memory time, six years in real time. Those six years had turned him from a zitty teenager to a powerful-looking man.

She tried to map the teenage face onto the one looking at her with intense curiosity. He came at Angie with thicker, stronger arms than she recalled and crushed her against his muscled chest.

'Look at you, all growing up,' he said into her hair. His body was hot and radiated the spicy scent of his body wash. His arm stroked her back, and she shivered.

The minor tune of 'All the Pretty Little Horses' rang in her ears, and a tiny, high voice sang along in her head. *Hush-a-bye. Don't you cry.*

Mom's words drifted as from a great distance. 'I've got lunch laid out in the kitchen.'

'I'll pour drinks,' Grandma said, and walked away. 'Everyone hungry?'

Angie heard the deep rumble in Yuncle Bill's chest as he answered. 'Mmm. Starving.'

He tipped Angie's face up to look at her. 'Prettier, I'd say.' He dusted her nose with a fingertip. His other arm still pressed her against him, and one side of his mouth smiled. Something about that smile . . .

Angie's heart began to race, for no apparent reason. She pulled back from his hug, felt his resistance. It was lasting too long. 'The — Everyone's in — ' she stammered, pointing to the kitchen.

He laid a finger across her lips. 'Hush,' he said. 'No tattling.' He winked, like there was a private joke in that. His eyes flashed in a peculiar, almost familiar way, and his face blurred, out of focus, swirling and dark and closer to hers. Her knees buckled. Her breath stopped. Powerful arms held her tight.

A little girl's voice called, *Quick, Angie. Hide!*

She twisted her head, searching for the speaker, but it was too dark to see. Something was wrong with her eyes. She closed and rubbed them. A pounding filled her ears, a galloping sound. An image of a pale child with long blonde hair streaming out behind painted the insides of her eyelids. The little girl bolted away from her on a huge bay horse.

'Come back,' Angie pleaded. 'Who are you?'

The little voice drifted back over the sound of pounding hooves. *Can't tell. No tattling.*

The front door slammed. The galloping stopped. Angie's eyes popped open. Her breath escaped in a loud sigh. The taste of chocolate ice cream was on her tongue.

'Well, that was a lovely visit,' Mom said.

Angie inventoried the house at a glance. They were alone. 'What? They're gone? Already?'

'I know. Time flies!' Mom said with a large smile. 'And since Grandma helped me with the supper dishes while you were out with Bill, you and I can put our feet up for the rest of the evening.'

'Dinner?' Angie glanced at the windows. It was completely dark outside.

'Come on. Let's order up a movie. It's just us girls tonight.' Mom linked an arm through Angie's and drew her to the family room. 'Did you find some cortisone to put on that rash? It looks like it's going down.'

Angie's right arm was covered with fading pink spots, all but one, which was bright red and painful, like a fresh burn. Appearing and disappearing spots? What next?

'Do you think it was the shrimp?' Mom asked. 'You were never allergic before.'

'No idea, Mom,' Angie said a little impatiently. There was no doubt she'd eaten. Her stomach was full and churning. But what? She couldn't remember. 'What happened to Dad?'

'He's doing paperwork in the den. Didn't you hear him complaining about the big presentation? Seems he has more work than ever these days.'

'Sorry. Guess I spaced out,' Angie said. Oh God. Spaced out for eight hours? How was that possible?

Mom handed Angie the remote. 'You choose.'

Gripping the remote to hide the tremor in her hand, Angie scanned the meaningless titles. Most of them were R-rated, and she was too young for those. Anyway, she didn't want to watch something too violent or sexy with her own mother.

'Want a blanket?' Mom said. 'You've got goosebumps.' She reached into the blanket bin for a pair of couch blankets and settled closer to Angie. 'So did you and Bill have a good catching-up chat on your walk?'

They walked? When? Angie spread the green chenille blanket over her lap, stalling for an answer. As she tucked her feet up, she noticed the hems of her jeans were covered in cobwebs. Her knees were dusty brown.

Mom rattled on. 'You two were always so close. He was your favorite babysitter, and he wouldn't even let us pay him.'

Thinking back, Angie couldn't remember him coming over a lot. Well, maybe she did. She remembered him arriving and leaving, just no idea of in-between. Maybe he let her stay up and watch inappropriate TV.

Her pulse was still rapid, her breath strained, her stomach sour, her arms red, her legs achy. What was wrong with her?

'Such a sweet boy,' Mom added. 'I know you missed him like crazy when he was deployed. You cried for a week straight.'

Funny. She didn't remember missing him at all.

7

PROPOSITION

'I contain multitudes,' Ms. Strang announced to the freshman lit class.

Angie's heart leaped in response.

The teacher continued, 'Does anyone know what Walt Whitman meant by this? It's part of the closing stanzas of his 'Song of Myself,' which you all should have finished reading last night. Anyone?'

Angie had. She'd loved it — the language, the images, even the parts she didn't understand at all but let them roll around in her mind. She felt her hand rising on its own and pulled it down abruptly. 'Figuratively,' she whispered to herself. 'It's just a metaphor.'

'I'm sorry, Angela. Could you speak up, please?' Ms. Strang must have the hearing of a bat.

Angie's fan club stared, waiting for her answer. What would the Gone Girl say?

She collected her thoughts. Her own thoughts. 'I think Whitman means that he contains all the ancestors who lived before him — like a huge human family tree that all comes to a point in him. And also, he contains all the world today, all of creation, because he's part of it and connected to it and stuff.' Fifty large eyes swung back to the teacher to see if that was correct.

Angie added, 'It's NOT like a multiple personality. It's a metaphor.' Why'd she blurt that out?

But I *do* contain multitudes, she thought. Literally. Whitman would probably think her version was pretty cool too. Maybe she'd write her own 'Song of Myself' once she got to know herselves better.

No progress there, unfortunately. After a couple of weeks of waffling, Angie brought her journal to a session, hoping it would help. 'Do not mention this to my mother,' she commanded as she handed it to Dr. Grant. 'She'd flip out.'

Dr. Grant read quietly for a few minutes, her placid face concealing her own reaction. 'Ah,' she said gently. 'So, the kidnapping hypothesis proves true.'

Angie felt a burst of gratitude for Dr. Grant's under-response. It was so much easier to deal with things on an unemotional level. 'Yep. But I still can't remember it myself.'

'That's okay, Angie.'

'Shackles. Suicide. Pretty heavy stuff,' she said flatly. 'I don't want Mom to have this in her head every time she looks at me. Okay?'

'I understand,' Dr. Grant said. 'What about Detective Brogan, though? This is valuable evidence, an eyewitness statement.'

Angie thought about it. 'There's not much there. No descriptions or anything.'

'Still,' Dr. Grant said. 'There might be enough to prevent wasting his time on false leads or wrong ideas.'

Point made. Angie shrugged. 'Sure. Go ahead

114

and make a copy. But I need to keep the original.'

'Of course. So, how do you feel about Girl Scout's story? Her experience?'

Angie rolled her eyes. 'It sucked. Obviously. But I kind of admire her spirit.'

The doctor allowed a smile. 'There's much to admire in a survivor, isn't there?'

Angie felt a twinge of jealousy. Some days Dr. Grant spent most of the session with Angie under hypnosis. How exactly was that helping her?

'So . . . what do you guys talk about? I mean when I'm 'not here'?' She made quote marks with curved fingers.

'Whatever Girl Scout needs to talk about. She's working through some of her own issues.'

'Oh great.' Angie digested that idea for a moment. Her problems had problems. Fabulous. 'But what about this Little Wife person she hinted about? Do you know who she's talking about? Does she have issues too?' Angie absently scratched her left hand. She frowned at the silver ring. There was something about it. Her chest tightened uncomfortably.

'I haven't met her yet,' Dr. Grant said. 'Or any others, for that matter.'

'What the heck? Is this like some mental hide-and-seek game? I mean, how am I supposed to get better if you can't even find these stupid alters?' She bolted up from the couch and paced to the window. She parted the drapes, pressed her forehead against the cool glass. A circle of moisture formed as she loosed a heavy sigh.

115

Silence stretched in the room behind her. Blinking away the almost-tears, she turned back to the doctor. 'Well?'

Only the faintest lift of her chest betrayed the doctor's answering sigh. 'Angie, therapy for DID takes a long time. Achieving complete integration, if that's what you want, will take a huge amount of work and dedication, on both our parts.'

Angie was back on the desk again, swinging her legs with agitation. 'What do you mean, 'if that's what I want'? What's the alternative? Go on like this? I want to be one person. Me.'

'I understand,' the doctor said. 'But realize, the negotiated blending of the separate personalities is going to result in you-plus.'

'Plus what?'

'Memories, feelings, shades of the alters. They're you too.'

Angie was silent, absorbing this idea. Her heels kicked against the wood.

Dr. Grant smiled gently. 'As I said, this is a very gradual process. Everyone will be evolving toward one another. You will feel like you, one you, in the long run.'

'What's the long run? It's been almost a whole month already! So when will I be one me? Like six months? A year or so?'

'Angie, dear. We're talking about several years. Potentially longer, depending on how cooperative everyone is feeling.'

'You're kidding.' Angie kicked the desk a little too hard, a new worry taking over from the last. Dad's insurance didn't cover this kind of thing.

She'd accidentally seen the bill for the first three weeks of therapy, nine sessions — Mondays, Wednesdays and Fridays: more than thirteen hundred dollars. There was no way Mom and Dad could afford that — not now, and certainly not when there was a baby coming. 'I can't wait for years. I need to be myself again now. Why should it take so long?'

Dr. Grant laid her pen down with a shrug. 'Hypnotism, reprocessing, and talk therapy, the work we've started together, is a gradual process of revealing, experiencing, and coping with the injuries and abuses you, the primary, can't remember. You can't rush it. But there's an excellent track record of success. I have no worries about your eventual success, especially as you have no alcoholism, no signs of depression. Angie, you're a very resilient personality.'

Angie huffed. 'I am *the* personality. The boss.' She ignored the sensation of laughter inside her skull. 'It's not that I don't, uh, admire and thank Girl Scout for taking one for the team, but it's time for the team to disband. I'm back.'

Dr. Grant sat back and twiddled her pearls. 'Hmm. I hear you. But we haven't heard from the rest of the team, have we?'

'Why do they get a vote?' She met Dr. Grant's unblinking and surprised stare.

'They're people. The citizens of your body. Aren't you curious, Angie?'

Typical. Why did she have to answer questions with questions? 'Curious? Isn't it better if the past just stays in the past? I mean, I'm doing fine in school. Things are okay at home. I'm beginning to make some new friends. I'm starting over fresh. Why would I want all the awful stuff dredged up from the bottom of my mental pond? Why would I want to remember it? Why can't it all just go away and let me be the old me again?'

Angie's eyes filled with angry tears. Dr. Grant's face smeared into a pink blur.

The blur offered her a Kleenex box. 'You know my primary concern is your recovery, but I have to ask you. What about the investigation? Do you want to help the investigation into your abduction? There may be other victims. Or potential victims.'

Angie imagined a new Girl Scout, chained up and frightened. Something in her mind wiped the image. 'NO!' The yell exploded from her mouth before she could stop it. 'I mean, no, that's not going to happen.' She knew it was true as she said it. She just didn't know why.

At her outburst, Dr Grant's eyebrows practically popped off her forehead.

Angie released a huge, irritated sigh. 'Fine. I get your point. I wish they'd all just tell you what they know. They're like ghosts, hanging around with unfinished business on earth. I wish they'd just spill their guts and move on. Get out of town. I don't need them anymore. I don't want them!' Her voice rose again.

'Angie.'

'You hear me?' she yelled, slapping her head with both hands. 'I DON'T WANT YOU! GET OUT!'

'Angie.' Dr. Grant grabbed her hands. 'Angie.

118

Don't hurt yourself.' Worry lines stood out on her forehead. It seemed she was mulling something over.

'What? What are you thinking?' Angie demanded, reversing roles.

Dr. Grant sagged back into her wing chair. 'Well, first, it's nice to see a little color in your cheeks. That's the most animated I've ever seen you.'

'Great,' Angie commented. 'I'll try to freak out more often. That's not what you were thinking, though.'

'I have a . . . a proposition for you to consider.' She was uncharacteristically hesitant.

'I'll consider anything. What?'

'I know of a psychiatrist at UCLA who's begun clinical studies with an experimental method. He's asked me several times whether I have any patients to refer to him.'

'Transfer? Oh. But . . . ' Angie felt silly. 'Start over with someone new? I'm sort of used to you.'

Dr. Grant clasped her hands together like a silent clap. 'Why, thank you, Angie. Fear not. I'd be a full collaborator. I'd be right there with you all the time. He'd run the fancy equipment, and I'd monitor you.'

'Equipment?'

'I have to tell you, in all honesty, I have no experience with his method. It's controversial, to be sure. It involves . . . eliminating, rather than integrating, the alters. But his patients can finish treatment in a matter of weeks, not years.'

Eliminating? Weeks? *Oh yes. Now we're talking.* Angie leaned toward the doctor, excitement simmering. 'Okay, that sounds interesting. Is it super expensive?'

Dr. Grant smiled. 'It's all being done under an NIH R34 award. The patients, of course, accept the risk of its experimental status in exchange for treatment.'

'But is it expensive?'

'There's no charge,' Dr. Grant answered.

'I'm interested,' Angie said. 'I'm way interested. How do I start?'

'We'll speak to your parents.'

★ ★ ★

At the next session, Mom and Dad were both present, hanging on the doctor's words. They perched on the edge of the couch. Angie slumped back in the beanbag chair.

'That sounds ideal,' Mom said.

'A win-win,' Dad added. 'She can be rid of these extraneous so-called personalities.'

The doctor frowned. 'With all due respect, Mr. Chapman, I wouldn't call them extraneous. They're unintegrated parts of your daughter's psyche, but parts that did play a critical role in keeping her alive and sane through her ordeal. They deserve your respect.'

Even the one that steals underwear? Angie thought.

As the sarcastic comment flitted through her head, she suddenly doubled over in agony, a knifelike pain radiating from her shoulders. No one noticed her, hunched over her knees in the corner of the room. The adult voices faded.

A picture forced its way into the space behind her eyes. On a bed, her thirteen-year-old body, cold and bare. On a bed, wrists red and scratched from the tug of coarse ropes. On a bed, looming over her, a pair of dark eyes too close together.

For a moment, she felt his weight. For a moment, she heard his heavy breathing. For a moment, she smelled his sweat. For a moment, paralyzing terror possessed every crevice of her being.

Then the image and the terror vanished, leaving shock waves behind, like the moment after a nightmare lifts. But words rang in her ears, the voice a low, female growl. *Don't ever disrespect me, Pretty Girl, after what I did for you. I saved your fucking life.*

'What was that, hon?' Mom gripped her trembling hand. She was crouched on the floor beside Angie. 'What did you say?'

'They saved my life,' she whispered.

A throaty laugh echoed between her ears. *You're welcome.*

The voice terrified her. It was like having a wild demon in her head. She squeezed Mom's hand and pleaded with her eyes. 'When can we start? When can we do the new procedure?'

★ ★ ★

Angie was late back to school because of the appointment, arriving just at lunchtime. She had stopped shaking from the glimpse of horror, and the memory was already bleeding away until she

121

couldn't quite remember what she'd seen — just that she was left feeling unsettled.

The cafeteria was filled with eating, joking, rowdy students. All she had to do was find a table of strangers and sit down so she could eat in peace. What she'd told the doctor wasn't entirely true. She wasn't making new friends. Sure, she had a crowd of followers, of fans, but it wasn't like she wanted to get close to any of them. Ugh. They were like fleas. Hopping onto her, touching her all the time, sucking away her energy.

It was much easier to float along, remain a mystery, keep them at arm's length. She didn't need to explain anything about herself that way.

She was still scanning the room with her food tray when a hand jostled her elbow.

Rebalancing her tray, she whirled to see Kate, or a three-years-older version of Kate, who made a quick sign of the cross on her chest. 'It *is* you,' she said in a hushed voice. She patted Angie, testing her solidity. 'Oh wow. I only saw you from the side a couple of times, and I wasn't sure. I mean, I heard the gossip, but I had to know for real. Come over here.' She grabbed Angie's tray and took it over to a table for two.

'Sit.' She leaned her head close to Angie's, foreheads almost touching. 'I can't believe it. I didn't hear anything on the news. When did they find you? Where were you? What happened?'

'Apparently I found myself,' Angie replied. 'I showed up at home — total amnesia.'

Kate's jaw dropped. 'Oh, my. I'm sorry. Do you know who I am?'

Angie rolled her eyes. 'Of course I do,

Katie-Latie. You were one of my best friends.' She noticed that she'd automatically used the past tense, like she was getting a sense of time — a *then* and a *now*. She didn't feel thirteen anymore. She felt — undefined.

Kate grabbed a baby carrot off Angie's salad, just like she used to. 'Well, you probably don't know it's social death to be seen with me. I should warn you. I'm a leper now.' She said it so matter-of-factly, Angie assumed she was kidding.

'I'm not kidding,' she continued. 'So if you don't want to — '

Angie shrugged. 'Because of the keg thing?'

Kate startled. 'See. You're back from the other side and even you know about it. Who told you?'

'Greg and Livvie,' she replied.

'So how come you're not hanging with them?' Kate's nose wrinkled. 'They're right over there.'

Angie looked in the direction Kate pointed with her chin. Liv had a sour look on, watching the two of them. Well, no wonder. If Greg had told her what happened, Liv had an excellent reason to look at Angie that way. She felt the color creep into her cheeks just thinking about it.

But if he'd kept it secret, then it looked like she'd just ditched them. She never called Liv that afternoon, and she'd blocked Liv's number after the fifth time Liv tried to call her. She didn't want to start her new life with an all-out catfight over something she hadn't even done on purpose. It wasn't like Liv would take 'It was my other personality' as an excuse.

And now Angie was eating lunch with the enemy.

Greg's expression was harder to read, more intense. Whatever it was, it made her hot and squirmy inside. 'Nah. Things have changed too much,' she said.

Kate raised her eyebrows. 'You could easily win him back if you wanted.'

'It's not a contest,' Angie said primly.

'Yes, it is,' Kate argued. 'Everything's a contest. Popularity, love, grades, success. You just have to learn the contest rules.'

Rules. The word struck a chord. 'Why'd you break the rules? Why'd you tell on them?'

Kate's smile was unexpected. 'I may have lost the popularity contest, but I won the integrity award. If anyone had crashed coming down that twisty mountain road from Kurt's house drunk, I couldn't have lived with myself or with Kurt. So I told, and no one got hurt.'

'Except you.'

'Except me. Acceptable losses.'

Angie wanted to hug her across the table, but salad dressing would have ruined her expensive T-shirt. She grabbed Kate's hand instead. 'Kurt was your boyfriend, wasn't he?'

Kate's smile slipped. 'Was. Yeah.'

'And you told on him anyway? I heard he got suspended.'

Kate's sigh was heavy. 'It wasn't easy. But what he did was wrong. Dangerous to himself and everyone else. So yeah. I tattled. Broke the first rule of the playground. No tattling on friends. But I had to in this case. That's the rule of self-respect.'

No tattling. The words echoed. *But I had to.*

124

What he *did* was *wrong.* Angie found a strange resonance in Kate's story. It clung to her.

'Can we be lepers together?' she asked.

Kate's grin was the brightest thing Angie had seen in days.

The best part of Saturday mornings was smacking her six a.m. school alarm and sinking back into sleep. But today, too nervous and excited about starting the experimental treatment, Angie's brain kicked right into wide-awake mode. She rolled out of bed and stretched, up to the ceiling, down to the floor. Her arms swung loose around her toes, and she noticed black smudges on the first two fingertips of her left hand, like pencil marks. Weird. She was right-handed. She rubbed her fingers together, and the black smeared into gray. A crumpled piece of paper on the desk caught her eye. Shreds of pink eraser covered the surface. She smoothed the paper and gasped.

Childish handwriting sprawled crookedly across the page and swerved diagonally at the end of each line. Some of the words had been written and erased and rewritten in a straighter line with a left-handed slant. The ghosting of the erased words made the note even more illegible. The writer must have crumpled it in frustration at the end. Angie dropped into her rocking chair and read.

Deer Angie,
This is very hard for me to rite but the big girl sayed I have to do it. I hop you can read my riteing Ok. I was the first girl you can hear. Onely some times.

But I am hideing from the scarey lady dr. I need you to get a tape recoding thing. It is to slow and hard to rite a letter.

Sinserely, Tattletale.

The big girl at the door sayed its Ok I have to tell you now so no body gets hurt any more.

A cold feeling dribbled all the way down Angie's spine as she read the note. She flipped her left hand over, awkwardly picked up a pencil, and tried to copy the letter onto a clean sheet of paper. Goosebumps raised the hairs on her arms. It wasn't her handwriting, for sure. She could barely form the letters left-handed. The child's writing looked polished next to hers.

The first one she could hear? What did it mean? And who was the big girl by the door? Was that Girl Scout or someone else? The gatekeeper, maybe?

Her life was a bunch of questions that no one else could answer. Instead of going away, the mysteries multiplied. Wonderful. Just like her personalities. All locked in her head.

What was so awful, so terrible, so frightening that she couldn't even tell herself? She'd survived, after all.

The idea of a little girl hunched over the desk in the dead of night, laboring to leave her a message, touched her in a way all Dr. Grant's wordy explanations never could. She was real — a child with her own dreams and fears. The scary lady doctor. Angie smiled.

126

Her smile faded as she thought about the new treatment. Dr. Grant had promised that all the alters would have their last chance to speak to her before they were erased. It was up to the alters to decide how much they wanted to tell. And it was up to Angie to decide how much she wanted to know.

She considered the crumpled paper in her hand and the little girl who wanted to speak directly to her, now, before it was too late.

Did they know about the treatment starting this afternoon? Could they hear and understand? Was this crumpled note a kid's desperate plea for communication before she was erased?

Angie pictured her, Tattletale, blonde hair streaming out behind her, blown by unseen wind, a pencil in her tiny hand.

She decided. It was time for secrets to come out of hiding. Ready or not, here I come.

8

COMMUNICATION

Twenty clear plastic boxes stacked four high and five across lined the garage wall. Clothes, books, toys, drawings — who knew what else? Good thing Mom was such a pack rat. Angie caught her in the kitchen, scrambling some eggs for Dad's Saturday breakfast. 'Hey, Mom. Do we still have that old Fisher-Price tape recorder I used to love so much?'

'Look in 'Toddler Two' on the left,' Mom suggested. 'Second row.' A pack rat with a perfect mental filing system.

Angie left the connecting door open behind her as she returned to the garage. She unpiled the boxes and dove into Toddler 2. Sure enough, the friendly recorder with the red-and-yellow microphone was next to the barn with the pudgy plastic animals. She cradled the pink pig in one hand, the rooster in the other, lost in the childhood memory.

'What do you want that for, hon?' Mom yelled out.

'I, um, was working on a song and I wanted to get it on tape before I forget,' she called back. She tossed Wilbur and Doodle-doo back in the bin, snapped the lid, and restacked the boxes.

Mom smiled to see her blowing silently into the microphone. 'Batteries dead?' She turned

128

away from the eggs and pulled open a drawer. 'Fresh ones in here. Hey, I'm glad to hear the sounds of guitar strumming in your room again.'

Okay, she wasn't exactly writing a song, but she had reunited with her guitar. Gradually fingering the chords and relearning the picking patterns she'd worked on so hard in the before-time was relaxing. It took her mind away from . . . from her mind for a while.

She glanced over Mom's shoulder at the steaming yellow fluff in the pan. 'Add a dash of thyme and some paprika,' she suggested. 'Dad'll love it.'

'Since when are you the master chef?' Mom's right dimple showed her amusement at the unlikely suggestion.

'I have absolutely no idea,' she said flippantly. 'Maybe a recipe I whipped up in captivity.'

'Oh Lord, I wish you wouldn't joke like that,' Mom said. Her cheeks sagged.

Angie was pretty sure she had Girl Scout to thank for that culinary suggestion. 'Mom, if I can't joke about it, I don't think I can live with it.'

'Just please, not around your father. He's having a hard enough time.'

'Work?' Angie asked.

Mom was silent.

A sharp pain cut across her chest. 'Me? Having me home again?'

Mom was more silent.

'Why?' Angie's voice rose. The words and fears she'd been holding back poured out with ugly urgency. 'He already had me dead-and-buried in his mind, didn't he? I am a ghost to him. He doesn't even see me.'

'What on earth are you talking about, Angie?'

'I saw it, Mom. I know about it. I saw the picture.' Her chin trembled, but she wouldn't cry. 'I found the scrap-book and I saw the grave.'

Mom's heated face faded to white. 'No, Angie. That was a mistake.'

'That was supposed to be for my body. My mangled, murdered body. Tell me the truth, for once.'

Mom's hand flew to cover her mouth. 'It wasn't like that,' she whispered between her fingers. 'Our grief counselor, she told us to do it. To begin to move on, because I couldn't. I wouldn't. We never gave up. I swear.'

Cold invaded Angie from head to toe. Her voice was pure ice. 'You didn't, Mom. But Dad did. He moved on. He started a replacement child. Is it a girl? A boy? Has he named it?'

In the last month, the size of Mom's stomach had grown from 'too much dessert' to 'no more tucking shirts in.' It was so obvious, Angie couldn't pretend it away anymore. They had to talk about it. But not now. She wasn't ready.

'Ange, please . . . ' Mom shook her head, reached out with the spatula. 'It's not that.'

Angie dashed it to the ground. 'Do you realize he's touched your stomach more in the last month than he's touched me? He hates me now.'

Mom studied the grease splatter down the front of her white shirt to avoid Angie's eyes. 'Oh, you silly girl. He's petrified, don't you see? He can only imagine what some anonymous maniac must have done to you. He's sick. He can't sleep at night.'

Angie felt a bubble of rage. 'Because his precious daughter is damaged goods? Because he thinks I would be better off dead?'

Mom pulled herself up to her full five foot six and glared. 'No. Because he failed to protect you. He lost you. He is burning up with guilt.' Her voice broke, and she looked away with brimming eyes. 'Do you want some of these eggs? I can't eat any. The smell is killing me.'

'You guys are killing me,' Angie said. 'As if I didn't have enough pressure.'

She dashed up to her room, slamming the door behind her. She leaned back against it and breathed as if she'd run a marathon, not a flight of stairs. It wasn't supposed to be her job to make her dad happy. It was supposed to be the other way around.

Angie flung the plastic tape recorder onto the bed. She collapsed facedown on her pillow and considered crying, considered not breathing. Neither one worked. The pillow-case gave off the faint, fresh scent of laundry detergent. It was such a happy smell, she couldn't follow through with tears or self-suffocation. So she got up and retuned her guitar, a process she could control, a discord she could fix. The flood of fury trickled away, leaving only a depressed puddle.

The honey-toned wood grew warm in her hands. She ran up and down a scale and began picking out an old tune — Grandma's lullaby. 'When you wake, you shall have all the pretty little horses . . . ' She closed her eyes, playing the

131

tune over and over till her fingers knew it without thinking. She disappeared into the music.

A hissing sound drew her back. Shoot. Had she turned on the tape recorder by accident? It was rewinding itself. She probably had fifteen minutes of pretty horses.

Angie held the toy tape recorder in her lap and pressed the big green PLAY button. The tape was old and had been recorded over and over again. Static ran for several long seconds, and Angie was just about to hit the red STOP button when she heard, 'Hello? Hello? I think this is working.' The child's voice was high and soft and breathless. Angie felt a jolt of recognition. Electricity ran all the way down to her toes.

'The big girl told me to say thank you very much for the tape recorder,' the child went on. 'It's really easy to use. I like it.'

Angie couldn't help smiling at the formal politeness. She sounded very sweet.

'This is my story,' the girl said. 'It's scary to tell. He made me promise I wouldn't tell. People who break promises go to Hell, he said, and they burn up forever. And I really don't want to burn up forever,' she said. 'He showed me how much a burn hurts with a match, and he said, That's just one little match. Imagine a whole world of flames. And he said, Friends don't tell on each other, see, like he didn't tell about me breaking Dad's best coffee mug. So I promised I wouldn't. And he said, The magic word is hush.'

Another few moments of silence. The coffee mug. Angie had a vague memory of an oversized,

132

brown-speckled mug teetering on the edge of the counter. The tape whirred another turn, and Angie imagined the little girl gathering courage to break her solemn promise of silence.

She resumed. 'We played a few tea parties, and we did dress-ups, like pirate and princess, when he came over to play with me. And it was fun. He showed me how to play Uno and Crazy Eights, and Slap Jack, too. We had lots of fun games while Mom and Dad were getting ready to go out to dinner all the Fridays. Then they kissed me good night and told me to be a good girl and do everything Yuncle said. Everything . . . ' The little voice trailed off. 'Everything,' she added sadly against the static hiss.

So literal, Angie thought. Little kids are always so literal. Yuncle? Why was her alter Tattletale talking about Yuncle Bill? That was so long ago. When her chest spasmed, gulping air, she realized she'd forgotten to breathe.

'So, this day Yuncle had an idea. He said, I'm tired of pirates. Princesses like horses better than pirates. Do you like horses, Princess Angela? Of course I do, I said. I love them. All the girls love horses. And he laughed so hard. He told me to hop on his back, and he crawled around on his knees while I yelled giddyup. And he said, all the best horse riders go bareback, so we had to take off our shirts so we had bare backs. And I rode around on his bare back, but it was hard to hold on without a shirt.'

Angie's mouth went dry. A creeping feeling of dread touched the base of her neck. She wanted to turn off the tape now, but the innocence in the voice compelled her to hear the rest.

'He said, I'm afraid you might fall off this horse, my princess, and he laughed and rolled us both over. I giggled at him, lying with his hoofs in the air, so he said, hey, I know. Let's make this a better game. Want me to show you how big girls ride? And I said okay, because I was getting kind of bored.

'Then he showed me. Then he showed me and he said, now you're a big girl too.'

There was a long silence. Angie filled it with a thousand questions. Yuncle? How could he have done it? That bastard. A tear rolled down her cheek. Mourning for the poor little girl and her awful, agonizing secret.

The voice came on again, sober and subdued. 'I didn't like the new game so much. He said, stop crying, you baby. Princesses don't cry. Next time won't hurt. And then he burned me with a little piece of Hell and made me promise not to tattle about our game. And it was the same next time and next time and next time.'

The recording finished. It was static to the end of the tape.

Next time and next time. Oh God. How many next times were there? Four years of Fridays? Right under her parents' noses?

Angie rolled up her sleeve to study the sore that had appeared without explanation the day Yuncle and Grandma had visited. The livid spot surrounded a swollen, oozing blister, just about the size of a match head.

And Angie instantly knew without knowing

134

— he'd done it again. That night. After dinner. That goddamn bastard had taken her for a sunset walk and done her. Or rather, done the trapped little girl inside he'd trained to be his sex toy. Poor, defenseless, silent Tattletale.

And where? In his car? In the shed? On the filthy ground in the cobwebs and dust? She couldn't remember a moment of it, like her mind had been wiped clean of his guilty fingerprints.

A sick rage like she'd never felt before surged inside her. Damn him to his own burning hell. Her hands reached for an invisible weapon, a blade to defend the child. A sound like the brush of a hundred dove wings filled her ears, almost blocking the sound of Mom calling, 'Time to go, Angie.'

Oh yes, Angie. Our Angel was very angry. Tattletale clung to his robes, ashamed and worried she'd done the wrong thing, telling you. Maybe it was too soon. Maybe you weren't strong enough. But you had to know, I told them, if you were ever going to defend yourself. I held the gate against Angel. This was your time. He stormed away with the look of heaven's own wrath on his beautiful face, denied his vengeance, denied his role.

If Angie's parents noticed her tense silence in the car, they never commented. They were so oblivious, they probably thought she was just nervous about starting the brain mapping procedure that Dr. Grant had convinced them to

135

try. She tried to cling to the hot, hard emotion, but the fury was draining away again, and a dull, gray calm spread through her. A smothering blanket of numbness pressed down on her head. Her eyes were achy dry.

Had her parents missed the signals of abuse? Or had she just absorbed everything deep inside herself and buried it in her mind — literally in a secret compartment? Either way, Yuncle had gotten away with it for years. Because she believed him, because she couldn't tell. It was impossible to imagine how much pain was buried in her head, like . . . what was the opposite of secret treasure? The rotting corpses of her innocence? Yeah. Like a mass grave. God forbid they should ever dig it up and examine it. She shuddered and prayed that the mapping would work.

Would they find the boundaries of all the secret compartments in her mind, empty them, and nail them shut? That's what Dr. Grant had promised. That was the goal, anyway. Step one of the experimental treatment — discovery before recovery.

The plan was that Dr. Grant would hypnotize her and hold the attention of one of the alters while the functional MRI machine mapped her brain. All the nerve pathways for that alter would light up with activity, and the computer would record their exact locations. Dr. Grant had arranged for a five-day stretch of recording slots at UCLA Medical Center, assuming that Angie could tolerate the one-hour sessions in the belly of the noisy, claustrophobic scanner. It was a

136

huge time commitment, an hour's drive each way in traffic, plus scanning time.

Dad hovered uneasily in the radiology reception area as they waited to get started — the downside of starting on a weekend so she wouldn't miss too much school. 'This shouldn't hurt or anything,' he assured her. 'It's all done with magnets.' He wasn't telling her anything she hadn't already heard. He patted her back in a stiff-handed way, transferring his own anxiety into her instead of the opposite. Why was he here instead of ignoring her as usual?

Angie bit her lip, holding in the tears that ached in her throat for the entire drive over. The numbness froze her. After what Mom had spilled about Dad's emotional meltdown, there was no way she could tell him the truth about his brother.

Hey, Dad. Guess what? Finally figured out why my brain knew how to break up into compartments. I had to build a wall between daily life and being molested by your brother. Over and over again. That's how I learned to keep pain and fear locked away in another place.

Oh yeah. That conversation would end well.

She chewed her cheek till she tasted blood, forcing herself to feel the pain. It anchored her as she followed her parents along the corridor into the imaging room.

'Ready, Angie?' Dr. Grant's smooth, cheerful face pulled her away from the echo of Tattletale's little voice and back to now. 'Let me introduce all of you to Dr. Hirsch, the guy in charge of the study.'

Now *he* looked like a typical 'brain shrinker,' from his black goatee to his bushy black eyebrows. Startling black eyes like giant pupils had a piercing quality, like X-ray vision into your psyche.

While he obtained formal consent from her parents, Angie mind-wandered. Who would come out today? Girl Scout seemed most comfortable with the doctor. But Tattletale was close to the surface. Little Wife was a total blank, just a name right now. And someone had growled in her ear. So that should be the four that Girl Scout had told Dr. Grant about. Or was Little Wife the growler, and there was someone else entirely? What a patchwork quilt she was — bits and pieces sewn together by disaster.

Dr. Grant's job was to bring out the alters one by one and hold them long enough to trace them. The bait she planned to use was inviting them to tell their stories as Girl Scout had already started to do, not to flood Angie with traumatic memories, but to give her an arm's-length look at her lost time. Of course, Dr. Grant didn't know yet about Tattletale's trauma, about what Angie had only just found out.

She tuned back in just as Dr. Hirsch said, 'Then ideally we will know the exact extent of the splintering, and can proceed with the therapy.'

'Which is what, exactly?' Angie asked.

'Erasure. In two steps. We'll block, that is, deactivate, the neurons used only by the alters after tagging them with special genes we can manipulate. And when that is complete, you will

138

have your unitary consciousness, one personality continuously in control. I have treated five prior patients with great success.'

That was what she wanted, wasn't it? Questions answered, gaps filled, and the alters could be retired. Girl Scout and Tattletale had already told her their worst, and she could handle it. Not *feel* it, exactly, but now she knew.

The machine room was intimidating, scary — the perfect place to send her primary personality fleeing in terror. A huge machine with a circular opening dominated the room. Her head was supposed to fit in the circle. She imagined invisible beams drilling into her skull and dissecting her, but then they'd promised her it was just a huge magnet.

In the dressing room, she shed her street clothes and put on the hospital gown. Her reflection looked back, pale and frightened. What secrets would she babble under hypnosis? She wasn't so much worried about what Dr. Grant would hear, but Dr. Hirsch was monitoring. He didn't know her. She didn't know him. And what if Tattletale came out and told Dr. Grant about Yuncle? Would she have to tell Angie's parents? There was some kind of law about teachers and health-care workers reporting abuse of minors if they found out or suspected. It was posted all over school. Did that law include psychologists?

Angie whispered to the mirror. 'Tattletale, you absolutely have to stay quiet. It's not time for you yet. Keep hiding from the scary doctor. Please.' Whether she imagined it or not, a feeling of agreement spread over her.

Dr. Grant was right outside the door when she came out. The doctor handed her a pair of wireless earbuds and lightly patted the back of her hand. 'Nothing to worry about, Angie. I'll be talking to you through these, since the machine is noisy. There's a voice pickup, so I'll be able to hear you. I'm sorry I have to be in another room. Now let's go somewhere quiet where you can become more relaxed and see who wants to talk.'

Dr. Grant took you into a dark, quiet room and sat you down. By that point, you were trembling. She talked in a soft, soothing voice about nothing at all until the fear drained away. Then she brought out a gleaming disc on a chain and asked you to follow it with your eyes until you surrendered yourself and allowed us to peek through the windows of your eyes. Doctor said, 'Girl Scout. We need to talk. We need to take away Angie's pain.'

It wasn't Girl Scout who came up spitting, though. I sent another through the gate — the Little Wife. It was time for her to lighten her burden, time for Dr. Grant to meet her. And time for you to know.

Angie, you thought you were making the right choice. Our mom and dad were completely won over by the doctor's sales pitch. In a way, they only wanted their Pretty Girl-Thirteen back again. They wanted their three years back, just like you did. They wanted to forget too. They didn't

140

want to know the full damage, to under-
stand all our scars. But you had to.

It was Monday, the third day of recording, and
Girl Scout had refused to come out, even under
hypnosis. Another alter insisted on dominating
the sessions. Dr. Grant gave a little 'aha,' as if
this was the one she'd been expecting all along,
the one who was closest to the trauma that had
splintered Angie's sense of self in the first place.

'I always knew there had to be someone in this
role,' she told Angie after the first two hours in
the clanking machine. 'The alter who personally
took on the physical abuse. I believe this one
who calls herself 'Little Wife' is at the heart of it.'
She frowned and twisted her pink lips in
concentration. 'Although I still find it remarkable
and somewhat baffling that a single event at your
age could have initiated this degree of dissociation. That's just so atypical.'

Dr. Grant was right, of course, but Angie
wasn't about to unload that secret. As she
prepared to go under for the third time, she
remained silent about Tattletale, the first little
splinter. Dad was so fragile; Mom was so
pregnant; Grandma was so completely depen-
dent on Yuncle. And Angie wasn't ready to deal
with the firestorm of accusing her 'favorite uncle'
of incest. Dad would probably kill his little
brother with his bare hands.

She would just never, ever let herself be alone
with him again, she promised. And at some
point, when she was whole and strong, she'd
deal with the bastard. That thought brought a

141

smile — the sudden image of an avenging angel with a sword. As Angie slipped under the spell of hypnosis, a satisfying fantasy of slicing Yuncle to ribbons filled her imagination. The sound of wings was the last thing she heard.

At the end of the session, Dr. Grant was cheerful and triumphant. 'We got another one,' she announced. 'A young man — very serious, very protective. He's also quite compact, neurologically speaking. Probably the newest and least developed. We got his entire range mapped out in a single session. Good work, Angie.'

Like she had anything to do with it. A young man inside. Great. Did that mean she was bi? The doctor quickly assured her that the gender of her alters had nothing to do with her own sexual identity. Thank God. She could *not* deal with any more complications.

In spite of lying still for an hour and dozing in the car on the way back, Angie was exhausted and begged to stay home from school for the rest of the day. Mom gave her a sympathetic hug. 'I have to go into work for at least a couple of hours,' she said. 'I'm way behind on shelving.'

'I don't expect you to stay home with me,' Angie said, a little more sharply than she meant to. 'Not if piles of books are calling your name. I just need to lie down for a while.'

She dragged up the stairs and collapsed into a tight bundle under the covers. Everything softened and blurred. Just as she thought she was drifting off for good, her hand crept under the pillow, the way it did when she was truly asleep, and her fingers hit something unexpected. She jerked awake. Her journal had been stuffed there, open and a bit crumpled. The top sheet was blank, but thick, jerky writing showed through.

Angie heaved up on her elbows and flipped the empty page. Her cheeks heated as she read the four words, carefully centered like a title page: 'Little Wife's First Journal.' Little Wife? Her left hand rose before her face, the fog bank lifted from her memory. She remembered the inscription engraved inside the wide silver band. How could she have forgotten something so simple? She slipped it from her finger and read it again. DEAREST ANGELA. MY LITTLE WIFE. Something trembled inside her, and she threaded the ring back over her finger, where it was supposed to be. The words made her feel loved and scared at the same time. But she was only sixteen. She couldn't be someone's wife. So what did it mean?

More words showed through the paper, small and dense.

With a flutter of anticipation, she turned the journal page again. Chills raised the thin covering of blonde hair on her arms. Once she started reading, she couldn't stop.

Hey Ange.

I know you've met Girl Scout, or at least she's had her chance to talk to you. Goody Girl Scout left a hell of a lot out, like the part where she freaked out and I came to the rescue. I mean, to listen to her, you'd think, 'Oh yeah, so she could make a four-course gourmet dinner with two ingredients and one hand tied behind her back.' Ooh. Sure, that saved our life. As if. Feeding the man's stomach, sure, that helped. But get real, bitch. That's not all he wanted from his little wife. Girl Scout could only handle the front room. Left it to me to conquer the back room, the bedroom. Want to know how it happened? Sure you do. You can't help yourself, wanting to know. Every girl dreams of her wedding night, right?

I'll warn you now, honey. It's no PG-13 story. Get it, Pretty Girl? We stowed you away safe, so you'd miss all the excitement. And now you're poking around? You really want to know? Are you sure? Here goes, then.

So Goody Girl Scout and the man finished their first dinner together. He made a point of telling her how dark it was outside the cabin, that there were cliffs and crevasses. The coyotes were howling like crazy, and he said, 'Hear that? Hear them hunting? Just remember you'll never hear the cougar before she gets you by the throat.' That's all he needed to say. She knew she couldn't run off in the dark.

Then he unlocked her bloody ankles and carried her through the door to the second room, the one she spent the whole day not looking at, not thinking about. The room was small and black. He put her down on that hard bed that was going to be my birthing place. I mean, that's where I was born that night. You know? No, of course you don't. Not yet. I'll set the stage for you, so you can really appreciate it, appreciate what I do for you, for all of you.

Girl Scout couldn't see a thing, just hear him moving in the room. She held her breath.

He lit the oil lamp on a shelf, and his face turned dark orange in the flickering light. Without speaking a word, he washed our feet with a wet cloth, rubbed the sores with some sweet-smelling liniment. He kissed our pretty legs. He treated her like a queen, and all she did was lie there like a stiff board. After he wrapped our feet, he leaned over her breathless, terrified face and kissed her on the lips. 'There you go, little wife,' he said. 'All better. Now, tell me how much you love me.'

She just lay there, the idiot. He smacked our cheek, gently. 'Tell me, Angela.'

She forced out the words. 'I love you.' She didn't even know his name.

'Show me,' he whispered. 'Show me

145

how much you love me.'

She looked helplessly into his dark eyes. 'I — I don't — I — '

'Don't love me?' His voice was cold, and his hand smacked our other cheek, hard enough to sting.

She cried out. The sound excited him, and he slapped her again. His eyes turned darker and closer together in the flickering yellow light. She rolled away from him, and he grabbed our hair and forced her to look him in the face.

'Angela, darling,' he said, but his teeth were tight. 'I wanted this to be a special night for you, but you are not cooperating, my little wife.'

She wigged out, freaked. She screamed. He slapped. She begged. He ripped at her clothes. She curled into a tight ball to hide her shivering bare body. He was reaching for this coil of rope he had ready on the bedpost, when she checked out. Yeah, Girl Scout just up and left the head.

So Ange, there you were for just a second, terrified, like, how did I get here? Then it was little Tattletale, but she opened her eyes and saw it was the wrong person, and it wasn't the horsey game, oh no. She scampered off screaming, and into the space she left behind I was born, tied down on that hard, hard bed with the man pushing and grunting and weighing me down. Well, that was done and over pretty fast, the first time. He shuddered and fell on me with all his sweaty body, and he said, 'you love me, little wife?'

And I didn't want to be hit, so I said, 'Of course I love you.'

And he rolled off, and smiled oh-so-sweetly and said, 'See, I knew it all along. You were just scared a little, weren't you, my shy thing?'

And I asked oh-so-sweetly, 'Could you please untie my hands?'

And he said oh-so-sweetly, 'Well, not tonight. We'll see how it goes tomorrow.'

And then, since I was in the middle of the bed, he lay down on top of me and fell asleep snoring, and I lay there awake till morning, trying to breathe and thinking about how I was going to get my hands untied.

And when the daylight came, he got up and went outside to pee. I asked, 'What about me? Can I please, please go to the outhouse?' And he untied me and showed me the chamber pot in the corner of the room.

Then he put me back on the bed and did it all over again, taking his time to pause and make me beg for *him. He told me how lucky I was to have a husband who wanted me so much. I didn't want to be hit, so I said, 'Oh yes, I know how lucky I am. I love you so much.'*

And he said, 'you are unimaginably sweet.' And he untied me and took me into the kitchen to start breakfast — her job. I left her to it with those heavy rings around her legs.

I knew if I said the right things at night, I could make things better for us. I knew if I did the right things in bed, I could make things better for us. And that prissy Girl Scout — I heard her saying, 'Stop pretending you don't like it. You're just a slut.'

Yeah. That's what she called me from the day of my birth. She called me Slut.

Ungrateful bitch.

Angie's ears rang with the blood rushing through them. She touched her wrist scars with gentle wonder. She had absolutely no memory of them — no memory of pain, of terror, of rape. She was innocent. Untouched. A miracle.

'Thank you,' she said quietly.

9

COMPETITION

The last two one-hour mapping sessions were a frustrating waste. Tattletale was clever at hiding, which was good. She'd had longer to practice than anyone. And Girl Scout was stubborn. She refused all Dr. Grant's invitations to step out, as if she knew the next step after mapping. And maybe she did. Angie had no idea how much of her life the alters watched, like movie critics in the dark of the theater, passing judgment on her choices.

Dr. Hirsch suggested moving ahead immediately with the next part of the procedure, at least with the alters they'd scanned. While Mom and Dad watched in awe and Angie in rapt curiosity, he pulled up a beautiful brain scan, a 3-D simulation spinning on his computer screen.

'That's me?' Angie asked.

Under a transparent shell that was recognizably the surface of a brain, bright-colored clumps marked the personality regions in the hippocampus. 'The red one is you, Angie, the dominant, by far the most extensive. The purple cluster is the 'Slut' — excuse me, 'Little Wife' — persona, and the yellow splash there is the male figure called, er, Angel. So now we introduce the modified light-sensitive genes into the neurons only being used by alternative personalities.'

Angie was fascinated. Did her sense of who she was all come down to a few cubic centimeters of cells in the middle of her head?

'What if you aim wrong?' Mom asked. 'Is there any risk of deleting Angie? I mean, that would be totally unacceptable, wouldn't it, Mitch?'

Dad didn't hesitate. 'Unacceptable.'

Angie let a small breath escape. Dad still cared, even if he couldn't make eye contact with her. He pressed the doctor. 'How safe is this procedure?'

Dr. Hirsch harrumphed a bit impatiently. They'd been through this before they signed consent forms. 'Optogenetic technique has been used extensively to treat the neurons involved in Parkinson's disease, epilepsy, spinal injury, and even certain forms of blindness. Using it for memory control is experimental — the new frontier. As I explained, the carrier virus will be injected only near the brain cells we want the new genes to enter. We can target with exquisite precision.'

Dad nodded. Mom asked, 'The virus itself? It's harmless?'

'Absolutely,' Dr. Hirsch assured her. 'Really the only function it retains is the ability to inject genes into a cell. And we've chosen those genes, haven't we? The only risk we run is that we will not succeed in silencing the alters, not that we will damage the core personality or Angie's brain. The neurons themselves won't even be harmed. We just eliminate their ability to send a signal by altering the membrane calcium channels and ion pumps.'

150

Mom looked baffled. Dad ran his hands through his hair. 'Now I'm completely out of my depth.'

Angie got it, sort of, thanks to seventh-grade Life Science. 'And how exactly do you get the virus into me? How do you put in the kill-switch genes?' she asked.

Mom frowned. 'Please don't use the word 'kill,' hon.'

Dr. Hirsch stroked his goatee. 'You know, I rather like the term. I may use it. 'The K-switch genes.' We'll only require three small bore holes for access.'

'Holes!' Dad jumped to his feet. His chair tipped over backward with a soft thud on the office carpeting. 'In her head? I don't remember anything about drilling through her head! You said *injected*. I thought we were talking about a shot!'

Mom looked just as alarmed. 'Will you shave off all her hair? I'm not prepared for that.' She smoothed her sleeves. And her face. 'We'll have to find just the right wig so no one knows. There's so much to prepare.'

Angie pulled back and let them handle all the anxiety. It wasn't worth obsessing about. Whatever they needed to do, they'd eventually do. As it turned out, though, she kept most of her hair, and it covered the tiny holes they drilled in her skull to lay in a channel to her hippocampus. The gene-seeding process was long and tedious, but much quieter than her hours in the scanner. Now they had to wait at least a couple of weeks for the genes to move in

151

and take control of these calcium channels or whatever before they could be turned off.

Should be a quiet couple of weeks, Angie thought. But she was wrong.

* * *

It was getting harder to get up in the morning. What was the point, anyway? It wasn't like she could concentrate on school with the constant clamor in her head. Before the stupid mapping procedure, she'd been fine. She'd been getting good grades and even thinking she might be able to move up in a few classes after Christmas. Now there was chaos. The alters were all stirred up.

She would dress and head into school, only to discover that Slut had slipped into the bathroom to put on thick eyeliner and dark red lipstick. Clearly Girl Scout had called that one right. Without warning, Angie would find her shirts pulled off the shoulder with her straps showing. Then Girl Scout would copy over homework in her own neat handwriting while Angie was asleep and reorganize her homework folders so she couldn't find anything. Tattletale would ride imaginary horses all night long, which left Angie's head pounding in the morning, as if hooves had kicked her repeatedly in the head.

Kate was an island of sanity for her. Lunch every day led to chatting every night. And if Angie ever said, 'I need chocolate ice cream or I'll die,' within half an hour Kate was there in her parents' ancient third car, ready to roll.

'You've got a lot of stress,' Kate said after the

third ice-cream night in a row. 'Maybe you should take up jogging or something. I'm gaining weight here. Look — look what I'm reduced to eating.' She pointed to her wilty cafeteria salad and bent a shred of purple cabbage like rubber.

'Sorry. I'm eating for five,' Angie said, testing the waters.

Kate laughed. 'I know you haven't been implanted with quadruplets. That excuse won't fly.'

Angie whispered, 'I've started remembering, in a way.'

Kate's smile instantly straightened. 'Oh, Ange. Oh wow.' She reached across the lunch table. 'Was having amnesia better?'

'Well, yes, in a way,' Angie said. 'See, we figured out that while my mind was checked out for three years, my body was hosting a bunch of multiple personalities.'

Kate gasped, her eyes wide. 'A bunch? Are you kidding?' She searched Angie's face for clues. 'Nope. You're not kidding. How disturbing and . . . and cool.'

'Cool.' An ironic laugh escaped. 'Sort of. Actually, they're the ones who remember what happened. Now they've decided to share. It's not pretty.'

'Whoa.' Kate sank back in her chair, arms crossed. 'Whoa. Okay, that's worth a lot of chocolate ice cream. Tonight I'm buying.' She hesitated. 'Do you . . . want to talk about it? I mean to a real person, not a doctor?'

'Eventually. Soon. I'm still figuring out how to wrap my head around kidnapping and bondage

153

and stuff. And three chicks and a guy sharing my body.'

'Hey, we've all got issues,' Kate said. 'Yours just have names.'

'And agendas,' Angie said. 'I don't know how to keep them under control.'

'Obviously,' Kate said. 'I mean, like, who dressed you today?'

'Oh no!' Angie remembered laying out embroidered blue jeans and the red sweater she usually layered with a black shirt. Now she had a flowered peach-colored blouse on top and a wide headband, courtesy of Girl Scout; tight black spandex pants and spike heels, courtesy of Slut; and a crazy glass bead bracelet, courtesy of Tattletale. 'Can't they at least talk to each other?' Angie wailed. 'I look like a hick country tramp!'

'Seriously,' Kate agreed. 'Can you give them different days of the week?'

'How?' Angie asked.

'Put up a calendar in your room and assign dressing days or something.'

'That's too weird,' Angie said.

'Like this isn't?'

'Oh God. You're right.' At least it was practical advice.

★ ★ ★

Angie wasn't getting any practical advice from Dr. Grant now. It was like the doctor was obsessed with this research, this experiment. Instead of therapy, she was trying too hard to pull everyone out. Angie could feel her

154

frustration. Five torturous sessions in the machine, and only two alters mapped. Well, to be fair, Angie had ordered Tattletale to stay low. But Girl Scout — what was her problem? And the other two were acting out. It was like they didn't want to get better.

They needed another breakthrough.

'I wonder if the Little Wife's preventing them from surfacing,' Dr. Grant pondered. 'She's a very strong personality. She's used to owning the night. Now she's been pushed to the side. I wonder if we should go ahead and remove her as soon as we can to make room for the others to step forward?'

Angie's stomach turned just a bit queasy.

The doctor picked up on her hesitation. 'You have her story. The police have her statement and her evidence. Clearly, she's suffered the worst of your trauma.' Dr. Grant still didn't know about Tattletale's secret. 'Don't you think it would be a mercy, to have all that off your mind? Literally?'

'Maybe so.' Angie picked at the new scar on her arm.

'I'm not pushing, Angie. I hope you know that,' the doctor said. 'It's only one option.'

'What's another one?' Angie asked.

'Here's the alternative. We can continue along the lines of traditional therapy. We'll work on breaking down the walls between you and this Little Wife. We'll encourage her memories to flow directly to you, and you'll reexperience the emotions for yourself. Then we'll work on helping you deal with feelings that were too charged for your younger self to manage. At some point down the road, you will try to arrange a compromise with her to give up her independence and merge into you.'

Merge? With the Slut? 'But I'd be changed, wouldn't I?'

'Life is change,' the doctor said.

Angie felt someone shove her aside. 'You can fucking embroider that and hang it on your wall, Lynn.' The awful words came out of her mouth.

'Well, hello again, Little Wife,' the doctor said.

'Either way, you want me dead, don't you?' Little Wife/Slut asked while Angie sat a million miles away, straining to hear. 'Not a goddamned person appreciates me. Not inside, not outside.'

The doctor reached out a hand. 'I appreciate you,' she said. 'But I think you're unhappy and spreading that unhappiness to Angie.'

'Then I'll just get happy. My way,' Little Wife/Slut said. She slapped the doctor's hand away.

Angie's hand still stung when she found herself back inside of it. 'Oh, Dr. Grant. I'm sorry.'

The doctor's eyes lit up. 'Did you actually hear that?'

Angie nodded, her cheeks hot.

'Then we're making some progress. The walls are thinning.'

No! Angie needed that barricade. 'I don't like her. I don't like her attitude. I don't like her clothes. I don't like her voice. I don't want her in me. Get her out. Erase her. Please.'

A piercing wail shot through her skull, and she

clapped her hands to her head. She felt herself pulled into darkness, the cabin at her back. Strong arms tried to force her into a rocking chair, and she resisted with all her strength. The doctor's office came back into focus.

'Angie. Angie. Are you okay?'

'Yeah. I am,' Angie said, breathless. 'I'm in control. But schedule it as soon as you can.'

Dr. Grant said, 'I'll give you a little longer to think it over. It's a big step. And irreversible.'

In the distance, she heard, *You have to sleep sometime, Pretty Girl.*

* * *

It was three a.m., and those words still haunted her. Terrified to close her eyes, Angie sat upright in bed, all the lights on. Her eyes burned, but she hardly blinked, as every blink got a little bit longer. Finally, her eyelids refused to blink up again, and she slipped into that weird state between waking and dreaming.

The angel figurine on her dresser swelled to full size. The white porcelain filled in with color — pale peach-toned skin, a splash of pink over the cheekbones, black, curling, flowing hair, dark eyes with the reflection of fire in their centers. Man? Woman? It was hard to tell. He/she stepped forward, a hand hidden behind. The wings rustled with thick, white feathers that reached impossibly wide and high, bigger than the walls and ceiling should have allowed.

'Who are you?' Angie asked.

'Fear not. I am Angel, the answer to a prayer.'

157

'My prayer?'

The angel shook his head. 'Not yours, Angie. Another's.'

'What do you want?' she whispered.

'Peace.'

'Don't we all,' Angie said with a little laugh.

'Justice. Vengeance. Completion.' Angel pulled his hands from behind his back, flourishing a long, silver sword. Flames from the point licked the night sky, where the ceiling should have been.

Thank goodness the ceiling is gone, Angie thought in her waking sleep. Scorch marks would have been so hard to explain.

★   ★   ★

When the alarm rang, Angie jolted out of the chair. She hadn't meant to sleep. A quick scan showed nothing out of place in her room. No new notes or strange presents waiting for her. She retained the strange impression of a dream about beating wings, but it faded quickly by daylight.

Extremely groggy, she got ready for school, double-checking her clothes and makeup before she left. No one had sabotaged her. It was only a one-mile walk to school, too close for the bus to pick her up. Mom had insisted on driving her every morning so far, as if letting her walk on her own for fifteen minutes of rush hour would expose her innocent daughter to mortal dangers. Right. Too late for that.

This morning, Mom had an early monthly

staff meeting, so Angie begged for a chance to be normal and walk to school. The wind was blowing crisply, but wrapped in a new down jacket, Angie was ready for it.

She wasn't the earliest one up and about. Mrs. Harris was out pushing the stroller. She waved to Angie and drew alongside her. 'How's your mom feeling these days?' she asked. The tone of her voice made it clear she was asking about the pregnancy.

Angie shrugged. 'She doesn't talk about it much. I think she's getting over the morning sickness. What a crazy thing to do, at her age. I mean — '

She cut herself off, realizing that Mrs. Harris was about the same age as Mom.

Mrs. Harris laughed. 'She's a brave one. Of course, George and I tried and tried for years. We eventually saw the light and adopted Sammy. He's been such a blessing.'

She pulled back the blanket to reveal a sleeping angel. Long, pale lashes brushed his fat cheeks. His lips were pursed with a little bubble clinging to them. Angie thought he was the most beautiful thing she'd ever seen.

'How old is he?' she asked. 'It would be so fun if he and Mom's baby turned out to be playmates.'

'Coming up on ten months,' she said. 'He's a fiendish crawler and just about ready to walk. He's rarely this still, believe me.'

'Do you ever need a babysitter?' The words were out of her mouth before she knew it. What did she know about babysitting? She'd never

159

even taken the Red Cross class, but it would be good practice before Mom saddled her with taking care of her own little brother or sister.

Mrs. Harris smiled. 'Why, yes, Angie. Thank you. George and I would love a night out, much as we love this little one. Maybe we could set up something regular. I remember how nice a little extra income was when I was your age.'

'Sammy,' Angie said, watching the little boy breathe. The bubble quivered.

'Samuel means 'asked of God.' We asked, and he sure answered.'

'Know anything about him? He looks American.' The only other adopted kids Angie knew had been picked up in Central America and China.

'It was a private adoption. His mother died in childbirth, and the father was too overwhelmed to raise him alone.'

'That's so sad. Poor little dude.' She couldn't tear her eyes away. 'Anyway, he's lucky to have you and Dr. Harris. I hope Mom's baby is this cute. Oh, gosh. I have to get to school. But call me anytime.'

Angie picked up her pace as she left the cul-de-sac. Socializing would earn her a tardy, but it was worth it if she got a steady job. A honk startled her out of her wits. A blue car idled across the intersection.

'Need a ride?' Greg's head poked out of the driver's window.

Angie hesitated. Things had been left very awkward, to say the least.

'Come on. Hop in. It's freezing out there.'

'Thanks.' Angie crossed over, walked around to the passenger side, and got in, stuffing her backpack by her feet. She buckled and studied the backs of her fingernails.

Greg pulled away from the stop sign. 'How's it going? We haven't talked. I think you've been avoiding me.'

Angie's embarrassment resurfaced as a burst of annoyance. 'Of course we haven't talked. There wasn't much left to say. I'm sure Liv wants nothing to do with me now.'

'I didn't tell her anything,' Greg said softly. 'Do you think I'm nuts?'

'Oh. Well, thanks. I, uh, I don't know what came over me. I mean I wasn't — ' No explanation sprang to mind, nothing that he'd believe, anyway.

'Ange. It's okay. Really. In fact, let me know if it ever comes over you again.' He dropped his right hand from the steering wheel to rest on her knee.

What? 'What?'

'I just . . . may have been a little nuts to stop.'

Now Angie was completely confused. 'But you were right. If you and Liv are — '

'Well, we're not,' he interrupted. 'I mean, not like we're committed or anything. We're just hanging together for fun. Only it's not that fun.'

He pulled over to the curb and killed the engine a few blocks short of school. He took her hand. 'Ange, I really missed you. Then you were back in my life for, like, two seconds and then gone again. Can we, I don't know, see if the old spark is still there?'

'But what about Li — '

Greg stopped her protest with a kiss. She closed her eyes and felt the swooshing of the lazy river again, felt the heat of a long-ago sun. Three years of forgotten time fell away and she was thirteen and caught in the incredible grip of first love. She sighed against his mouth. His hands slipped around her and pulled her toward his seat at an awkward angle. The gearshift poked her in the ribs. 'Ouch,' she muttered.

'This is majorly uncomfortable, isn't it?' he commented. His eyes flicked to the backseat. Angie's flicked to the clock. They had fifteen minutes to make out before school started. Was it worth it? *Hell yes*, a voice inside urged her. Well, the good doctor had told her to listen to her voices! Why not?

They scrambled out their own doors and met in the backseat. 'Duck,' Greg whispered, staying below window level. 'Duck.'

'Goose.' Angie giggled and pulled him down to cover her. 'You're it.' Her arms wrapped his neck. Her legs wrapped his waist. Daring. But how else would they fit? It wasn't a big car.

He sank his face into her neck and kissed the skin all the way along the edge of her V-neck shirt until he got to the cleavage point.

Her skin fizzed with every touch. 'Are we sparking yet?' she asked. Her breath was shallow. Just looking into his black olive eyes gave her goosebumps.

'All eight cylinders, you bet!' He laughed and rubbed his cheek on hers. His face was just a little prickly, and it gave her the strangest feeling of déjà vu. She licked his lips with the tip of her tongue. That sure got his attention. The kisses deepened, and his hands slid up inside and found her bra. Then the kissing stopped. His face took on a look of concentration, and he was rocking his hips harder against her. His sweater scratched the soft skin of her stomach where her shirt pulled up, and his belt buckle gouged against her. She whimpered, and he laughed, misunderstanding, and pressed harder through his jeans. A wave of terror shot through her. What was she doing? He would be out of control soon. No! School was starting. But yes, she had to, had to have him closer and more. Little animal sounds in her throat begged him. His breath came in gasps. He groaned a word that might have been her name. Then he was done with her, leaning back and resting his head against the car window. 'Oh wow,' he gasped. 'Oh wow.'

Angie was cold, exposed, her top pushed up around her neck, her body confused, throbbing, still stretching for something out of reach. 'What . . . ?'

He slapped the ceiling and hooted. 'Angela Gracie, you are the best-kept secret. You may look like a domestic Chevy, but under the hood, you're a hot, fast Porsche. What an awesome ride.'

Perhaps he thought that was a compliment? Angie didn't know what to say.

He threaded his hands into her hair. 'And that's with everything on. I knew we still had it.'

Angie found a tiny voice. 'Does that mean

. . . does that mean you'll tell Livvie now? About us?'

Greg's face turned slightly confused. 'Oh, uh, yeah. I . . . just give me a little time to figure out how. I don't want to upset her. You understand. That's what's so great about you. You know Liv.' He kissed her on the nose. 'Come on. Hop up front. We're really late for class.' He shot her a white grin that sent lightning flashes straight to her toes.

Angie unfolded from the backseat and straightened her clothes, before she opened the door to move. Greg still liked her, all right. The problem was, she didn't know whether to feel wonderful or stupid. And her body ached for him.

10

DELETION

Unfinished business. Why was it always unfinished business between her and Greg?

'Well, he obviously hasn't told her yet,' Kate whispered across the lunch table. 'I mean, look at them.'

'I'd rather not,' Angie said, peeking anyway. Of course, she had wasted no time confirming Kate's prediction, that with only the slightest encouragement, Greg wanted her back. But three days later, Greg was still eating lunch with Liv and tossing Angie only the most sideways glances to let her know he knew she knew he hadn't officially broken up with Liv. Ugh. Why did it have to be so complicated?

'It's getting awfully close,' Kate said.

'What is, their knees under the table?'

'No, you jealous voyeur. The fall formal. I mean, he has to uninvite her if he's going to take you, right? We're starting ticket sales tomorrow.'

Until this moment Angie hadn't even considered it. 'Are you going?'

'I have to. Student government VP and all that. Noblesse oblige.'

'What does that mean?' Angie asked.

'My position obligated me, more or less. Plus Ali asked me. Can't say no to my president!'

Just an obligation? Kate's dimple suggested it

was more than that.

Angie followed her gaze to the table where Ali and his twin brother, Abraim, usually sat alone for lunch. As the only two Muslims in the senior class, they were two peas in their own pod, identically handsome and smart — perfect for Kate. Angie teased her. 'You like him too. Don't you?'

Kate shrugged, failing to wipe the smile off her face. 'At least I don't have to worry about him getting drunk.'

Angie snorted. 'Bought your dress yet?'

'That's on the agenda for Saturday. Come with me tomorrow and we'll shop for you, too.'

Great. Another expense for Mom and Dad. But if she got a regular babysitting job Friday nights, she could at least contribute. She'd talk to Mrs. Harris as soon as she got home.

Mrs. Harris was thrilled at Angie's offer. 'That would be just wonderful, dear. If I get Sammy off to bed at seven, we can pop out for a quick dinner.'

'I'll come at six,' Angie insisted. 'It's your night off. Just tell me his bedtime routine, and I'll take care of everything. Make it dinner and a movie, even. I'll be fine.' The more hours, the more dollars.

★ ★ ★

'He's a little tricky to settle down,' Mrs. Harris warned as her husband went to start the car. It was already six fifteen. Her instructions had been thorough, covering every possibility from diaper

166

rash to Martian landings. 'Don't hesitate to call if there's a problem.'

Angie hoisted Sam on her hip. His fingers tangled and pulled her hair. His breath was sweet and carroty. 'Go. Don't worry about a thing.'

'You seem very confident,' Mrs. Harris said. 'Do you babysit a lot?'

'Actually, not a lot,' Angie said. In fact, never. 'But we'll be fine. Mom's just across the cul-de-sac if I need advice.'

Mrs. Harris relaxed. 'Oh, yes. You're right. What am I worried about? And of course, if you were his big sister, I wouldn't think twice. Your mom's going to be so lucky to have you to help her out.' She leaned forward and kissed the baby in the middle of the towhead fluff standing straight up on his head. He made a grab for her hair, but it was safely pulled back in a sleek blonde bun. 'Be good, Sammy. Be good for your honorary big sister.' She chuckled.

'I think he looks like you a little,' Angie said.

'How sweet of you to say so, Angie. Of course, only a coincidence, after all. See you in a few hours.'

Angie lifted a tiny fist from her hair and waved it. 'Say bye-bye, Sam. Bye-bye, Mom.'

'Ba-ba ma,' he said, waving. 'Ba-ba ma.' He crowed with pride and buried his face in Angie's neck, giggling. She cuddled him close, thinking for the first time that it might not be so awful for Mom to have a baby. Sam fit into her arms like he belonged.

★ ★ ★

Next morning, when Kate arrived to pick her up, Angie was hollow-eyed and exhausted. She couldn't explain it. It's not like the Harrises had gotten home too late. And she'd slept in till after nine. Only one hint — her room was spotless, and her rocker was halfway across the room, facing the window, with the blanket neatly rolled like a mini sleeping bag. Looked like Girl Scout had gone into a cleaning frenzy and sat up the rest of the night, rocking. At her next therapy session she would ask Dr. Grant to please find out if Girl Scout was her mad rocker — so they could 'communicate and negotiate.'

'Shopping, shopping, shop-ping!' Kate sang to a cha-cha beat. 'We are going shop-ping.'

'Groan.'

'What's the matter, Ange?'

'I am possessed by a rocking demon. She seriously gets me out of bed for hours.'

Kate clamped her hands on Angie's forehead. 'Out. I cast you out, rocking demon,' she muttered in a deep voice. 'Out!' She flung her arms apart. 'There. Did it work?'

Angie tossed her a twisted smile. 'We'll see tonight.'

The hunt for dresses was frustrating at first. Kate wanted something not too short, not too strappy, not too plungy for Ali's sensitivities. Of course, everything she discarded as inappropriate, Angie's hands grabbed. At least Angie had a clue what was going on now. Slut wanted a party dress. Slut wanted a private party with Greg. Angie was having trouble telling where Slut's

168

feelings for him left off and hers started. Maybe they were the same, but she wasn't sure.

'Here, try this,' Kate said, thrusting a satiny dark blue thing at her.

'It looks so boring,' Angie argued.

Kate stuffed it into her hands. 'Just try it.'

Angie came out of the dressing room with a new appreciation for Kate's taste. 'Oh, girlfriend, just look at me,' she commanded. She twirled, full-skirted in front of the triple mirror, and the dress, which hung below her knees at rest, flared into a spinning shimmer. The sapphire color turned her skin milky white, her cheeks rose pink, and her gray eyes twilight blue.

A dressing room at the far end opened and out stepped a girl in ruby red — Livvie, in a strapless crimson mini. Her cleavage was legendary. 'I guess jewel tones are in,' she said with a tight laugh. 'Nice dress. Who's taking you?'

Angie's mouth dried up. A week away, and Greg still hadn't straightened it out.

Kate came out of another room to save her life. 'It's a surprise, Liv,' she said. 'Apparently.'

'Why, it's Glinda the Good!' Liv commented.

Not entirely fair. Kate's dress was a pale blue gauze monstrosity with puffed sleeves, but not totally good-witch-in-a-bubble material. 'I'm going to alter it.'

Angie was impressed. 'You know how to do that?'

'Oh yeah. Piece of cake,' Kate said. 'I like yours, too, Liv. You look like a Twizzler with tits.'

'Oh, stuff it,' Liv said over her shoulder as she flounced back into her dressing room.

169

'Is that her secret?' Angie whispered with a giggle.

Kate yelled down the row of dressing rooms, 'Don't cut the tags off too soon.'

Angie nudged her. 'You are soooo bad.'

'Ridiculous,' Kate replied in a high voice. 'Don't you know I'm Glinda the Good?'

★ ★ ★

By Wednesday, it was getting completely irksome. Greg hadn't called her, hadn't changed his lunch-with-Liv routine. She finally had to break down and stalk him to get him alone after school. When he opened his car door to leave, she was in the passenger seat, waiting. 'You never lock, do you?'

'Safe part of town,' he said. 'What's up?'

Ugh. How awkward. Again. 'I — you haven't — I haven't heard from you,' she said lamely.

'What do you mean? I see you every day. I haven't heard from you, either.'

Angie frowned. 'I mean, I — you — have you talked to Livvie yet?'

A shadow of annoyance crossed his face. 'It's only been a few days. I will. Hey, don't nag me about it.'

Angie shrank into the seat. 'It's just, I was thinking, with the formal coming up and . . . ' She trailed off.

His jaw tightened. He exhaled loudly. Angie stopped breathing.

'The formal. Oh. Right.' He turned back to her and rested his hand on her arm. 'So, like, Liv and I already had a date for the formal. I made dinner reservations a long time ago. She already bought an expensive dress and everything.' He smiled apologetically. 'I knew you'd understand.'

Angie started, 'I bough — ' and stopped herself.

'But right after that, I'll tell her, I swear. It's bad timing now, is all.' He took her face between his hands. 'I still . . . you're still really important to me. God, don't look at me like that. You make me crazy for you.'

He glanced at the windows and sank his lips into hers like a bee diving headfirst into a flower.

You opened your mouth and invited more. Behind your eyelids, sparkling patterns danced. Oh yes, he wanted you. You could taste it, smell it. His urgency made you tremble. But this was good, right? He had to want you more than Livvie. We had to win. That was vitally important. You could hear the pounding of his heart, feel his pulse race against your chest. A deep voice in your head said, Step aside, Pretty Girl. I've got this covered.

You tried to hang on, but the messages from your lips, from your skin, got fainter and farther away. You were pulled away from them, dragged back to the old, derelict porch. Some faint sounds reached you — sighs, groans, zips, clicks. You turned your head away. You had no part to play. You sat in darkness and wondered and rocked until . . .

171

'So that's okay, then?' Greg's voice.

Angie was home, standing by the rolled-down driver's window of his car.

He tugged a strand of her hair to pull her face in close and kissed her with his tongue. He tasted weird. 'But after the dance, I promise. I'll tell her then.'

Angie nodded numbly. What had happened? And what had she agreed to? Clearly, he wasn't taking her to the dance. He was still taking Liv.

She had to call Kate.

'That cowardly bastard,' Kate declared. 'Sorry. I guess you still want him?'

Angie shrugged, then realizing that her gesture didn't transmit well across the phone, added, 'I think so. I mean, all I can think about is kissing him.'

'Oh, great. That's your libido talking, not your brain. Sure, he's a hottie with a body, but how does he treat you?'

Damn, she wished she could answer that question first-hand.

'Silence?' Kate commented. 'Excuse me for being a buttinsky, but here's how I see it. You guys have a history, of a mild sort. Now you're like the all-American cover girl, and he wants to keep you in reserve for when he gets tired of Livvie and her attitude. So he'll do just enough to keep you enthralled, and I do mean enthralled like enslaved.'

'I'm not his slave,' she said indignantly.

'No? You're not his slave, but you'll just . . . just hop into his car and do him in the parking lot without a commitment?'

All the blood drained from Angie's head. She collapsed back onto her bed, phone pressed to her ear. She whispered, 'How, uh, why do you think . . . '

'I saw you, crazy girl. I can recognize the back of your head.'

'Oh my God. That's impossible. I've never . . . I wouldn't even know how!'

'Ange. Apparently you do.'

Or someone did. That damned Slut. It was definitely time to pull the plug on that part of her brain before she got her into deeper trouble.

Angie breathed hard, no answers coming. 'Kate, what do I do now?'

'Ask yourself if a guy who'd use you like that is worth it and come to the obvious conclusion.'

'You don't mince words, do you?' Angie said, a small piece of her innocence in tatters. She didn't want to give him up. He was a link, a bridge across the lost time.

'I don't have to,' Kate replied. 'I'm already a leper. Gives me the freedom to be honest.'

Angie sighed deeply. 'Nope. You're a friend. Gives you the responsibility to be honest. Damn. You're right, of course.'

'Come with us,' Kate suggested. 'Happiness is the best revenge. Double-date with me and Ali. You'd actually be doing me a favor, since Abraim was going to tag along with us anyway. He can be your escort. Two problems solved, since you already have a dress.'

'Okay,' Angie said. 'Since I already have a dress.' And although she knew she shouldn't go there, part of her wondered how jealous Greg would be seeing her with another date. 'Talk tomorrow. Bye.'

She lay back on the pillow and experimented with her emotions. She tried to be deliriously happy that she had a friend like Kate. She tried to be furious with Greg. She tried to cry. A tear or two squeezed out, but mostly she felt numb. Shell-shocked. God help her if any of this got back to Livvie. She'd tell the world.

★ ★ ★

Friday morning, she told Dr. Grant she had absolutely, positively decided. No take-backs. She was ready to go ahead with the procedure. While she waited, Dr. Grant called and confirmed arrangements with Dr. Hirsch for first thing Monday morning. Angie's head pounded through the rest of the school day and all night.

★ ★ ★

Saturday afternoon, Kate drove over with a set of hot rollers to do Angie's hair. 'You are going to need major makeup,' she said. 'More mad rocking?'

'That, and headaches, too,' Angie said. 'I hope I make it through the evening tonight.'

Kate smiled. 'Once the party starts, you'll be great. The boys are picking us up here at six.' She found an electrical outlet. 'And now, let the magic begin.'

She rolled Angie's long hair and went to work on her nails and makeup. By the time she'd finished, soft blonde curls of hair framed the face of a porcelain doll with wide gray eyes. Angie stared in the mirror at the beautiful girl who supposedly was her.

While Kate did her own final tweaking, Angie tore herself away to dress. She had figured out the hideous scar issue, she thought, crossing her fingers that Kate would approve.

She twirled in front of Kate in high-heeled ankle boots and sheer black stockings. 'Okay?'

Kate tipped her head, giving her the once-over. 'Yeah. Different, but kind of sexy. That'll work. Here, let me show you mine.'

Kate tossed her shirt and jeans aside, slid her own dress out of the garment bag, and wriggled into it.

Angie was amazed at the fashion makeover. 'How'd you do that?' Gone were the puffy sleeves and gauze overlay. The pale blue under-sheath was now a strapless, backless satin dress. Kate had turned the blue gauze into a wrap that concealed her back and shoulders in a way that was both mysterious and hot.

'Get this,' Kate said. She reached into the bag and pulled out a long, silvery scarf, which she draped over her dark hair, crossed under her chin, and threw back over her shoulders to hang down her back like a pair of silver wings. 'Think he'll like it?'

Angie giggled. 'Chah. Though if that's supposed to make you look modest, I bet all he'll think about tonight is how to unwrap you.'

Kate gave a smug smile. 'Good.'

'I so can't believe Liv called you a prude,'

Angie said. She clapped a hand to her throat. 'Oops. Sorry.'

Kate shrieked with laughter. 'Livvie kills me. She's the one who needs a couple of shots to loosen up enough to let a guy near her.'

Angie had an aha moment. She chuckled low in her throat. 'She's not a hot, fast Porsche?'

'Huh?'

'Something Greg once said. Explains a lot. No wonder he's obsessed with my inner slut.'

Kate's jaw dropped. 'You have an inner slut?'

Angie rolled her eyes. 'Surely you remember the wardrobe sabotage? The black lace? Et cetera?'

'The fire-red lipstick? Cleopatra eyes?'

'Oh yeah. That's her.' Angie snorted.

'The no-bra white stretch top?'

'Oh, no. Please tell me you're making that up,' Angie begged.

Kate's mouth turned down. 'Sorry. You didn't know about that?'

'That was definitely her.' Angie sighed. 'Anyway, she's totally history Monday morning.'

'Wait, what do you mean? Are you getting cured?'

If only it were that easy. 'Well, there's this experiment — ' Angie started.

'Hang on. An experiment? With your brain? But I love you the way you are!'

A rush of happiness flowed over Angie. 'Hey, don't worry. I'll be — '

The doorbell rang, and Kate scrambled for her shoes. 'Oh kill me. This is so to-be-continued . . . '

Ali's eyes nearly dropped out of his head when

Kate answered the door in her sparkling, homemade head scarf. At least, Angie hoped that one was Ali. She didn't want her date ogling her friend instead of her. Of course, his eyes went straight to Kate's neckline after that. Boys will be boys.

Angie watched for Abraim's reaction. Would he approve of his blind date? He gave her a shy smile as he stepped forward with a corsage box, the twin of the one in his brother's hand. 'You look pretty, Angela,' he said. 'Thank you for saving me from being such a hanger-on.' He had the slightest hint of British in his diction. 'I hope roses suit you?'

Angie held out her wrist without thinking. She was completely used to the scars, but she saw them again through the boys' startled eyes. Abraim hesitated just a second too long with the corsage elastic.

Kate plunged to the rescue. 'Old Girl Scout hunting accident,' she improvised on the spot. 'Ran into a bear trap. She had to gnaw her own hand off to escape.'

Angie picked up her cue. 'That's where the doctor sewed it back on.' She gave a light laugh.

Abraim gently took her fingertips and bent her wrist back and forth. 'Fascinating. I didn't know microsurgery had reached this advanced level.' He adjusted the trio of roses on her arm, just hiding the strip of scar tissue. 'I am planning on medical school. After college.'

'Where are you applying?' Angie asked.

The boys chanted in unison, ticking off the colleges on their fingers as they went: 'Harvard,

177

Yale, Stanford, Tufts, and Hopkins.'

Angie's eyebrows rose to her hairline. Quite a list. 'What are you going to do if you get into different ones?'

The boys looked at each other like they'd never considered that possibility.

'How about you?' Abraim asked Angie. 'What are your plans?'

'To get through Monday. I'm kind of living a day at a time. Long term? No clue.'

'Hungry here,' Kate said. 'Shall we?'

Abraim put a hand under Angie's elbow in an old-fashioned, gentlemanly way to lead her to the car. 'How about college?'

Angie shrugged. 'That's a long way off. I'm only in ninth grade.'

Abraim's hand abruptly dropped from her arm. 'So young?' He looked frantically at Ali.

'Sixteen,' Angie said quickly. 'I'm sixteen.'

It was strange to hear herself say the words, and stranger still, for the first time she actually meant it. She *was* sixteen. She was moving forward. 'I, uh, was abroad for a couple of years. I didn't go to school. So now I'm catching up.' Yeah. She was. Catching up. The unfamiliar emotion of sheer happiness made her light-headed.

* * *

Dinner was amazing, a Middle Eastern all-you-can-eat buffet. It was a long drive to get there, but the guys promised it was totally worth it. They were right. Angie rolled the new foods around on her tongue, trying to guess the spices.

178

Help me out here, she thought deep into her brain. She imagined the creak of wood on wood, the sound a porch rocker might make.

A tentative thought came back. *That's cumin. Turmeric. That sweet one is cardamom. Garlic, of course.*

'Thanks,' she said, filing the tastes away in her own memory.

'Thanks for what?' Ali asked.

'Oh, uh, for passing the water,' Angie. improvised. Talking to herself was 'a new hazard of the thinning walls,' as Dr. Grant had informed her. Great. It could be awkward if she didn't watch herself.

On the long ride back to school for the dance, Kate and Ali chatted in the front seat, loudly enough to make up for the slightly delicate silence in the back. Angie studied the stars through the window until a touch startled her.

Abraim held her hand gently in his. 'Did it hurt? The surgery?' he whispered.

Angie's eyes filled unexpectedly with tears. 'Yes,' she whispered back. 'I believe it did.' Abraim lifted her arm to his lips and kissed her inner wrist, his dark eyes soft and compassionate. Then, as if shocked by his own actions, he jerked his head away to look out his own window. But he never let go of her hand.

★   ★   ★

The decision was made. There was no going back now. Angie sat motionless in the surgical suite, her head secured in place with cushioned

179

clamps. The room was very, very white, and the lights hummed at a high pitch that didn't seem to bother the doctors and nurses.

Dr. Grant's eyes poked over the top of her surgical mask. The corner crinkles suggested she was smiling underneath. She gave Angie two thumbs-up.

Angie smiled weakly. The mild sedative kept her calm enough to hold still, but she was alert and awake. The tiny holes in the top of her head were hidden under her hair and filled with sterile biological putty. Three weeks ago they had prepped her brain by letting a virus carry those special genes into the web of neurons where the alters Slut and Angel lived. Who could've dreamed that a gene from an archaebacteria would save her sanity?

Dr. Hirsch confirmed that the genes were absorbed and working, making these special light-sensitive membrane proteins called opsins. So far, so good. Now, finally, Slut's neurons were at the mercy of the laser lights on fiber optics that would be oh-so-carefully threaded through Angie's brain into just the right places. Yellow light would blast aside the total darkness inside her skull, and those opsins would stop working — would shut down the ability for communication. Painlessly. Instantly.

Angie was almost surprised that Slut hadn't taken over by force and hitchhiked out of town. She'd been strangely quiet about this whole thing, and that worried Angie. Was she resigned to her fate or biding her time for some dramatic explosion?

Dr. Grant had warned her about the possibility of memory cascade. 'Often in therapy,' she cautioned, 'there may come a point where the walls are fractured. Something will add the final stress, and the whole structure will come tumbling down, flooding you with memories. Repressed and hidden stories will whirl through your mind with hurricane force. If Little Wife unloads her personal history of abuse on you all at once, the overload could be devastating. But,' she advised, 'if that happens, I promise I will be here to help you clean up the mess and rebuild.'

'Great,' Angie answered. 'You're my personal disaster-response team.'

So Angie held tight to the hope that this would all be uncomplicated, that Slut would leave her, not with a bang, but with a whimper; that the worst of the experience would forever remain someone else's memory — not hers.

Gowned and gloved, Dr. Hirsch stood behind her where she couldn't see his expression. She knew he was excited, though. Another success, and his technique would be on its way to a major medical journal. There were whispers among the techs and nurses about a future Nobel Prize in Medicine.

She felt only the slightest jostle as he threaded the optic bundles with their microfibers deep into her hippocampus, the location of all her memories, good and bad. Angie had time for one moment of complete terror. What if the genes had leaked? Would anything else be wiped out? And then the doctor said, 'Roll the laser.'

Angie, while you sat immobilized in the surgical chair, amber and green light traveled down the slender filaments deep into your brain. The tiny glow penetrated the folds of matter that taken together were not one but many consciousnesses. One by one, the specially prepared cells began winking out. Your eyes rolled back, and immediately you were with us at the cabin. You stepped toward the broken porch, your attention sweeping the group, recognizing us one by one.

Little Wife clutched a hand to her throat as pieces of memory were stripped away. She sat frozen in her rocking chair, her black lace camisole fluttering in the breeze. Her face, your face, was melting away before your eyes.

Girl Scout watched in terror, knowing the same execution was in store for her. Her sash lay abandoned in her lap, a pile of merit badges spilled at her feet.

Tattletale watched from the meadow, seated high on a large black horse. The horse trembled, ready to bolt.

Angel manifested suddenly above the cabin. He stood before Little Wife, threatening you with his sword. 'Are you the destroyer?' he demanded. He spread his enormous wings to hide her from your view.

'No,' you said. 'I am the survivor. Step aside and let me live my own life.'

Angel furled his wings, sheathed his sword, and stepped behind Little Wife's chair.

Her legs were gone now, her body translucent. She reached toward you with her arms, her face a pale blur.

Angie, something moved you to step forward, to take her hands. You braced for anything, a flood, a hurricane. Her voice came from a lipless face. 'Take these.'

A picture. Your journal, hidden in your desk drawer. There was a final message.

And this. A memory. Of the last time she stole control. The sweet taste of it filled your mouth:

Abraim held you close on the dance floor while the slow music played. She slipped into your place and nestled tighter into his arms. Safe, comfortable. He kissed her brow. She kissed his neck. Later in the night, when the party was done, Ali drove you all up the mountain to watch and wait for the sunrise. He surprised Kate with a couple of blankets from the trunk, and they laid a fire in the stone fire ring and sat together close to the glow, wrapped up in each other, literally.

Sparks rose on hot air currents and flew up like stars. Beautiful, but it made us nervous, the untamed flecks of fire.

Abraim took you back into the warm car and you watched each other with shy glances. The firelight reflected on the windows and into his eyes. Little Wife looked through you and read his thoughts, his desires. She knew how to read men.

She moved your hands to your back

183

zipper and pulled. The shoulders fell open, and Abraim sucked in his breath. Speechless, he understood her offer. Then he stroked her arms twice, kissed you above the heart, and settled the dress back together again. He zipped the back and pulled her/you into his arms. 'I just want to hold you,' he said. His arms were trembling and his heart was racing, but it was a safe place. A harbor for the shipwrecked soul. She/you settled into the fold of his shoulder and slept deeply until the sky turned red.

She gave you the memory, of love, of peace, of rest, of comfort. And then she was gone.

'All done,' Dr. Hirsch said. 'The effect should be instantaneous and permanent.'

Angie felt around in her brain for any sign of . . . of Slut. A wave of shame rocked her. How could she have thought of that lonely, broken girl that way? She searched her brain for any sign, any hint of Little Wife.

She was gone.

As soon as Angie got home, she rummaged through the bottom drawer of her desk. Under a layer of theater programs, she found it — the journal Little Wife had hidden again. She opened it to a new entry, dated from the Friday before, from the day Angie had signed her death warrant. Angie's stomach clenched. Yeah. Death warrant. Be honest. Because for all her problems, at the last moment, Angie had recognized Little Wife as both a part of herself

184

and as a separate person with her own wants and needs, history and present. But no future. In that moment she had understood.

Angie's throat closed up painfully, and she thought about burning the note unseen. What would the condemned person say to her in the only way she could?

She spun Little Wife's silver ring on her finger. She could take it off now, and she started to, but something held her back — maybe just the guilt.

The journal demanded her attention. It was all she could do to make herself go on, but she did.

Ange,

That Lynn is a persistent one, and patient. You've gotta give her that. She's been trying hard to get me to answer her questions but, sneaky as she is, I've managed to keep her off. You have to hear it from me. Because I know what you need to know and what you don't. There's things you've gotta understand about the man. And me.

No, first of all, I don't know his name. Never did, and that's true. What did I call him? She asked me that a hundred times already, like she's the freaking police detective or something. I called him 'Husband.' That's what he wanted, so that's what I did. Whatever he wanted, I did. That's how you don't get hurt.

The ring was my idea, early on. It

made things righter, you know what I mean? He made this huge deal about giving it to me, down on one knee. And that was when I convinced him I didn't need to be tied to the bed when he did his thing on me — not if I was his Little Wife. I mean, if my hands were untied, I could make it better for him. My freedom at his price.

He only trusted me so far. Still tied me for sleeping. Not that I slept much, spread out on my back with his snoring self half on top of me.

Did I ever find a piece of paper with a name? she asked. No. Did I ever look? Yes. I tried. He brought a briefcase home with him, but it was never in the same room as me. He was very careful about that, no matter how much he trusted me in the end. There were a few books in the bedroom, *Leaves of Grass*, a few westerns, some Shakespeare, and a Bible. None of them had a name in them. I'd put them in a pocket when he wasn't looking, so Girl Scout could read them in the daylight. Kept her busy and out of my domain, not that she wanted in, at least at that point.

All I was, all I knew, all I felt — it happened within those four walls, with only a narrow doorway between my world and hers. But we learned to exchange a word at the threshold as we passed through and exchanged places. Yeah. A word. At night she'd say, 'your turn, Slut.' In the morning, I'd say, 'your turn, kitchen bitch.' Not exactly the best relationship for two people who completely depended on each other.

All she had to do was keep the front room clean and put a decent meal on the table. Boring as hell. And she had the nerve to look down on me.

Little did she know, that bedroom was my heaven. The man, he brought me the most beautiful things to wear for him, lace and satin. He dressed me up and stroked and admired me. He made me gorgeous. My only mirror was his eyes. He loved me. He was the only person I ever knew for a long, long time.

That bedroom was also my hell. The man, he told me I could never leave him. He tied me to sleep. He feared me. And yes, Ange, I feared him. Hated him too. I especially hated him that time when I started getting fat. It had to be Girl Scout's fault, because I never ate. He put me away and had no use for me. I don't know what I did to make him so angry. For months, I was all alone, so lonely, and she took my place. From our porch, I couldn't see her, but I heard her crying. She screamed a lot — for something, for

187

someone. She disturbed him. Finally he called me back, and things went on as before. I was thin and I was happy again.

What happened after that was all her fault. She was the one who let the Angel in while I slept. Always remember that, Ange. It was all her fault. It had to be her. I could never have harmed my husband. And yes, Ange. I loved him.

I'm so tired. I know you hate me now too. So I don't mind going away. I just wish I could feel a little love again before the end.

Angie closed the notebook.

She began to sob. All the sadness, all the regret, all the pain of three years exploded with shoulder-heaving, gut-wrenching wails.

What had she done?

11

APPARITION

Tuesday morning, Greg was on the lookout for you, Angie. In fact, you found him leaned casually up against the wall right inside the school entrance, striking a pose. 'Mornin', beautiful,' he said.

You weren't beautiful, you knew. Especially not this morning, after spending the whole night tossing, far removed from actual sleep. Much as you usually avoided mirrors, you had actually spent a full five minutes admiring and trying to conceal the puffy circles.

'Mornin', Greg.' You were surprised that the sight of him didn't give you any kind of warm, buzzy feelings. In fact, you just felt vaguely annoyed.

'I told her,' he said.

Your mind went blank. Was that supposed to be important?

He stepped up to you and put his hands on our shoulders. He gave you a little shake. 'Get it? I told Livvie about us. I was going to tell you yesterday, but you weren't here.'

'What about us?' you asked.

'Well, not all the details,' he said, pressing close and grinding his hips against you suggestively.

189

You took a step back so that his hands tumbled from our shoulders. You studied him curiously. Why had you been so attracted to him?

He sensed your distance. 'What's the matter, Ange?' he asked you. 'I did what you wanted. I broke up with Liv. Ho, boy. When I saw that senior with his paws all over you at the dance, I nearly lost it. Point made. It should have been me. I get it.' He took a step toward you, a simpering smile on his face.

To his astonishment, Angie, you whirled away, avoiding his touch. 'No, Greg. The moment's gone. It probably wasn't meant to be, after all.'

You go, girl, we cheered in our silence.

But then Greg grabbed our right arm from behind, squeezing his fingers hard into our bones. 'What? You tease! You manipulative tease!' His fingers tightened.

Pain radiated from the grip on our shoulder. A loud rushing sound in your head — the sound of enormous white wings unfurling — nearly drowned out his next bitter words.

'You just wanted to break us up! You played me.' He yanked our arm, hard. 'Damn you. Look at me when I'm talking to you.'

With narrowed eyes, you rotated slowly to face him. Our left hand clenched into a fist. A terrible brightness filled your field of vision. You stepped aside, inside, and let

190

another take your place. Angel. We swelled with power and grace.

Greg's eyes widened in surprise.

Without warning, we backhanded him across the face. Our sharp knuckles cracked against his cheek-bone.

He shrieked in surprise. 'Shit!'

Greg dropped our elbow and retreated, one hand clasped to his face, bleeding where the ring cut him.

Angel's deep voice dropped an octave and commanded him, 'Don't you ever touch her again.'

'You're fucking nuts!' he shouted over his shoulder as he ran off. 'And you're going to regret treating me like this.'

We laughed at his back. You, too, Angie. You laughed. Together, we were invincible.

Angie rubbed her bruised fingers, wondering what had come over her. She'd never hit anyone before in her life! Still, it felt good somehow, knowing that she'd gotten one over on Greg. Served him right. He'd used her and set her aside until he was jealous. He deserved more than a punch in the face.

It still mystified her what the powerful attraction had been. Probably Little Wife's desires on top of Angie's crush had led to . . . possibly disastrous results. Angie could only imagine what she had done to win Greg, but thankfully she would never have to remember the intimate details. To the end Little Wife had kept to herself exactly what had gone on in Greg's backseat.

191

A twinge of guilt and sorrow pierced Angie's moment of triumph. She felt just a little emptier without the raw energy of Little Wife, the first alter to leave.

The first one. Now Angie had a decision to make. Who next? Tattletale was most bruised, most injured, most betrayed. It would be a mercy to erase those firsthand memories of Yuncle so they could never return, wouldn't it? And then there was Girl Scout, competent, practical, and actually skilled. Angie almost hated to think of losing her. What about Angel? The protector. It was kind of cool to have a personal protector, a strong friend who stood up for her — except this one was inside, which meant she could stand up for herself.

In the end, the decision was made for her.

★　★　★

Greg and Livvie found their own form of revenge faster than Angie thought possible. During lunch break, they called the press. By dismissal time, a crowd had gathered as close to the school grounds as they were allowed. Two news trucks were parked in the faculty lot. The local five o'clock news anchors were drooling for an interview with the lost girl, now found. They were staked out with their camera crews, just waiting in the cold November afternoon.

The moment Angie walked out the front doors of the school, flashes popped, and a bouquet of microphones unfurled in her face. The questions hit her like a hail of bullets. Who? What? Where?

When? Why? And, of course, How do you feel about your ordeal, Ms. Chapman?

She blinked in confusion, blinded by streaks from the flashes. She felt a tug on her arm, and Abraim and Ali were pulling her back into the building. 'We know a sneaky way out of here,' Abraim said. They hurried her away to their car, parked right behind an obscure side door that opened off the science lab.

'How'd you know it was about me?' she asked.

Abraim took her hand. 'I must admit, I Googled you after the dance. I wondered how I could have missed seeing you around all these years. When I realized you were the legendary missing girl and there was no public commotion about your return, I thought maybe it was deliberately suppressed. Are you in witness protection or something?'

Angie slipped into the backseat and buckled lying down. 'I have an identity crisis, but not that kind of identity crisis. Everything I know about those missing years is secondhand. I don't actually remember any of it. So even if I wanted to, I couldn't answer their questions. Can you get me home without anyone seeing me?'

'Sure. That was the general idea.' Abraim peeled out and took the side streets to Angie's neighborhood. 'Oh my,' he said as he pulled close. 'You've got police protection.'

Angie popped up. Two squad cars were parked in her driveway. No news vans. She felt a sudden tightness in her chest. The timing was too close. They probably weren't here about the press, or they would have shown up at school. 'Just drop me off, guys. You're the best.'

She walked into the house to find Detective Brogan and both of her parents home in the middle of a work day. Three other officers stood uneasily in the kitchen, shifting their weight from foot to foot, hands clasped behind their backs. Brogan was in a suit, all serious.

'Hi, everyone,' Angie said as normally as possible. Her pulse was just a little too fast. 'What's up?'

Brogan replied without a pause. 'We've had a major break in the case.'

'That's great!' Angie said with joy — at least, she meant to say it with joy. Suddenly her heart felt incredibly heavy. It was hard to catch her breath. 'What . . . what is it?'

'We found it,' Brogan said. 'We found the cabin.'

While Angie had been fighting her way toward normality, Detective Brogan had been pursuing the thin leads that her alters had offered. Not much to go on, but he was a man who didn't miss much, as Angie had already realized.

In therapy, Girl Scout had given a good description of the rustic cabin where she had lived — the physical cabin, that is. She had recalled some landmarks along her home-bound route. And she gave Dr. Grant permission to pass on the information. It was enough.

The two Forestry Service special agents assigned to the Angeles National Forest had finally located the site of the remote hand-built cabin deep in the thousand square miles of the San Gabriels. The cabin was off the grid and far from any known trails, farther still from the fire access roads that crisscrossed the mountains.

Brogan was sober as he told her, 'A sophisticated scrubber was attached to the chimney to conceal evidence of smoke. Without that, we might have found you years earlier.' Regret deepened his voice.

'We've found positive forensic evidence of your presence there, Angie. Matching hairs and fibers. Ropes and shackles. We're sure it's the right place.'

Her hair and fibers. Bits of herself. Left behind. Angie felt queasy instead of elated.

Brogan went on, unusually oblivious. 'Judging from the dust and cobwebs, it's been abandoned for weeks.'

Mom gasped. 'So he's gone? Just vanished?' She sank into a chair and buried her face in her hands.

Brogan rested a hand on her shoulder and squeezed gently, like a friend.

It occurred to Angie how much of a lifeline he must have been for her mom during the last three years.

Dad threw his arms up in dismay. 'That's it? No arrest? No trial? No punishment?' he roared right in Brogan's face. 'That guy should hang for what he did!'

'This is far from over,' Brogan assured him. 'Now we switch to a manhunt. No personal information was found in the cabin, so we're searching the area for more clues as to the identity of the abductor. Hang in there. I'm sure we'll soon have all the answers.'

Ropes and shackles. Scabs and skin. Angie's stomach lurched. Mom yelped and reached for her. But it was too late. She found herself covered in vomit.

'Oh, no,' she said. 'I'm sorry.' She spun as her legs threatened to buckle underneath her. She breathed slowly through her nose, trying not to let the dizziness knock her down.

Brogan patted her back and pulled out a clean white handkerchief. He offered it to her lamely. 'My fault, Angie. I'm sorry. Too much, too fast. I wasn't thinking.'

Mom reached around Angie's waist. 'If that's all, Phil, I'll take Angie upstairs to clean up.'

Angie glanced back to see Brogan watching her with sad eyes. His shoulders heaved once with a deep breath. Then he dropped to the mess on the carpet and began dabbing at it with his handkerchief.

Mom started the shower running. 'I'll wash your clothes, hon. Just hand them out to me.'

Angie stripped off her sour-smelling jeans and sweater and passed them through the cracked door. She locked it tight, against intruders, against the world. Her stomach still churned like an epic battle was taking place inside her body.

The mirror wasn't steamy yet, and she couldn't help being drawn to it. She stared herself in the eye, except it wasn't herself she was looking for. 'What do you guys know?' she asked the reflection. 'I know you're holding out on me. Why?'

She thought about the derelict porch where everyone had gathered for the moments before

Little Wife was shut off. The walls between them had been down for just a few minutes. It had felt like total honesty. Now they'd walled her off again.

'Where are you?' she whispered. 'Please.' A presence stared at her from her own eyes, and behind her back, a shimmer in the shower mist suggested that a larger person stood behind her. Hallucination?

She blinked hard, and the mist was only mist. She climbed over the edge of the tub, pulled the curtain, and let the hot water cascade over her shoulders. Then she sat on the rubber shower mat, closed her eyes, and invited the water to rain down on her. Heat flowed over her like caressing arms, and she had the strongest feeling now that someone was willing to talk to her, to meet her on another plane. Eyes tight, she dived back into the image of the porch. She summoned up her memory of the railing, the pillars, the rough, splintery floor. The patter of the water faded away. Birds were singing, faraway song sparrows and warblers.

'Who's here?' Angie asked, trying to focus.

Gray wood, chipped boards. A porch. They gradually resolved into a setting Angie recognized.

Girl Scout raised tearful eyes from her sewing and glanced toward the empty spot where Little Wife's rocker used to sit. Tattletale was nowhere in sight. 'She's too young for this,' Girl Scout explained. 'I sent her to ride. I have to leave too. Angel's coming now.'

A sound like trumpets and wings broke the

197

stillness, and the terrible whiteness of Angel arrived. His cheek-bones were cut from crystal. His brow was tall and smooth, a halo of thick black hair rising from it. Snowy wings closed behind his back, and at his side hung a jeweled sheath. The gold handle of a short sword rested close to his waist. His black eyes held pinpoints of flame that settled on Angie. She trembled inside. What was this magnificent creature doing in her head? Surely he hadn't come from her.

'Angela, Pretty Girl, you cannot call me to your aid again,' he scolded so gently.

'But . . . but I didn't call you,' she protested. 'You just . . . you just came when I needed you.'

His lips tightened into a grim line. 'Then you must destroy me.'

Angie gasped. 'No. I could never do that!'

'You will,' he said firmly. 'You must. You will do to me what you did to the other one, the Little Wife.'

Angie felt compelled to argue. 'But you're so strong and beautiful. I need you. I don't want to delete you. Can't you stay with me? Forever? You're my inner strength.'

The angel shook his dark curls. His voice was pure music. 'You have your own strength and beauty and beyond that, innocence. I am only a danger to you now. It is far better if I go unremembered.'

'But why?' Angie demanded. 'Because of Greg? That's ridiculous. He had it coming.'

Angel stood glowing before her. He didn't reach for his sword this time. His hands were tucked behind his back, hidden in his folded wings. 'Angela, our Pretty Girl, please listen. Girl Scout and the Little Wife suffered much, and for so long. Then the lonely one called me into existence. It was finally unforgivable, what the man had done. She called me out of herself, out of her pain, out of the strength of her love. She sat and rocked in the dark, alone, locked in. She rocked and sang and sobbed and prayed.

'I was the answer to her prayer, her avenging angel. When I appeared before her, she said only, 'Save us.'

'And I replied, 'Arm me, and my hands are yours.'

'From the folded blanket on her lap, she pulled a sword of silver brilliance. 'Save us,' she said again fiercely. 'Swear it.'

'I held the sword high and gave her my oath. Strength filled my arm. Sun shone around me, and I spread my wings in the heat of the day. I had no heartbeat drum to follow yet, or eyes to truly see. I was only her thought, but it was good to be alive. It was nearly my time.

'I waited while the others won his confidence, so he would never see my black eyes watching him from within, planning salvation. Girl Scout, so clever, won some release from the shackles. I put a glow on her pale cheeks, which he believed a glow of love. Little Wife made him happier, more secure in her love. He slept so deeply the night I came for him. And what Little Wife told you was true. She never woke as I severed her bonds.'

Angel stopped speaking, and the rainfall patter of the shower grew louder again.

She felt the weight of her body enclosing her. 'What did you do?' she asked.

But Angel was fading away. His eyes were large and full of remorse.

'Come back,' Angie called. 'Don't leave. Please.' She reached for him, grabbed for his sword belt to hold him.

'No!' His wings unfurled, impossibly huge and white. He thrust out his hands to push her away. Blood dripped from his fingertips.

'What the hell did you do?' Angie cried out in her mind. 'Oh God. What?'

The musical voice became hard and brittle as porcelain. 'You can't be allowed to know. If you know, then they will know. Before the questions come, before the walls come down, I have to die.'

Abruptly, the presence was gone and an icy-cold sensation took its place. Chill all around her. Chill raining down. Angie shivered, aware again of her surroundings.

Oh, the shower. The water had run cold. And she'd lost her connection.

With a regretful sigh, Angie opened her eyes. A shocked moment later, she screamed. The water lapping around her legs was red with blood.

12

REPUTATION

'Hon, hon. Angie. Calm down. It's okay.' Mom patted Angie through a thick blue towel. 'Just terrible timing, is all. Welcome to womanhood.'

Angie still trembled, as the last of the water slipped down the drain. She had a hideous feeling that it was more than her body maturing. It was a message of some kind, a parting message from Angel. They were bathed in blood, together. Her heart pounded, still reacting to the rush of adrenaline.

'I have to call Dr. Grant.' Maybe her psychologist could help her understand what had just happened. Whatever it was, it was bad. Of that she had no doubt.

'Are you that upset?' Mom asked. 'We've never bothered her on a non-appointment day.'

'Considering how much you guys pay her, I wouldn't call it bothering,' Angie snapped. 'She said she'd be there for me if I had aftereffects. Well, I'm having them.'

'Okay. Of course.' Mom hesitated. 'Is it something you can talk to me about?'

'No way, Mom.' She wasn't about to share her worst suspicions with her mother.

She retreated to her room, clutching the mini-pad Mom had handed her wordlessly. When she came out again, dressed, Mom was on the phone in the master bedroom. 'No, I'm sorry,' she was saying. She put a finger to her lips when she noticed Angie peeking through the door. 'No. No comment . . . No, we will not be making a public statement today . . . Yes, that's true. September eighteenth . . . How would you feel? . . . Because we needed our privacy. We still do. Please don't call again.'

She slammed down the phone on her nightstand. 'Blasted reporters.'

'What?'

Mom ran her hands through her curls. 'Oh, the questions. That's the third call today.'

Angie's heart raced. 'What are they asking?'

'Crazy stuff,' Mom said. 'Just ridiculous. You don't want to know.'

'Yes I do. I had to ditch them at school today. I need to be prepared.'

Mom huffed impatiently. 'All you have to say is 'No comment.''

'Mom. Just tell me.'

She plopped into a chair and rubbed her cheekbones hard. Her fingers left red streaks across them. 'They want to know why we didn't contact them sooner. Why we've had the 'lost girl' home for two months and haven't shared the news with the public. They want to know whether we're hiding something.'

Angie's heart skipped a beat. 'Like what?' Her vision darkened for a second, but she pulled herself back. No one was taking over for her. She had to handle this. Still, she couldn't shed the image — Angel's hands dripping with blood.

She heard male voices in the living room,

raised in excitement.

She and Mom hurried downstairs to see. The living room was full of policemen. Why were they still here? Brogan was on his cell phone, and Dad was pulling the curtains across the front window. 'News trucks,' he said. 'Right on our street.'

'How absurd,' Mom said. 'Detective, can you get rid of them?'

The doorbell rang. One of the policemen went to answer it.

'Get rid of those damned reporters, will you?' Brogan said to him. He slipped a hand into his pocket. 'We've called in the L.A. County coroner's forensics team for the next step. Forensics will go over everything with a fine-toothed comb — working the cabin, working the site, looking for graves.'

'Graves!' A small shriek escaped Mom.

Brogan pinned his gaze on Angie with a sad twist to his mouth. 'Angie beat the odds, however she escaped. You know that.'

She tried not to flinch. Yeah. However. She had the weirdest feeling. She broke away from his sympathetic look. She couldn't take it.

Brogan misunderstood. He dropped a hand on her shoulder. 'I'm so sorry. Angie, is there anything, anything at all helpful you can tell us before the report comes in? If you can handle it, I'd like to take you up to the cabin when they're done — see if it triggers any memories. Or more confessions from your inner informants. Anything that would help us find this guy.'

Knees weak and feet filled with the urge to flee, she tried to shrug nonchalantly. 'Maybe. I

203

don't think it would help. I don't remember anything.' It was true, literally. *She* didn't remember anything. Surely Angel did, however. Angel with blood on his hands, begging to be deleted before his memories infected innocent Angie. Oh God. She'd never get that picture out of her head, even if she did erase Angel.

She wiped her hands on the seat of her blue jeans.

Brogan's eyes narrowed slightly. 'Right. Okay. We'll be in touch.'

'What do I do about the press?' she asked. 'They were all over school this afternoon. Now they're all over our lawn. They're going to follow me everywhere, aren't they?'

'Don't tell them anything,' Brogan advised. 'Call me if you need to.' He left, taking all the oxygen with him.

★ ★ ★

Greg and Livvie had declared an all-out war on Angie — calling the press was only the first shot across the bow, ushering in a week of torture. Now her phone number was showing up in the bathrooms, both male and female. There were graphic descriptions of what she would and wouldn't do with boys, girls, and animals, plus crazy claims of what turned her on — all untrue, all disgusting.

Angie started carrying around a small can of red spray paint to wipe out these little bombs of cruelty, as well as the crude drawings that often illustrated them. Now she wished she'd made

204

more friends at school so she'd have more defenders, or at least more people who would recognize this as a hate campaign. But having painted herself as a blank, she left herself open to being painted in whatever colors Greg and Livvie picked.

Her friendship with Kate the leper didn't help, but no way would she give up Kate. Kate held Angie's head above water every day and yelled, 'Just keep kicking and breathing.' Figuratively, that is.

'Did you see the new one in the stairwell?' Angie asked, threading her hair through her palms over and over. Her lunch tray sat untouched, as it had all last week, ever since the discovery of the actual cabin.

Kate rolled her eyes. 'That's not physically possible,' she said. 'Not even for gymnasts.'

Angie groaned.

'It'll pass,' Kate assured her. 'It did for me. Worst case, they'll repaint over the summer. The school is starting to look like it has chicken pox with all your tagging.'

'What I don't understand is, why Liv? I mean, sure, I can understand why Greg would be pissed. But why is she helping smear me? She won. She's got Greg. And . . . we used to be friends.'

'It's the only way she can deal with taking Greg back and not feel like she's eating your leftovers, so to speak. It's how she changes the story of you dumping him into him dumping you because you're trash — sorry — in her words.'

'Pathetic. How long till it all blows over?'

'Hey, relax,' Kate advised. 'We've got our beloved five-day Thanksgiving break starting in a few short hours. They'll lose momentum.'

'Doubt it,' Angie said. 'They'll stuff themselves on turkey and pumpkin pie and come back mean as ever.'

Darn Thanksgiving weekend anyhow. Dr. Grant was already at her sister's out of town. Although Angie had pleaded with her about erasing Angel, Dr. Grant told her they couldn't possibly do the next deletion any earlier than next Monday after the holiday — the facilities simply weren't available. So Angie had to brood on her worries like an old hen until they were fully hatched. Any second now, Brogan would have a story put together, right or wrong.

Here's how it would read. Angie had clearly lived in the cabin — hair and fibers everywhere. She'd been carrying a shiv away from the scene. Then a body would be found, with his throat slashed, or his wrists slashed, or his torso stabbed, or some other cause of death requiring a sharp, pointy implement — only Angel knew for sure. All the DNA evidence would come in next, linking the man to the cabin and Angie to the man. It made a neat, tidy package suggesting that Angie killed her captor (because who would blame her) and was faking amnesia and DID to get herself out of whatever they do to juvenile murderers. They'd stuff her under a lie detector. They'd hypnotize her and force Angel's confession.

It would never stay secret. And even if what Angel did was ruled self-defense or justifiable

206

manslaughter or something like that, no one would ever, ever look at her the same. Her life might as well be over. It was all coming down soon. She could feel it looming.

Kate snapped her fingers in front of Angie's face. 'Hey. Snap out of it. You're sinking into self-pity again.'

'Not pity,' Angie said. 'Just a reality check.'

'The guys want to double-date later tonight, but I'm not taking you along if you persist in acting like you're getting hanged in the morning. I'll take one of your other personalities. Who's the funnest?'

'Depends on your idea of fun,' Angie said. 'If you want to play dolls or dress-up, I'd suggest Tattletale. She's six. If wreaking dreadful vengeance with a flaming sword is more your style, I'd send Angel. But he's a guy, so perhaps not exactly right for Abraim. And if cooking over an iron-bellied stove trips your trigger, Girl Scout's your girl.'

'Aw hell,' Kate said. 'We'll take Angie. She just better be in a better mood.'

Angie scowled. 'Okay. I'll try.'

But what she learned at home that afternoon didn't help her lighten up. Exactly the opposite. Grandma and Yuncle Bill had been invited for Thanksgiving.

'Mom, can't we make it just us, the nuclear family?' Angie pleaded. 'I mean, it's the first Thanksgiving I've had with you in a long time. Could we just enjoy it together?'

'It's Grandma's first Thanksgiving without Grampy,' Mom reminded her. 'She needs us.'

'Can't Dad pick her up, then? Or could she take the bus?'

'Angela Grade, what has gotten into you?' Mom asked. 'Yuncle will bring her.'

'But . . . ' Angie stopped dead. She couldn't put into words, at least not acceptable words, how much she dreaded seeing Yuncle again. The only consolation was that she was prepared this time. There was no way he would get her alone. She'd make absolutely sure of that.

★ ★ ★

At eight o'clock, the guys' car pulled up in the driveway. Angie wondered how they decided to split driving since they were twins.

'Ali is twenty-six minutes older,' Abraim informed her. 'So he claims the right of the firstborn. However, if I grab the keys first' — he dangled the keys in front of her — 'I do not yield.'

Ali and Kate were snuggled in the middle of the backseat. From the looks of it, Ali didn't object to having a chauffeur. Angie buckled herself into the front passenger seat and wrenched her neck around to say hi.

'Are we cheerful?' Kate asked.

Angie forced a smile. 'Working on it.'

Abraim put his right hand on her shoulder. In a surprisingly in-tune tenor voice, he started doing Mick Jagger: ''Angie, Angie, when will those clouds all disappear?''

Angie blushed and giggled. 'Oh, please. That's a sad song, isn't it?'

'That depends on your perspective. Sure it's kind of haunting, but think of the refrain.' He leaned toward her and crooned in her ear, ' 'Ain't it good to be aliiiiiiiive?' '

'Well, no doubt it beats the alternative,' she said.

Abraim rocked back into his seat, his face instantly contrite. 'Oh, forgive me.'

'What? Oh,' She punched him gently in the arm. 'No worries. As what's-his-name said, the rumors of my death were greatly exaggerated.'

'Mark Twain, I think,' Ali supplied from the backseat.

Abraim still looked like he was beating himself for saying something foolish.

Angie found herself in the reverse position of cheering up someone else, forcing her to make light of everything, which made her feel a lot better herself.

They snuck into an R-rated movie — not sneaking for the boys, but sneaking for Kate and Angie. They were almost seventeen, sort of. Through whatever magic, whether it was Dr. Grant's expensive therapy or Kate's free therapy, Angie was growing into her age. She didn't feel awkward about seeing a sexy spy thriller with a guy. In fact, she was looking forward to it. Abraim was very sweet, probably the right speed for her first real boyfriend. And if things didn't work out, well, he'd be leaving for college eventually.

Angie wasn't at all hungry so soon after dinner, but she happily shared the popcorn Abraim bought for the excuse of bumping hands in the dark. Two inches away from her, Kate was missing the whole movie, locked in a quiet kissing marathon with Ali. When the popcorn was gone, Abraim stowed the bag and pulled her against his shoulder with a long arm. Angie rested against him comfortably for a moment; then with a jolt she recalled the last time she'd snuggled up like this, right after Slut had started her striptease. Oh God. Angie flushed in the dark. What did he think about that? Explaining to him 'I'm not that kind of a girl' required too many other explanations. Best not to bring it up unless he did.

After the movie, they went for ice cream, so by the time Angie was dropped at home, it was close to midnight. Abraim walked her to the front door and paused as she fumbled under the mat for the key. 'I had a great time,' she said as she fitted it in the lock.

'Me too.' He dropped a quick kiss on her cheek and ducked his eyes. 'Thank you for coming out with me. I hope you don't mind that you got the slow, shy brother.' He glanced back to the car where Ali and Kate were making out again. Poor Abraim would have to play the chauffeur, avoiding the rearview mirror.

Angie rested a hand on his arm. 'No. Not at all. You're just right for me.'

A slight tension in his shoulders loosened. 'Ah, I'm glad of that. The other . . . well, I wondered . . . I hoped I didn't disappoint you.'

Oh hell. He'd brought it up. 'That wasn't me,' Angie said. 'That was like another girl. And you knew exactly what we both needed. Just a long hug. So thanks for being the slow, shy one.' She leaned closer and kissed his cheek back. He smelled fresh and spicy at the same time.

His confused and startled expression made her giggle long after she'd gone upstairs. She'd managed a perfectly normal date, no blackouts, no lost time. A small victory.

She indulged in the treat of sleeping in, so that by the time she worked her way out of the warm covers, through a hot shower, and down to the kitchen, Mom had already put the stuffed bird in the oven and had an apple pie cooling on the countertop. Angie peeked out the window, happy to see that journalists had their own family obligations on Turkey Day, too. No sign of satellite trucks and roving reporters. Everyone was watching parades and football games.

'Can I help?' she asked. 'What are you working on now?'

'The outside stuffing,' Mom said. 'You know, some like it in and juicy; some like it out and crispy. And cranberry cobbler.'

Angie grabbed the stuffing bag and read the back. Melt tons of butter. Sauté tiny pieces of onions and celery, toss them with the seasoned croutons, and add broth to perfect moistness. 'Simple enough,' she said. 'I'll do this.' It was nice to feel competent. And confident. She could handle stuffing, especially with Girl Scout on hand to advise.

'That's great, Angie,' Mom said. 'I've always said that if you can read, you can cook, but you were always so reluctant to try . . . before.'

Angie waved away Mom's flustered expression, 'True. I was. But I had to learn a lot of practical skills. One of the unforeseen benefits of being kidnapped, right? I don't expect there are many.'

'Uh, no.' Mom made a pained sound. 'So how do you feel about fruit salad?'

'Point me to the fruit,' Angie said. 'I've got it under control.'

Mom showed her the collection of canned fruit on the counter — peaches and pears and apricots, as well as the bananas hanging on the monkey stand and a pair of green apples. 'Cutting board is in the drawer, and the paring knife is right next to you.'

Angie found the manual can opener and got to work slicing and dicing fruit into a large bowl. She didn't even hear the doorbell ring. Next thing she knew, there was a tall, strong someone behind her. Yuncle. She recognized his scent. He had his hands on her waist. A foot away, Grandma was kissing Mom, careful not to get flour on her visiting clothes.

'Smells wonderful, Margie,' Yuncle Bill said, but his nose was pressed to Angie's hair. 'Hey, Angie baby, turn around and say hi.'

Angie's skin prickled, not with her own memories, but with others rising to the surface. She squashed them down. She'd handle this.

'You're crowding a woman with a sharp knife,' she warned in a playful voice. 'Bad move.'

He chuckled and stepped back.

Grandma tsk tsked at him. 'Bill, darlin', stop making a nuisance of yourself and get out of the

212

kitchen. There's women hard at work in here. Go watch the game with Mitch. I hear cheerin' from the other room.'

'Yes'm,' Bill said with a slight chuckle. 'I'll bother Angie later.'

Was it only her imagination or was he sending her a coded message? Damn him, playing that game in front of everyone. Had he always pushed like that? She didn't remember him well enough to know.

She shook off the gross feeling where his hands had wrapped her waist. She could handle this. She *would* handle this. She sent a message deep into her head, hoping Tattletale was receiving. *You don't need to come out today, honey. I won't let anything bad happen.*

She hung out with Mom and Grandma in the kitchen, set the table with the best china and crystal, started a load of laundry — anything to avoid coming into contact with Bill again before she had to.

Everyone was totally oblivious at dinner. Had it always been like this? Bill stared at her intensely the whole time and no one seemed to notice. Her heart ached for Tattletale — how lonely and scary and unfair it must have seemed.

Angie picked at the banquet on her plate and forced herself to eat enough to avoid attention. Finally, when Bill declared he couldn't eat another bite, Grandma offered to do cleanup.

'Don't be ridiculous, Ma,' Mom said. 'Angie and I have it covered.'

Bill stepped up. 'Will it go faster if I help dry as well?'

Mom smiled broadly. 'Well, of course it would. Come on in.' She tossed a dish towel at him. 'Isn't that sweet, Angie? You don't see a lot of men volunteering to help with dishes.'

'No, ya don't,' Angie said. Crap. He was on the prowl.

Mom grinned. 'He'll make a fine catch for some girl.'

Angie's stomach burped up a little bit of dinner. She forced it back down.

Bill snorted at Mom's comment. 'Angie's my best girl. You know that, Margie.'

Mom was charmed, as usual. She snapped her towel in his general direction.

Angie found herself scowling at the dishwater. Damn, he was smooth with the grown-ups. He probably always had been. The china plates clinked together under the suds.

'Careful with those, Angie,' Mom said. 'Would you rather dry and put away?'

No, she'd rather not make eye contact with Bill. Washing the breakables gave her the perfect excuse to be glued to her work. The hot water ran in a gentle stream as she passed the soapy dishes through it and into the rack. Mom and Bill alternated grabbing plates to dry.

'So, how's school going?' Bill asked her in a perfectly normal voice.

'Fine,' she muttered.

'Fine? That's it?'

Angie imagined the look he gave Mom as he said, 'Kids.' There was a shrug in his voice.

Mom, unfortunately, volunteered more information in a singsong voice. 'Angie has a boyfriend.'

214

Angie heard his intake of breath. Soft and menacing. But his question came out in all innocence. 'Angie! Is this true? Why didn't you tell me?' And then pretend-hurt. 'I thought your heart belonged to me.'

Mom leaped in to worsen the tension. 'Well, she's a bit shy about it. Besides the formal dance, they've only gone out once. His name's Abraim.' She pronounced his name about as foreign as she could make it, with a long rolled *r* and the syllables stretched out. 'Nice-looking boy. Angie tells me he's very smart, applying to Harvard and all.'

The pride in her voice made Angie want to scream, *Shut up, Mom. Just shut up.* No-college Bill didn't want to hear about Angie's intelligent boyfriend. But of course, she didn't. She just kept washing and passing the long-stemmed wineglasses.

Mom picked up the stack of dinner and bread plates. 'I'll stow these,' she said, walking toward the dining room.

As soon as Mom's back was turned, Bill pressed up against Angie's back, pinning her against the edge of the sink. His hands reached around and below her breasts. She froze.

'Boyfriend, huh?' Bill whispered against the side of her head.

Angie felt a pressure building inside. A flutter of panic. A tiny voice saying, *Hide.*

'No,' she said aloud to Tattletale. And in her head, *I'm not leaving. This stops here and now.*

Bill heard only the 'No' and nuzzled her neck.

215

His hands moved higher and squeezed. 'Has he touched you here?'

The frantic feeling in her head increased. *Go. Go now! Quick.*

'No!' she said to Tattletale. And 'Stop it' to Bill.

Mom's return was seconds too late. Bill was innocently back to drying silverware. With his probing hands gone, Angie's body tingled with feelings she loathed. Ugh. He had her body trained to respond to him while her mind resisted with all her strength.

Angie plunged her bare hands in the water. Red spots appeared on her arms, like oil spatter burns. She touched them, feeling nothing.

Mom had grabbed the four crystal stems between all of her fingers. The bowls touched with a gentle *ping*. She headed back to the china cabinet in the dining room. 'You two finish up,' she called over her shoulder.

And Bill was back again, lifting the hair from her neck and pressing a kiss behind her ear. 'We'll sneak away as soon as we can,' he promised.

Angie shivered and whirled around, meat fork in hand. 'No, we won't,' she hissed. 'Ever. Keep your goddamn hands off her.' She waved the fierce prongs under his nose.

'What's wrong with you?' he asked in a hushed voice. He raised a fingertip to his lips. His eyes darted to the dining room door.

'She's reclaiming herself,' Angie said. Her voice came out deep and strange.

'Aw, come on, Angie baby. Don't play games. You were burning hot for me last time. Oh yeah, babe.' He grabbed her shoulders and did a little

216

hip dance. 'Your little boyfriend doesn't need to know you got a real man.'

Angie shuddered. Invisible wings opened on her back. She clung to her core, but with the threat level rising to red, Angel was roused and angry.

Mom's voice came from the living room. 'Anyone want coffee with their pie? Mitch? Ma? I'll put on a pot. Who was ahead at the half?'

Angie followed it with her ears.

Distressingly normal sounds from the other room — Dad urging the team through the TV, Grandma asking for decaf, if it's not too much trouble — can't have real at this hour, or I'll be up all night.

Angie's hearing was supernaturally amplified, her consciousness elevated outside the room, moving into the distance. Fragmented. Part of her was the little girl trembling before this man, who was her beloved Yuncle — anything to avoid the fire, she was thinking. Part of her had white, rustling wings, and a sword at the ready. Part of her stood aside and watched, wondering what her role was supposed to be.

'That's better,' Yuncle sighed. 'That's my girl. That's my pretty girl. You want it.'

Angie snapped back to find herself running her hands under his shirt. She snatched a handful of hair between her fingers and ripped. 'Like hell,' she screamed.

'Shit,' Bill grunted. He raised a fist.

Mom's voice penetrated from a distance. 'Angie? Everything okay?'

Angie's arms rose to protect her face. He

captured her wrists and squeezed so hard, her hands started to go numb. 'Don't . . . say . . . a . . . word.' His mouth was only four inches from her face. His spit rained on her cheeks.

The deep voice of Angel broke through again. 'I will not permit.'

'What?' Bill's face was a riot of confusion. His hesitation was a definite mistake.

Angel twisted his right arm out of Bill's hold and smashed his elbow down through Bill's grip on Angie's left. Bill shook his battered arm, and Angel grabbed the fingers, twisting them backward till there was a snapping sound.

Bill stared in disbelief at his deformed hand and gasped, loud enough to carry. 'Why, you bitch!'

He moved to take a full-fisted swing at her, but Angel moved Angie's hand to reach for the meat fork and plunge it deep into Bill's forearm. She felt the sharp points scrape bone, and a sick, triumphant feeling surged through her.

Bill's roar brought the others running from the living room. 'Look what she did! Look what she did to me!' he hollered. 'She's insane!'

Her parents pulled up short, confronted with the stranger in their daughter, the hard, glittering eyes of the Angel, the set of his jawline.

Angie's heart swelled with certain knowledge. He would never touch her again. She was free. Angel grinned.

Your victory was short-lived. A moment later, your father tackled you to the ground. 'Call the doctor, Margie! No, call 911! She's

218

having a total breakdown.'

Angie, you tried to breathe, tried to explain, but the fall had knocked all the wind out of you. You gulped for air, like a fish pitched out of a bowl.

Above you, Grandma already had a clean towel around Yuncle's arm, staunching the blood flow. 'Oh, Bill, how lucky she missed your torso.'

Dad's chest heaved with short, quick breaths. 'Thank — thank the Lord she grabbed the fork. Not the carving knife.' He pinned your shoulders against the hard kitchen tiles.

In total disbelief and unable to say a word, you lay there gasping. There was only hatred and fear in Grandma's face. You blinked your eyes pleadingly at Mom, who was dialing the phone. Mom reached out her other hand to you, but Dad stopped her.

'Margie, keep away,' he barked, his voice cracking. His hands dug into you with strange energy. 'God only knows what she might do to you and the baby. I knew this would happen. I knew . . . she's been too calm . . . just waiting to break.'

You finally grabbed enough air to wheeze, 'Dad, please. Let me explain.'

Dad's head snapped around, and he looked straight into your eyes for the first time. His breath caught. 'Angel? What — ?'

'No, Daddy. Angel's gone. It's me, Angie.' You tried so hard to make him understand.

Bill's good hand grabbed Dad's shoulder from behind, and he loomed over both of you, there on the floor. 'She nearly killed me, Mitch. She hit an artery. My goddamn fingers are broken.' His voice was level, but his eyes promised revenge. You flinched away, and the connection with Dad broke.

'Restrain her. Keep her calm,' Bill ordered.

Dad tensed and pinned you tighter. Sweat beaded on his forehead. His mouth was a pale slash in his dark red face. He looked like he was about to have a stroke. And his fingers pressed lines into your shoulders.

You twisted weakly, trying to escape his grip.

'They're coming immediately,' Mom said. 'Angie, hang on, honey. Help is coming.' She reached out again, met Dad's warning glare, and retreated, twisting her hands. She looked away, toward the front of the house. 'And thank God there aren't any news trucks today. An ambulance would put them over the top.'

'Ambulance?' you squeaked. 'I'm fine. I don't need an ambulance.' Then you were babbling. 'Maybe Yuncle the creep needs one. Yeah, I hope he needs one.' Babbling out Tattletale's delight at the turn of fortune. 'Now who's gonna be in trouble?' she taunted.

'Oh, Mitch. Let her up. Let me hold her,' Mom begged.

'Margie, please. Just . . . I've got her.'

'Daddy, you're hurting me,' you pleaded.

Tears filled his eyes, and his hands loosened slightly, but still he kept you under his control.

Bill stared down at you with false pity. 'Poor child. Complete psychotic breakdown. I've seen it after combat. She doesn't even know what she's saying.'

Angel pushed to the front again. His growling voice tore through the confusion. 'You lying bastard. You molested her. For years.' He twisted away from our father's hold with renewed strength and broke free. He jumped to his feet, a towering fury. He reached to his side for the jeweled sword that hung there in the inside world, found only belt loops on your blue jeans. His dark eyes fixed on the knife block next to the sink.

'What is she saying?' Grandma demanded.

Angel reached for the knife block.

'Watch out, everyone!' Bill yelled. 'Get back. I've got her.'

The sound of an ambulance siren drew closer. Mom ran to the front door.

Bill sprang at you, at Angel, at Tattletale, all messed up together in a tangle. He socked you in the stomach and wrenched your arms behind your back. 'Sedative,' he called toward the approaching paramedics. 'Quick. Knock her down.'

We felt a sharp pinch in the arm, and everyone collapsed into unconsciousness.

221

13

CONFRONTATION

Angie woke in a clean white bed, in a clean white room with green curtains. She felt dulled, empty. Where was she? Within moments of opening blurry eyes, she zoomed in on the chair next to the bed. A woman slept in it, her head tilted on her shoulder. 'Mom?' Angie's voice croaked between dry lips.

Mom leaped from the chair to Angie's side. She clasped Angie's hand. Angie noticed soft restraints on her wrists. A tear slipped out of the corner of her eye. She hardly sensed it. 'What happened? What did I do? Am I under arrest?'

Mom stroked her forehead. 'No, no, hon. You're under observation. Something happened to trigger a very violent reaction. We were afraid you'd hurt yourself or someone else. You've been sedated for a day. Dr. Grant rushed back from her sister's, bless her heart, and they did another one of those procedures that seem to help you.'

'Is she still here?' Angie desperately needed to talk to her, to process what had happened.

Mom tipped her arm to check her watch. 'She said she'd check in very soon. I think she went to get some coffee. It's been a long vigil.'

Angie winced. 'I'm sorry, Mom.'

'Well, you'll be glad to hear that Bill's arm will be just fine. No nerves or arteries hit after all, so

222

two stitches, antibiotics, and a big bandage is all he needs. Of course, the broken fingers will take a little longer, but they'll heal straight, the doctor said.'

Angie was silent. Stone-faced.

'Angie, aren't you glad? You didn't do any permanent damage, and he forgives you.'

Angie's stomach did a double flip. 'He forgives me?' She tugged at the restraints in frustration. 'What the hell!'

'Calm, Angie. Or I'll send for another sedative,' Mom warned.

Angie froze in place. 'Mother — that guy molested me for years, every time he babysat me. He molested me again a week after I came back. He's just plain evil. I didn't know how to tell you and Dad.'

Mom's expression softened, but not in the way Angie expected. 'You poor confused girl. Bill said he thought it was something like that. You've got him confused in your mind with the man who abducted you, who raped and abused you.' She cupped Angie's cheek with her hand. 'Remember? It was that evil man, not your uncle Bill.'

Oh, that sneaky bastard. Tears washed down her face. Someone's tears, not hers. She was too tired to cry. 'Mom, get this. Yuncle Bill, who I loved and trusted? He raped and abused me. For years.'

Mom shook her head dismissively. 'You were only six, hon. He was a little boy. You're trying to make me believe he molested you every Friday night for four years?'

'Yes.'

Mom's head still shook slightly. None of this was getting through to her. 'And you never said a word? Never hinted? Never told us not to go out? Why not?'

A question Angie had asked herself a hundred or more times since she'd learned Tattletale's story. 'Because he made me promise not to.'

'Oh, hon. You're really, really confused.' Mom's forehead creased with concern. 'Our Bill would never do anything to hurt you. You should have seen how worried he was for you, even while he was bleeding like crazy. Somehow your wires have gotten crossed, is all.'

She reached out to stroke Angie's hair.

Angie pulled away. She could read the verdict on Mom's face — entirely unconvinced. Damn. Why did she believe him, not her own daughter? Angie turned her head as far to the side as she could. 'I want to see Dr. Grant,' she said into the pillow. 'Please leave.'

A pained gasp came from Mom's direction. Then she was gone.

The next ten minutes felt like ten hours. The leg and arm restraints reminded her too much of the memory flash from captivity that Little Wife had shared with her in a fit of anger. She felt around in her head for the presence of the others, but they were scared into corners. Everything was quiet inside. Maybe the sedative had that effect too.

Finally, Dr. Grant knocked and entered. She took the same seat Mom had vacated. 'That must have been terrifying for you,' she said, 'to have your alters manifest so blatantly in front of your family. What happened? Was it a memory cascade?'

'I feel so stupid telling you this now,' Angie said. 'If I'd spoken up sooner, none of this might have happened.'

'Well, now is now,' Dr. Grant said. That was the great thing about her. No judgment in her voice. No blame. 'What should I know that I don't?'

'Can you unstrap me? I feel sort of vulnerable like this.'

Dr. Grant peeled back the blanket and saw the restraints. 'Good heavens. Of course you do. Why did they do this? It wasn't on my orders.'

'I assure you you're safe. There's no sharp cutlery around here.'

Dr. Grant smiled gently. 'No. There isn't.' She unbuckled Angie's right wrist. 'So. I'm listening.'

Angie felt the strength of Tattletale's inhibition. No tattling allowed. She opened and closed her mouth a few times. Nothing came out.

'Angie, child abuse is one of the few exceptions to our doctor-patient confidentiality. I am required by law to report within twenty-four hours. Do you want to go on?'

How did she know? 'Yes. Yes, I do.' Angie blurted it all in a rush — the history of Tattletale and Yuncle.

Dr. Grant pursed her lips. 'Ah,' she said. 'I had wondered. That makes much more sense now. Your mind already had an escape hatch. Creating new ones was a natural defense in a similar situation.'

'Yeah. I get that,' Angie said. 'So you believe me?'

'Of course I do,' she replied.

'My parents don't,' Angie said glumly. 'They'd rather believe in Bill and think I'm insane. Isn't that so twisted?'

'It rocks their world to think the other way around. Think of the burden of guilt on their shoulders if they let themselves believe you. They let it happen. That's awfully bitter to swallow. I'll help you talk to them about it, if you wish.' She smoothed the sheet over the side of the bed. 'When did you find out?'

Angie swallowed. 'The first week I came back, Grandma and Uncle Bill came over to see me. I lost eight hours — pretty much the whole visit — but I didn't know why. Then, a couple weeks later, Tattletale left me a message asking for a tape recorder. As soon as I got one, she told me the whole story.'

'Do you remember it for yourself?' the doctor asked.

'Not directly. And I'm positive that during those dropped hours he got me to switch and raped her all over again.'

'Her or you?'

Angie understood the question immediately. 'Her. All I had to show for it was a small burn on my arm. No memory.'

Dr. Grant frowned. 'Are you on birth control of any kind?' she asked carefully.

Angie's stomach swan dived. 'Oh. My God, no. But hang on. I started my period after that. Yeah, way after that.'

'Started, you say?'

Angie blushed. 'Yeah, I kind of freaked out since it was so unexpected.'

Dr. Grant patted her hand. 'Well, not exactly started. Girl Scout once told me she had terrible cramps and very irregular periods.'

'Oh? Oh. Maybe I should be thankful I missed that,' Angie said lightly.

'Why do you think you had such an aggressive response with your uncle this time?'

Angie grunted. 'Well, for one thing, I knew Tattletale's secret, and I was already pissed off. I was determined not to let him get to her again, and yet there he was, so smug and confident and weaselly, I wanted to vomit. Also, Angel knew I was mad and wanted it to stop. Angel didn't exist for her when she was little and alone.'

'Angel. The protective male alter. Yes, I knew he must have come to the front. A physical attack was so unlike you.'

'I felt him trying to get through. It was so bizarre. A power struggle.'

Dr. Grant had that listening look on. She didn't interrupt again.

'Tattletale was trying to get me to leave so she could take the abuse for me; Angel wanted me to get out of the way so he could teach Bill a permanent lesson; I was stuck in the middle trying to protect Tattletale. Eventually, Angel won. He protected all of us. He can't help himself, right? I mean, that's what he was born to do. He is strength. He is vengeance. It's his only job.'

'Yes, of course. And that's why you wanted

227

him eliminated next. Right?'

'I'm so worried about what he's capable of doing.' She looked at her own hands, imagining them streaked with red. 'About what he might have done. I have . . . you can't say anything, right? About what I tell you?'

'Not unless you grant me permission.'

Angie's voice shook. 'Even if it's criminal?'

'Are you planning to commit a crime?'

How she could ask that question with such a bland, neutral expression was amazing.

'Not planning, no. Dr. Grant, I didn't know I had that kind of violence in me. And yesterday, everyone saw it.'

Dr. Grant made a *hmm* sound.

Angie's throat tightened. 'You should have seen the look in my grandma's eyes. She was terrified of me. And Dad . . . even worse. He hates me. He hates what that man made me into.'

'It wasn't only your abductor, Angie. It didn't start there, remember.'

She clenched the sheet with white fingers. 'He will never in a million years believe that about his little brother. And I'm going to be forced to see him year after year. Although he probably won't wait long to find a way to get revenge.'

'No way, Angie. We'll get a restraining order. Trust me. Now, what are you really afraid of?'

She bit her lip. 'It could have been the knife. It could have been his chest. If I, Angie, hadn't blocked Angel, I think he would have killed my uncle. Right there in the kitchen on Thanksgiving. Without hesitation or remorse. And — '

Angie stared at her hands. She couldn't say it. All that came out was, 'But only Angel knows.'

'Ah.' Dr. Grant sighed. 'Knew, I'm afraid. While you were heavily sedated, I called Dr. Hirsch and we went ahead with the deletion procedure you had scheduled for Monday. He was willing, under the circumstances. So you don't need to be afraid anymore, my dear. Angel is gone.'

Angie felt a tremendous tearing inside. Heard a wailing scream. Felt a stranger.

Nothing showed on the outside, though. She turned her face to the wall, a tear escaping.

The hospital smell was strangely comforting. Angie hung on to one thought only. What she couldn't remember, they could never get out of her, even with a lie detector. Even with hypnosis. Angel had stayed self-contained and taken his guilty memories with him. No last-minute confessions when he went. She was safe. She was just done. Her breath pulled in and out more easily.

Dr. Grant said, 'Well, that's two down. How are you feeling?'

'Quiet. Empty.'

'I'm glad. All right then. I'll set up some mapping time to go after the other two.'

'Oh.' Angie hadn't thought that one more step ahead. Erase Girl Scout? Erase Tattletale? That was the next logical step, she supposed. Still, it seemed sort of ruthless to delete them. They weren't harming her.

'Dr. Grant. Actually, I was wondering if we could take a stab at doing more therapy, maybe

229

that integration thing you were talking about. Do you think they'd cooperate?'

Inside her head, a voice said, *Oh, yes. Better than dying!*

14

RENOVATION

Angie relaxed into the sofa, ready for the alter team meeting. Dr. Grant had helped her come up with this plan. There was a lot of mess to clean up. She and the other two girls would work together in the imaginary world where they'd met before, the derelict cabin in her mind. Tattletale didn't live there like the others had — she only visited — but Angie felt that with the threat of Yuncle neutralized, she'd be able and willing to join them. They had some serious personality renovations to tackle as a team. A building project together was a perfect metaphor for reconstructing Angie's unitary mind. Not more shortcuts, not more losses and erasures. Girl Scout and Tattletale had been issued an invitation — let's talk about complete integration.

The pine knots in the wall paneling no longer looked like threatening eyes to Angie. That had to be a positive sign. The girls were much less afraid than they had been.

Dr. Grant brought out the light bar to initiate the deep visualization; she would begin the guided meeting, but Angie would have to do the heavy lifting once things got started. She fell under the sway of the bouncing light within moments.

Of course, I was there to help you, Angie. I heard every thing you hear. I saw everything you see. I stood outside it all, recording and watching, controlling the walls and the gates. I supported your goals. We would have a happier and calmer, and certainly more predictable life if we worked together instead of taking turns.

You came to the porch, ready for action, holding a broom and a bucket of paint. Daylight shone on the cabin, and the dry boards and rusty nails stood out. You began by sweeping the cobwebs that hung from the rafters and fresh webs that wrapped the runners of the rocking chairs. Tattletale crept out of the shadows to see what you were doing. 'Come help me?' you suggested. 'We need to clean these before we put them away.'

'Away?' Tattletale asked. 'Why? Where's everyone going?'

'Into the sunlight,' you said. 'We're not going to sit in the darkness anymore. We can all be in the light. Would you like to come too? Would you like to be with me all the time?' You were careful not to show how anxious you were.

'Will there be horses? Real horses?' Tattletale asked.

Sure. Why not? There were stables and a riding school nearby. If Friday night babysitting became a regular thing, you could take riding lessons and pay for them yourself. 'Yeah,' you promised her. 'If you come with me, we'll ride beautiful horses.'

Tattletale gave you a huge smile. She took the broom and started dusting the rockers. 'Then as soon as we clean up, can we go?' she asked.

So soon? You'd expected this to be harder. 'As soon as we've put everything right,' you said.

Girl Scout had been silent the whole time, rocking and sewing. She lifted her feet when Tattletale got to her chair.

'Aren't you going to help us?' Tattletale asked.

'Why should I?' Girl Scout snapped. 'We'll just disappear like Slut and Angel.' She crossed her arms around her chest and frowned.

You hurried to reassure them. 'No, no. I don't want you to disappear. I decided to take you with me. Please. I want you with me.' You handed a hammer to Girl Scout. 'You look kind of mad. Would you like to pound some nails?'

Girl Scout rose reluctantly, but she took the hammer and began taking huge whacks at the rusty nails poking out of the wall boards.

I brought a can of cornflower-blue paint out of the shadows where nobody went. Angie, you noticed and said, 'This is just what we need.' Three brushes were next to the can, so after you opened it, the three of you could stand side by side, painting the wall of the house — the only wall you had. The paint covered the weathered wood, making it fresh and vibrant again. Progress *on the wall was quick. Soon, it was blue as the sky.*

Girl Scout stepped back and admired it. 'That's a good day's work,' she said. 'We're a good team.'

You understood the message. She wasn't yet ready to merge, but she was considering it. That was great progress for one session, Dr. Grant told you. We were closer than we had ever been to integration.

Angie was out of school for that full week, daily sessions with Dr. Grant and the girls taking all her time and energy. They made a ton of progress, both on the imaginary porch and on their mutual understanding. The rockers had been replaced by flower boxes filled with blooming chrysanthemums, appropriate to the colder weather. The front railing was painted a bright and welcoming yellow. The floorboards had been firmly nailed back into place and refinished, providing a firm foundation. The metaphor worked. Angie felt herself standing on firmer ground.

'Any day now,' Dr. Grant said. 'I think Girl Scout is ready to come aboard.'

'That would be pretty cool,' Angie replied. 'And will I actually absorb all her knowledge of cooking and living off the grid?'

'The good and the bad,' Dr. Grant replied. 'Be prepared as well for firsthand memories of the captive experience.'

'She's told me all about it. I've got the scars to show for it,' Angie said somewhat defensively.

Dr. Grant twisted a pearl earring. 'It's not going to be a walk in the park. You're in a good place right now, which is great. Just be aware that incorporating what's coming may set you back a little emotionally. I'm not saying you can't handle it. Just don't underestimate.'

Angie sighed. Even without Angel, she felt strong. She could handle it. It was time to put the rest of her life in order as well. She signed up for riding lessons as promised, shopped for the ultimate riding outfit, and took her first lesson on the Sunday afternoon before she was due back at school.

They gave her the most gentle horse in the stables. Even so, as the pace picked up a little, Angie felt herself flying. The wind blew her hair back where it hung below the riding helmet. Her knees gripped the bounding animal. Her heart pounded. 'Take it, Tattletale,' she whispered, and slipped aside. From a close spot, she watched the little girl take up her body and gallop the horse around and around the corral. The smile in her mind was priceless, worth handing over control for a while.

'Excellent progress,' the instructor said at the end. 'Are you sure you've never ridden?'

'Only in my imagination,' Angie told him.

'Well, you must have an excellent imagination,' he said.

'So I've been told.' Angie smiled inside. Tattletale squeezed her hand in thanks.

Angie, I was so proud then, of you and what you'd done. And you finally realized, that

235

*evening as you sat on your bed rubbing
lotion into your sore muscles — you had
opened the gate to Tattletale yourself, on
purpose, and you had brought her back in
again. You didn't need me to do it for you.
You could handle this job. I was fired.*

*At that moment, your heart swelled with
strength and joy. You never even felt me go,
as I vanished and blended into the whole we
would become.*

'What is up with you?' Kate said when Angie
went back to school the next morning. They
caught up at the bank of lockers. 'You look
great.'

'Oh, thanks a lot,' Angie said. 'Why so
surprised? You were expecting me to look
hideous?'

'They said you were out with the flu — that's
why I didn't call — but obviously not.' Kate
pulled two heavy textbooks from her locker.

'Hey, if that was the rumor, go with it.' Angie
tapped her chest and faked a cough.

Kate eyed her skeptically. 'So what, really?
Hiding from the press? Taking an unauthorized
family vacation?'

Angie laughed. 'Not in the sense you mean.
I've been communing with my other selves,
doing some housekeeping and renovations.'

'What the hell does that mean?' Kate
demanded, shouldering her backpack.

Angie grabbed her history book and slammed
her own locker shut. 'Mostly a lot of hypnosis
and visualizing and internal conversation stuff.

236

We're negotiating a merger. Harder than it sounds.'

Kate snorted. She set off down the hallway with a quick stride. 'I didn't think it sounded easy. Jeez. Your life is way complicated.'

'But there's a pot of gold at the end of my rainbow, a light at the end of my tunnel.'

'A dawn at the end of your day?'

Angie snickered. 'Well, something like that. Have the reporters stopped hanging out at school?'

'They finally gave up Friday. Thank God for the short attention span news cycle. Hey, here's where I get off. See ya at lunch.' Kate ducked into her Spanish class.

Therapy sessions hadn't taken all day. Angie had kept up with the schoolwork while she was out, so settling back into each class was no problem. Several teachers asked if she felt better, and she answered as if they meant the flu.

She dreaded lunchtime, just a bit. She figured the best strategy with Greg and Liv was to pretend nothing had happened, that is, if they would let her. She could stand up to them. She could endure. Considering what else she had been through and survived, their petty meanness was nothing. The question was, would they let her?

At the end of the first day, it seemed they might. She was invisible to them at lunchtime, and with no classes together, she thought she had skated by when she heard her name called, and Liv jogged up behind her.

'You're back,' Liv said bluntly.

'Did you hope I'd changed schools?' Angie asked. 'Well, I didn't.'

Liv scowled. 'If you think you're — '

She didn't get any further before Angie interrupted. 'Liv, before you say anything else, I want to apologize for going after your boyfriend. It was rude and stupid, and I was partially out of my mind.' Wasn't that the truth! 'You can be sure I have no desire to repeat the experience.'

Liv stepped back with a strange expression. 'Why not? What's wrong with him?'

Oh God. 'Nothing. He's just not the right guy for me,' Angie said. 'I don't know what I was thinking.'

'Hmm.' Livvie seemed to be considering the merits of the apology. 'I couldn't have told you that?'

'You never had the chance. You stopped talking to me after the first day. Remember?'

'You stopped talking to me,' Liv shot back.

Right. What could she say? Try the truth? 'I guess I felt guilty — '

Liv cut her off. 'You know, I sensed something, right off. Like there was still this chemistry between you.'

'All physical,' Angie said. 'And that's way over. Emotion-wise, there's nothing there. You're the one he likes.' For better or worse, she thought. 'He never really wanted to break up with you.'

'Really?' Liv's shoulders rose a little. 'He said that, but I didn't know whether it was true. You know guys. They'll say anything they think you want to hear.'

Didn't she know it! 'Yes, they do. But in this

case, it was true. He's all yours, Livvie.' Take him. Please.

Livvie's lips closed in a self-satisfied smile. 'Good. So, whatever. See you round.'

She took off for the parking lot with a bounce in her step. Angie watched as she headed straight for Greg's car, climbed in, and grabbed him for the public display of affection that was banned in school. Making quite a point of it, actually.

She tested her emotions. Any regrets? Any jealousy? Not a hint.

15

INTEGRATION

'Ready?' Dr. Grant asked.

'Maybe.' They'd done all the work they could on the cabin — a wall and a porch with no interior. At least, Angie couldn't open or see past the doorway to the inside. She couldn't walk around the corner to the other three sides, assuming they even existed.

'Watch the light,' Dr. Grant said softly. 'Watch the light and relax. Sink back into that place, the meeting place. How does it look?'

'Beautiful. Cheerful. Ready for company.' Bright sun beamed on the red and orange flowers. The yellow railing sparkled with morning dew. A broom leaned up against the corner, but there was nothing left to sweep away except the walls between the girls.

'Has anyone arrived?' Dr. Grant's voice came from a distance.

Angie looked again. Tattletale leaned against the porch railing, dressed for riding in a miniature riding suit.

Angie spoke aloud for the doctor's benefit. 'Just Tattletale so far. I think today's the day. She looks ready to move on.'

'Are you?'

Angie thought hard. This was what they'd been building toward — unity. Would she still

240

feel like herself? Would she feel smaller or larger? Losing Little Wife and Angel had been abrupt, and their private knowledge had been stripped away. This would be completely different.

Angie extended her hands to Tattletale, who smiled shyly and stepped into Angie's arms. Angie hugged her. 'No one's ever going to hurt us again,' she promised. 'And you don't have to take care of me — we'll take care of each other. Okay?'

The little girl raised her face to the sun. The wind lifted a strand of golden hair and blew it across her lips. With soft fingertips, Angie brushed it away and felt the brush across her own lips. It was her own hair, and the little girl was her and she was the little girl and they were apart and they were together, standing in the rays of the morning sun, hearing the meadow birds singing, touching the dew on the railing with ten fingers, not twenty.

Angie was dressed in the blue jeans and pink sweater she'd worn there, but a riding crop was in her hand and tall boots were on her legs. 'Yes, we'll ride today,' she said, but of course there was no one else to hear her.

★ ★ ★

She probed the new memories gingerly. Yuncle. Somehow she didn't hate him. Or fear him. Of course there was confusion and pain and embarrassment and even boredom. Now she remembered the day when he left for the army. Her tenth birthday, and he'd promised her a

241

special present. He looked so handsome in his uniform. Grampy and Grandma were so proud, they said, that he had found a calling after drifting through high school — whatever that meant. It was her birthday, and everyone was making such a fuss about him. No fair.

Grampy took pictures of the family in all the different possible groups. Angie wanted one just of her and her soldier, like the pictures she'd seen of ladies sending their boyfriends off to war.

'Ready, Grampy? Take this!'

She threw her arms around Yuncle's neck and kissed him like the pictures, arched backward, one foot up, long and hard. She clung to his lips and waited for the sound of a click, but it never came. Yuncle pushed her off him, and she fell on the floor.

Everyone was staring at her with strange, disgusted looks on their faces.

Mom gave a nervous giggle. 'Too much television, I guess. Gives them crazy ideas.'

Yuncle left for the war without speaking directly to her again. She never found out what the special present was. And that was why she had cried for a week.

Tears of childish regret rolled down her cheeks in Dr. Grant's dark office.

★ ★ ★

'Angie, how do you feel?' Dr. Grant's office came back into focus.

Angie rubbed her cheeks and answered hoarsely. 'I feel, um, enlightened.' In both senses.

242

Lighter and informed. 'I have this irresistible urge to eat sugary breakfast cereals.'

Dr. Grant's eyes widened. 'Really?'

'No, just kidding. I . . . it's great, though. She's part of me now, but woven into me everywhere instead of apart. I can't describe it. I just feel more settled. But I don't understand why Girl Scout didn't come.'

'Maybe she's still scared of losing her independence,' the doctor suggested. 'Or maybe she has unfinished business.'

Angie picked a loose pill off her sweater and rolled it in her fingers. 'She's the only one who never took me over except in therapy. Or redoing my homework.' The pill dropped to the carpet. 'At least that stopped. You know, she's never been out in the real world.'

'That's an interesting point. She lived her whole life in that rustic kitchen. What do you suppose she would like to do?'

Angie wracked her brains and immediately heard the answer shouted at her. 'Go to a restaurant!'

Dr. Grant broke into unexpected giggles. 'Of course,' she said. 'Let me see what I can arrange for tomorrow.'

For the rest of the week, therapy was scheduled during the lunch hour. Angie got only thirty minutes for lunch, but her after-lunch class was studio art. She could easily make up the work with a long day at the easel, so Mom agreed to let Dr. Grant pick her up from school right after morning classes. 'I can't exactly say I understand it, but Dr. Grant seems to know what she's doing. You've been so much calmer lately.'

Angie swallowed a snippy retort. She didn't want to blow it.

Tuesday was the best Italian spot in town. Angie sat across the booth from her therapist, feeling self-conscious. 'How will I make sure Girl Scout gets to enjoy the food instead of me?'

'Look at me,' Dr. Grant said. She lifted her spoon and twirled it slowly to catch the light.

'Now what?' Angie asked. 'What's that supposed to do?'

Dr. Grant smiled. The table was covered with empty dishes, and Angie's stomach felt hugely distended. Her top jeans button was unsnapped.

'Oh my God. Don't tell me she ate all that!' Angie wailed. The taste of oregano and thyme hung in her mouth.

'Should we go for a walk?' the doctor suggested.

'Yeah. Like a 10K,' Angie said. 'Better yet, let Girl Scout walk it off.'

Wednesday: Chinese. Thursday: barbecue. By Friday, Angie was scared to step on the scale. Dr. Grant assured her that the eating binge was almost done. She told Angie that Girl Scout had been taking a scientific interest in the dining experience, asking to speak to the chef, quizzing him or her on ingredients and techniques. 'I saved the best for last. There's a lovely French restaurant she'll especially enjoy.'

Angie felt a twinge of jealousy. Her alter was spending all this quality time with Dr. Grant, and all she had to show for it was three extra pounds and garlic breath.

'I've booked the entire afternoon with you, Angie. We'll have the drive over to talk and set the stage. I think this might be the right time. We're on the verge. Can you feel it?'

'I just feel hungry,' she answered. 'I used to eat salad for lunch. What have you two done to me?'

The atmosphere of the French restaurant was cheerful and formal at the same time. Crisp white linens on the tables were set with china plates and crystal glasses. The waiters wore black suits and addressed them as *mam'selle* and *madame*, thinking that they were mother and daughter. A spray of pink camellias floated between them as a centerpiece.

Angie wanted to stay. She'd never been to such a nice place. Was Dr. Grant sending the bill to her parents every day? Still, a deal was a deal.

A glimmer of reflected light caught the dessert spoon Dr. Grant was lifting to begin the transfer. Angie reached over and stopped Dr. Grant's hand mid-twirl. 'Wait.'

'Oh, I'm sorry.' Dr. Grant lowered the spoon. 'I should have asked if you were ready.'

'I am,' she said confidently. 'But I think I can do it myself.' She felt it, now, deep inside her head, a meeting place, a swinging gate. She reached for it . . . and there it was, and her hand was guiding. She felt the smile stretch her real cheeks on the outside as she headed in.

While Girl Scout took over, Angie waited on the porch, sitting on the railing, swinging her feet and watching swallows catch flies in the field. Funny how the real cabin had been buried deep

245

in the woods, while her mental cabin sat in this open field. Now and unexpectedly, she remembered the first time she'd come here, thrown into pitch black, terrified and out of control, unable to move or turn her head. Gradually, light had seeped in along with the ability to get up and move around, to talk to the others. Funny also how the cabin sat like a Hollywood front, barely three-dimensional, nothing on the other side of the wall as far as she knew.

On a whim, she knocked on the door. Nothing. She tried the handle, but it was locked securely. She pressed her ear to the door. A faint creaking sound, but that might have been her feet. As soon as she noticed it, the creaking stopped. She had the oddest impression that someone was inside, holding his or her breath, hiding.

'Angie.' The voice behind her made her jump back with a guilty feeling, like she'd been caught snooping. 'Don't go there,' Girl Scout said. 'We're not allowed.'

'Why not?' Angie demanded. 'What's inside?'

'We don't know. We can't get in either. Only Angel could. Leave it alone. Come on with me.' Girl Scout held out her hand, taking the lead. She pulled Angie away from the door, the porch, the cabin front, and into the meadow. 'Take off your shoes.'

'But the grass will give me a rash!' Angie argued.

'No, it won't.'

'It'll tickle.' She hated seeing her legs.

'Oh, come on.' Girl Scout took off her own

shoes and socks and rolled her khaki pants up. The wounds around her ankles were raw and chafed. Angie's were tight bands of scar tissue. She felt foolish for hesitating. The ankles were Girl Scout's legacy, the wrists were Little Wife's, and the burns were Tattletale's. What a road map of pain was written on her skin. Angie released a gust of breath. She took off her shoes and socks. Then, in the warmth of the inner afternoon, alone with herself, she stripped off her clothes. She lay down in the grass with all her scars exposed to the light and said, 'I contain multitudes.'

Beside her, Girl Scout quoted another line of the poem they both loved. 'Who wishes to walk with me?' They turned their heads to each other and smiled.

Touching fingertips, they recited in unison: 'For every atom belonging to me as good belongs to you.'

They embraced, soft white arms in long green grass, and held each other so tightly that no one could tell where one left off and the other began. And with a shudder and a swelling and a joining and a sigh, there was only one girl, collapsed into herself in harmony.

Pictures flashed through her head, the man's face both loving and angry. The heavy chains so binding for so long, then unlocked and discarded in a corner, yet still binding. The familiar handle of the well pump. The chipped brown pitcher. Her iron pots and skillets. A book tucked in the pocket of her apron. The bottle of oil for refilling the lamps. The scant pantry filled with canned

247

and dried goods and spices. The mossy pine trunks that led her down the mountain, away from the cabin, away from the cabin, away from the cabin, clutching a bag of a few precious items. The store where she stole the map, having no money at all except the four quarters she'd found under the stove. The quarters bought a Coke to fill her hungry belly after days of walking. Nothing had ever tasted so wonderful.

★   ★   ★

Nothing had ever tasted so wonderful. Angie's mouth filled with the sweet, creamy texture of a crème brûlée. The caramel flavor melted on her tongue.

Her eyes flicked up to meet the doctor's. 'This is amazing, Lynn. You should have ordered some.'

'Angela?' The doctor's eyes were filled with tears.

Angie's brow wrinkled. 'Why did I call you Lynn?'

Dr. Grant grabbed a napkin and dabbed away the damp shimmer. 'Girl Scout always calls me Lynn. Is she . . . with you?'

'Completely,' Angie said. 'Hey, what's wrong? Why are you crying?'

Dr. Grant — Lynn — sniffed. 'Oh dear. How silly. In the middle of dessert, she said, 'I'm saving this for Pretty Girl.' She just said, 'I'm going now,' and here you are. I never had a chance to say good-bye.'

Angie laughed. 'You don't have to say

248

good-bye, Lynn. I'm still here.' She devoured another spoonful of the crème brûlée and sighed.

'Oh, Angie. Welcome to unity.' Then Dr. Grant broke into blubbering tears, a totally unprofessional and hugely gratifying display of affection.

PART III

I

16

CONFESSION

I came waltzing home from school with the taste of crème brûlée in my mouth, floating about a foot off the ground. Mom had been watching me curiously ever since she got home from the library. I was bursting, just waiting for the right moment, the right way to tell her. She gave me the perfect opening as I helped her set the table for an early dinner.

'Is there anything special you want for Christmas?' She handed me three sets of silverware.

I grinned at her, bouncing on my toes. 'I've already got what I most wanted,' I said. 'Me, myself, and I. All glued together, more or less.'

Mom gasped. 'No! Yes? Really? Already?'

I nodded, my cheeks threatening to snap with joy.

'Oh, Angie. Oh my.' She squeezed me hard, her body shaking. 'That won't fit under the tree,' she said stuffily in my ear, off on another crying jag. She was so sensitive these days.

'Mom, Mom, Mom.' I returned her hug, a laugh bubbling my voice. Silverware jangled in my hands as I avoided stabbing her. 'You're right. How about riding boots?' I recognized Tattletale's influence, but what would once have felt like separate thoughts were my own now.

253

'That's all?' She pulled back, her face pink and wet.

'They're crazy expensive.' I knew. I'd checked in the tack shop at the stables.

'Do you need those weird pants, too?' she asked. She wiped her eyes.

Also expensive. 'Nope. I'll be fine with skinny jeans for now. Oh, one other thing.' I hesitated. Two weeks out from Christmas, only one thing had me worried, and that was the question of who would be sitting around that dining room table for Christmas dinner.

I wanted more than anything to see Grandma again, to make things right between us. When I thought of the last look on her face, I went hollow inside. She'd never visited me in the hospital. She'd never even sent me a card. I was too nervous to bring it up with Dad.

So now I got up the guts to ask Mom. She unhugged me, holding my shoulders and looking as serious as I've ever seen her.

'Since we got the restraining order on Bill, Grandma has refused to come. She scolded me for a good half hour about forcing her to choose between her sons. It wasn't pretty.' The grim line to Mom's mouth told me this was probably the watered-down version.

'She doesn't appreciate that we're not throwing his ass in jail?'

'Not a bit. She refuses to believe your — our story. And don't say ass, hon.'

'Ugh. How's Dad doing?' I asked.

'Not taking it well. As you'd expect. He loved Bill.'

An echo in my head prompted me to reply, 'Chah. So did I.'

Mom cringed. Her hands dropped.

'I'm so sorry,' I said. 'So at least Dad believes me?'

Mom nodded without looking up. 'Dr. Grant was mighty persuasive. If we could get her in front of a jury — '

'Stop. We've talked this to death. Bill was a minor, except for the last time.' And there was no physical evidence, just he-said, she-said. And even if we had proof, incest had much lighter penalties than stranger rape, for whatever stupid reason. We'd done what we could. 'Anyway, now he has to stay away from me. That's good enough.'

I walked around the circle of the table, placing the forks with precision. 'I wish it didn't have to be like this. I wish I could take back my life and start over.'

'Don't get me started on do-overs,' Mom said, tearing up again. She grabbed a folded napkin and mopped her face. 'I have been asking and asking myself about all the warning signs we must have missed. You just seemed like such a happy, contented child. Even looking back, second-guessing myself like crazy, I can't find it.'

'Look, Mom. I hid it so deep, even *I* had no clue till I started therapy. I don't blame you and Dad.'

Mom watched me with a half-hoping, half-skeptical expression.

'Really. I mean it.' I hugged her to prove the point and felt her growing belly press against me.

It lurched and bumped. 'Mom! He kicked me!'

'Oh, yes. It's kind of early.' She patted her bulge. 'You actually felt that?'

'That's so weird,' I said, laughing. 'He has big feet.'

'Sounds like you're betting on a little brother.'

'I don't know why I said that. It doesn't matter. I'd be happy with a sister, too.' As I told her, I realized it was true. Having another new little life in the family would give us all something wonderful and positive to think about instead of going around in circles with the 'Sheesh, we totally screwed up on Angie' thing. I was ready to move on. I just needed Mom and Dad to catch up with me. Mom was close, but Dad was still a basket case ever since the Thanksgiving massacre.

In spite of missing a week of school and going short last week, I was more than ready to move on there, too. The school counselor had given me a couple of exams and said that with the recommendation of my teachers, I could move up to tenth grade after Christmas break. After three months with the thirteen- and fourteen-year-olds, I was definitely psyched for more mature company, even if it meant starting over with a new set of peers. Especially if it meant starting over. Time to come out of my own isolation. Kate was wonderful, my north star, but I needed to expand my social set, and maybe bring her back into the fold along with me.

And there was one more thing I had to put back on track. I hadn't seen Abraim in two weeks. Kate had arranged the double dates.

Abraim and I had never actually called each other or gone out without Ali and Kate. The extra company didn't make those two shy — maybe they secretly liked an audience to their make-out sessions — but I had a feeling that Abraim and I would be stuck in the same place forever unless we spent time alone. Plus, I was ready to be a bit more truthful with him now. He had to realize a bear trap hadn't chomped off my hand, after all. And now that he was dating only one girl, maybe, just maybe I could tell him about the others.

I took a deep breath and forced myself to be brave. I called Kate and asked if she had his cell phone number.

Abraim's phone didn't finish ringing once before he answered. 'Angie!' He sounded a little breathless himself.

'Hey.'

'Hi. Um. Yeah, it's me.' Ugh. A moment ago I'd had a speech prepared, but unfortunately, it erased itself at the sound of his voice.

'Are you well?' he asked.

That broke the ice. 'Oh yeah. You don't know how well,' I said. 'Can we — '

'Do you want — ,' he said at the same time.

I wimped out. 'You first.'

'Do you want to go out tonight?'

'Absolutely,' I said. Could he hear my smile? And then I remembered. It was Friday, and I'd already promised the Harrises. 'Do you mind starting late? Like nine? I'm baby-sitting for the neighbors. But they usually get home at nine. We could go for pizza or ice cream or something.'

'Sure, that would be great,' Abraim said. 'I already claimed the car. I was . . . I was planning to call you.'

My heart warmed. I knew it. He'd been sitting on his bed too, practicing his speech. 'So, I'll see you later.'

'Until . . . until tonight, my Angie,' he said with what he must have thought was a romantic flair. Funny thing — he was right.

★　★　★

Sammy was in a rowdy mood when I arrived at the Harrises. With four teeth on board, he had graduated to the life of real food and sippy cups and Cheerios. Locked into his high chair, he was banging wildly with a spoon into a bowl of scrambled eggs. Most of them were flying into the air and landing on the floor, nowhere near his mouth. 'Annee, Annee,' he crowed when he noticed me.

'Who's my favorite guy?' I prompted.

He raised his right arm, a trick I'd spent two weeks training him to perform. 'SSSammmmm,' he yelled. Yellow eggs floofed out of his mouth.

I dived in to clean him up and pick some off the floor.

Mrs. Harris appeared behind me. 'Oh, sweetie, you don't have to worry about that. I'll get it.'

'Not dressed like that!'

She was wearing a wine-red silk dress with a sparkling gold wrap. She twirled for my approval.

'Gorgeous. Special occasion?' I asked.

'Dr. Harris's departmental holiday party. I

hope they don't remember this dress from last year.'

'Wouldn't matter if they did,' I said. 'It's great.' By this point I'd cleaned up the floor so she wouldn't be tempted to try. 'How about some Cheerios cars, Sam?' I suggested.

'O's,' he repeated, which I took to mean yes.

'I'll leave you to it,' Mrs. Harris said. 'It's so nice that he never fusses when we leave him with you. He was so awful with his other babysitters before — ' She broke off awkwardly.

'Before I came home,' I supplied.

'Right. Before you came home.'

'Well, he was a lot younger then,' I suggested.

Mrs. Harris tilted her head. 'Maybe. But there's more to it than that. There's just something about you. Anyway, lucky for us.' She bent over and kissed Sam on his head, risking her dangly diamond necklace and silk neckline close to his greasy little paws.

Dr. Harris poked his head into the kitchen. 'Night, Angie. Help yourself to pay TV if you'd like. You've got my pager number if you need me.' He took two huge steps and ruffled Sam's fluffy hair. 'You're the man of the house now, Sam. Be good.'

'Nice tux,' I said. His vest matched the color of Mrs. Harris's dress perfectly.

They disappeared out the door to the garage, and moments later, I heard the powerful engine of his Maserati, the nicest car in the neighborhood by far. It was great that they were such down-to-earth people when they obviously could build themselves a custom mansion in a fancier

259

area with an ocean view.

'Okay, little Sam. Fast cars for you, too.' I pulled a block of cheddar from the fridge and Cheerios from the breakfast cupboard. Four Cheerio wheels pressed into a cheese cube looks like a car to a hungry toddler. I vroomed a car across the high chair tray and into his hand.

He stuffed it into his mouth. 'Mo,' he demanded. So I made mo.

We had a routine. After supper, a warm bath. At first, I'd been really nervous about the whole drowning possibility, but after Mrs. Harris introduced me to the suction cup bath ring, I was fine. Sam soaked clean and played for a while with rubber ducks and pouring cups while the warm bath got tepid, then chilly. Only at that point was he willing to leave the water. I bundled him up in a thick towel and sang the rubber ducky song while I dried him off and stuck on a diaper before anything bad could happen. I plopped him safely on his bedroom floor and rummaged around in his dresser for the Batman pajamas, which I knew were his favorites.

'Annee, Annee!' he called.

I whirled to see him tottering to his feet in the middle of the room, arms outstretched. He took three steps toward me and plumped down on his padded butt.

'You walked! Sam! You really walked! Do it again!'

'Ahden, ahden,' he said. He got back into crawling position and rocked himself to his feet. This time he made five steps before collapsing.

I picked him up and whirled him around. 'You

did it, you did it!' I sang. 'You walked all on your ow-wn.' The Harrises would be so excited and so ticked that they'd missed the first steps. 'Darn. I should have taken a video,' I told him. But there was something extra special about having the memory all to myself.

'Ahden, ahden,' he said, squirming to get down.

So for half an hour, we played 'again, again' with walking and twirling, until we were both totally exhausted. 'Reading time,' I insisted. 'After we brush your four little teeth.'

That was a household rule, always read before sleeping. Both the Harrises had bookcases next to their sides of the bed — detective novels on her side and medical thrillers on his. Sam had all the Dr. Seuss collection, and tonight he grabbed *Green Eggs and Ham* before he climbed onto my lap. It was his favorite, for obvious reasons.

'Fam Am fam!' he chirped. 'Dih-doh. Dih-doh.'

'Hmm? What's dih-doh, little guy?' Oh, the doorbell was ringing. Weird. I hitched him onto my hip and went down the hall and around to the front door. I peered through the peephole at the looming, distorted face of Abraim.

A blast of cold air swooshed in the door. 'Hey, what are you doing here?' I asked.

Blinking Christmas bulbs reflected in his black eyes. 'It's nine o'clock. Your mom said you were still working. She thought it would be okay if I came over, but I can wait in the car if you'd rather I didn't come in, and your employers might misunderstand, so I should probably — '

'For goodness' sake. Come in. I'm sorry. I forgot they had an actual party, so they may be a while.'

He stepped in uneasily, but his eye was drawn to the collection of old medical books on the front hall table, part decor item, part hobby. 'Very nice house,' he said.

'I know. One day you'll have a house like this, future Dr. Rahim,' I teased. 'Come on. I was just about to put Sam to bed with a book.'

Abraim's eyebrows rose. 'He can read?'

'No, you nitwit. I'm reading. He's listening and hopefully not tearing the pages.'

Abraim sat on the floor. Sam sat on my lap, thumb in his mouth, glued to the story of Sam-I-am and his picky nameless friend. Forgetting I had a double audience, I totally got into the book as usual, and by the time I hit 'And I would eat them in a boat. And I would eat them with a goat' et cetera, I was reciting from memory in quite a dramatic rendition. Abraim applauded at the end, and I blushed all over.

'Night-night time,' I told Sam. He yawned hugely. The power of suggestion.

He rolled onto his side in his crib, and I tucked him in tight. 'Night-night, sweetie,' I whispered, and kissed him on the ear.

'Need this?' Abraim asked. He was reaching under the rocker for Sam's blue-and-white-checked blankie.

'Thanks.' I took it from him. As my fingers sank into the soft baby fleece, my vision darkened for just a second, and my head swam.

262

Knees buckling, I grabbed the crib railing for support. 'Whoa. Head rush. Got up too fast, I guess.' I blinked away the darkness and rattled my head. 'Here, Sammy. Blankie.' He reached out with his eyes closed, already working away on his thumb.

We tiptoed out, closing the door with a soft click. The smell of baby shampoo still lingered on my shirt and hands.

'Want anything to eat or drink?' I asked. 'I'm sure it would be okay.'

'No, thanks. I'm fine.' Abraim hovered awkwardly. 'Are you sure you don't want me to wait in the car?'

I just rolled my eyes. 'Don't be ridiculous. Come check out the sound system in the living room.'

I led him to my favorite room in the house. Two leather sofas and a matching pair of chairs were a soft butter yellow, the color of sunshine. A multicolored rug in a modern design covered much of the pale hardwood floor. The lamps and end tables were stylish and metallic. Two enormous speakers flanked the fireplace, and the rest of the surround sound was ceiling mounted around the room. Although the rest of the house was single-story, this room was vaulted, with a dramatic full-height window facing an unob-structed view of the mountains.

The window created the perfect backdrop for the twelve-foot Christmas tree the Harrises had put up over Thanksgiving weekend, a real cut tree, decorated all in white and gold balls, angels, and stars and lit with clear twinklers. I dialed down the track-lighting dimmers to show the full effect. The scent of pine filled the room, familiar and comforting.

Abraim traced the height of the tree, from the brightly ribboned packages beneath to the crystal star on top, almost brushing the redwood beams. 'Fantastic,' he said. 'That makes our stubby six-foot tree seem extremely inadequate.'

'You have a tree?' I asked.

'Well, it's the common culture, after all. And I don't mind the accumulation of presents under it.'

The twinkle lights flickered off, and I dived under the tree to fiddle with the twitchy connections until they lit again. A shower of dry needles pattered to the ground. 'Bad strand somewhere,' I explained.

Abraim dusted a couple of needles out of my hair. 'I think they must be cutting these trees at Halloween these days. I almost pronounced ours DOA, but we managed to resuscitate it with sugar water.'

'And now you're planning a career as a tree surgeon,' I joked. I picked up the media remote. 'What kind of music do you like, doc?'

'You choose,' he said immediately.

'Well, something quiet as long as Sam's falling asleep,' I said, and selected a soft-jazz station. It was sort of make-out music, if you liked that kind of thing, not that I was thinking in that direction. Exactly.

'You're very good with him,' Abraim said, an admiring note in his voice. He sat down in one of the deep chairs and ran his hands along the

264

creamy-soft leather arms. 'Very natural.'

'Good thing, isn't it? I mean, we'll have one of our own soon.'

His eyes popped. 'We will?' he squeaked. His face turned bright red.

I giggled. 'Oh God. Not . . . us. My family. My mom's pregnant, believe it or not.'

I think he started breathing again. 'So you'll be a sister.'

'Yeah. But Mom's so old, everyone's going to think the baby is my accident, at least everyone who doesn't know us.'

'Oh. Uh.' He fished around for a reply and apparently gave up.

It was painfully quiet for a moment while both of us wondered how to go on from here. I had an opening to tell him what I wanted to tell him, but I just couldn't do it to his face. I lay down on a sofa with my head on the armrest, staring at the grain in the redwood planks high above my head.

My voice quivered just a touch. 'See, I have a lot of unexplained time to account for.'

I felt a warm hand on my shoulder.

'You were missing,' he said. 'I know. Your parents were still here in town. I told you I read all the old newspaper articles and YouTubed all the news reports.'

Right. 'When I first got back, I couldn't remember anything. Not a single thing.'

'How . . . awkward,' he offered.

'Totally. But I do remember some of it now,' I said, fixing my gaze on the faraway ceiling. 'The truth is, I was kidnapped.' I held up my scarred

265

wrists. 'And I was obviously held captive, at least for a while.'

'Stockholm syndrome?' he asked.

'What's that?'

'When the captive eventually identifies with the captor and doesn't try to leave.'

I wrenched the silver wedding ring off my finger. It wasn't that I wanted to honor that lie, but somehow I still needed to see it on my hand. Maybe Abraim was right — it was a syndrome. 'Read this,' I said. 'It's so creepy.'

Abraim was silent.

Crap. It was too much, too weird, too soon. Yes, Abraim was very silent.

So was I, while I waited for him to get up and leave and never speak to me again.

But he didn't. He came over and kissed me upside down, leaning over the couch. His eyes were moist. 'Are you okay?' he whispered.

'Oh. I think so. Yeah.' My eyes went all swimmy too. His tenderness touched me deep in the center of my fast-beating heart.

He knelt next to me so he could see me better, his hand cradling my cheek. 'How did you not go crazy? How did you survive? How did you not kill yourself? You must have the strongest will to live.'

My mouth crumpled a little. Did I dare tell him? Now?

While I searched for the right words, the music swelled in a particularly emotional way, and the next thing I knew, Abraim had slipped both arms around me and tugged me into a fierce hold against his chest. His voice crackled.

'I wish I could have saved you. I wish I had known where to look.'

'No one did,' I whispered. 'But thank you.' My arms went around him, too, and then we were surrounded by music and soft leather, and he was kissing me, and I was kissing him. And the wonder of it was that it felt new and good. I felt like I'd never been kissed before, except by this sweet, gentle, protective guy who wanted me even though he knew how damaged I must be.

Tears of happiness trickled from the corners of my eyes. He tasted the saltiness and sat up with a questioning look on his face. 'What?' he asked. 'I'm sorry. Too much?'

I smiled and wiped my eyes, which kept on streaming anyway. 'I'm just so happy, so lucky,' I said. 'You're too good to be true. I'm afraid of waking up.'

He flushed, with a pleased grin, and I pulled his head down to mine to demand more happiness, more luck. Time evaporated as we explored the curves of each other's lips, cheeks, throats with soft kisses.

The mantel clock chimed eleven, and he pulled apart from me. 'Oh dear. So late. I should probably go before your employers return, because, Angie, if you look at me like that for much longer, I'll have to kiss you again and again, and I am afraid of what they might walk in to see.'

'Oh. Our date . . . I'm sorry.'

'Now you're the nitwit,' he said. 'I wouldn't trade tonight for a movie and popcorn. Are you kidding? But how about tomorrow we get together for pizza and maybe something weird, like bowling?'

'I bowl about a ninety-five, at least I used to,' I warned him. I wrenched myself out of the groove I'd worn into the couch.

'Uh-oh. If you're that good, I'm in trouble.'

I refrained from pointing out that I was that bad. 'You want to pick me up at six?'

'Delighted to,' he said. As we walked to the door, he had an arm around my waist. His jacket hung on the coat-rack, and after he shrugged into it, he leaned over me and gathered me into his arms again for one more good-night kiss. Somehow, it lasted until the clock chimed eleven fifteen, at which point, I was dizzy and breathless.

I watched him drive off before going in to check on Sam. He'd rolled onto his back and thrown off all his covers. I tucked him in, smoothing the binding of his plaid blankie between my fingers. The silkiness was hypnotic, and I watched him breathe his baby breaths in and out, the rise and fall of his tiny chest.

The sound of the garage opening startled me, and I hurried back to the kitchen to greet the Harrises.

'Oh, Angie,' Mrs. Harris said. 'I so apologize for how late it is. The night just got away from us.'

'That's okay,' I said. 'We had a big night here. Sam took his first real walking steps.'

'Oh! Wonderful!' She gave me a hug. 'How fun for you. Did you hear that, dear?' she called as Dr. Harris came in from the garage. 'Our little

268

guy is up and running.'

'Hey, hey, hey!' he cheered, giving Mrs. Harris a hug. 'I can't wait to see him in the morning. TG it's Saturday tomorrow. Shall I walk you home? Did Ginny tell you? We were having so much fun dancing to the moldy oldies, the time just got away from us.'

The clock chimed one in the morning like an exclamation point on his apology.

One? Wow. Somehow the time had gotten away from me, too. Had I actually fallen asleep on my feet by the crib side?

★　★　★

Saturday morning was supposed to be a day of sleeping in, waking up refreshed. But when Mom came and woke me for the third time at two thirty, my eyes still felt like they'd been sandpapered. I didn't drag my butt out of bed until she threatened no late babysitting ever again if I couldn't handle it. Considering the crisp new hundred-dollar bill in my wallet (double time after midnight, Dr. Harris explained, as he'd pressed the overpayment on me), I wanted to prove I could handle it. Besides, I'd been asleep for more than twelve hours. I should be bouncing out of bed.

I greeted the afternoon by opening my curtains. I had to push my rocker aside to reach, and my stomach flipped as it dawned on me — the rocker had moved. In the night. On its own. The blanket that usually sat folded on it was rolled into a tight sausage-shaped bundle.

Deep tread grooves were worn in the carpet. I touched the seat, and to my horror, it was still warm.

Holy crap. The mad rocker. She wasn't one of the others. She was her own person. And she was still with me.

17

POSSESSION

Yesterday Lynn and I had talked about cutting back to one day a week, both of us thinking that most of the hard work was behind us. Guess we were wrong. Way wrong. I needed her now.

My heart pounded with the realization that as exhausted as I was, as heavily as I should have slept, the mad rocker still had the power to wake up my body and take over. And that was unacceptable.

Mom called again from the top of the stairs. 'Are you actually out of bed, at long last?'

'Yes. Down in a minute,' I grouched.

'You said that last time.'

'I'm up!' I yelled.

'Dad's out in the garden, cutting back the roses. Maybe you could help him,' she called. Like that would make me enthusiastic about getting out of bed. 'It's a beautiful day,' she added in a singy way.

Maybe for her. She was still on an emotional high from yesterday. But not for me — everything had shattered overnight. I had to consult with Lynn, privately, where Mom couldn't overhear. Between Dad, the baby, and Christmas, she had enough on her mind. Telling her I wasn't as well as we thought I was — No, Not yet.

So when she retreated to the kitchen, I grabbed the upstairs phone from Dad's den. Safely behind closed doors, I called Lynn's emergency patient contact number.

She answered immediately. 'Is this Angie?' Right. Caller ID.

'Hey, Lynn. I have some news.' My voice came out soft and strained. 'Remember the trouble I used to have with the mad rocker?' It was a rhetorical question, but I waited anyway.

'Sure I do, Angie. Of course.'

'And remember how none of the alters ever confessed to doing it, even though we were pretty sure it was Girl Scout? Well, guess what?'

'It wasn't,' she said. 'Of course.'

'Bingo. It wasn't. Because it's someone else. I lost time again, Lynn. Last night. I lost almost two hours — and that's just when I was awake. She stole my whole night's sleep. I don't know what to do.'

Lynn's soothing voice had just as much effect over the phone. 'We can deal with this. It's going to be okay, Angie. Don't panic. Do you need to see me before our regular time? Can your Mom drive you in for an extra session? Today? I can meet you any time. The only thing I had planned was Christmas shopping, and, of course, that can wait.'

'I'll check. Can you hang on?'

I ran downstairs, trying to think of a reasonable excuse to tell Mom why I needed an emergency session. Inspiration struck on the landing, so by the time I got to the kitchen, I was ready. 'Mom, can you please take me in to see

Dr. Grant? I had an awful nightmare last night. That's why I didn't sleep well. It brought up all sorts of scary thoughts, and then I couldn't get back to sleep.'

'You poor thing,' Mom said. 'Of course.'

We hopped into the car half an hour later, my hair dripping wet from the shower. I could tell she wanted to ask me more about the dream, so I made up a story about being stuck inside a cocoon with the air running out. My chest did feel tight and breathless with anxiety. That much was true.

★ ★ ★

'Haunted!' I told Lynn. 'That's how I feel. I'm an old house with a spirit still rattling around in the attic.'

She gave me a gentle and sympathetic smile, her specialty. 'Any clues at all?'

I wracked all the corners of my brain. Spit it out, I told myself. No more secrets. But the memories I'd absorbed didn't cover this. If there was another alter, Girl Scout and Tattletale didn't know her. The literal doorway of communication Girl Scout used to share with Little Wife convinced me that Little Wife hadn't known about her either, although come to think of it, Little Wife had mentioned being sent away and replaced for some time. That was suspicious. Very suspicious, because now I knew Girl Scout wasn't the one who replaced her. How did I know? Because I held no memories at all of that time.

273

And Angel — he'd said something weird. What was it? Called forth by one of the other alters, he said, when the man did something so unforgivable. Which led me to ask, what could be more unforgivable than what he'd already done to me?

I knuckled my eyes till swirly patterns covered the insides of my eyelids. I reached and explored inside, while Lynn waited patiently. At last, I found the wisp of a possibility. 'The Lonely One — that's all I know,' I told her. 'Angel said he was called forth by the Lonely One. I didn't hear it with capital letters when he said it, though. I guess I just thought he meant one of the others. Little Wife, I guess, since she complained when the man left her alone.' I pictured his beautiful face and gleaming whiteness. A lump rose in my throat. There was only silence where his presence used to be. The emptiness turned my stomach queasy. 'It's too late, Lynn. We can't ask him. He's totally gone.'

I flumped over my knees and hugged them, feeling small and weak without him. 'We screwed up.' Tears dribbled onto the carpet.

Lynn patted my back in a sort of maternal way, but more awkward. 'I'm sorry, Angie. I thought we were doing the right thing. Don't worry. We'll get to the heart of this, one way or another. It'll just take more time without Angel's help. Do you want to try a hypnosis session?'

'Maybe Monday. Can we just talk?' I asked. 'I really, really don't want to go away from my head right now.'

So we talked about whether I missed Little Wife and Angel. And I suppose from the amount

274

of tears that ended up on my sleeves, the answer was yes.

★ ★ ★

Kate caught up with me right after my Earth Science exam. 'You look horrible,' she said, in the way only a best friend can. 'Trouble in paradise?' She motioned with her head to where the guys were exchanging one set of books for another at their lockers.

'What? Abraim? Trouble? No. He's great. That's great. We're great,' I stuttered. 'We saw each other twice this weekend.'

'Make any progress?' She elbowed me with a wink.

I blushed, remembering the feel of his warm hands on the small of my back, darting under my sweater to explore as we kissed good night. I could still imagine every fingertip tracing gentle circles.

Kate took one look at my expression and snorted a laugh. 'Never mind. You already answered.' She glanced back to see the twins heading our way. 'Is that why you look so exhausted? Too much loooove?'

'I wish,' I whispered next to her ear. 'The mad rocker is back.' She'd spent all Saturday and Sunday night dragging me out of bed, torturing my body, which should have been in bed resting up for exams.

'What? I thought that was all taken care of.'

'Me too.' I couldn't help heaving my shoulders dramatically. 'But no. Apparently, my demons from the past aren't done with me. I'm still possessed.'

'Wow, that sucks. I wish there was something I could do to help.' She gave me a helpless, sad smile. 'Maybe we could go running later? That always clears *my* head. I mean . . . oh, how stupid. I didn't mean — '

If only it were that easy. 'Shush. The guys.' I waved her to silence before they were close enough to hear.

Ali planted a kiss on Kate, regardless of the PDA rules. Abraim raised his eyebrows at me, kissing me only with the light in his eyes, but I felt my lips tingle, all the same.

'How was your exam this morning?' he asked.

'Easy,' I replied. 'Hardly interesting enough to keep me awake.' A huge yawn burst from my mouth. 'Thank God I'm done for today. Two harder exams tomorrow, though. World Civ and English. I've got pages of vocab to review.'

'Need a ride home?' Ali asked. 'We're done too. We could take you.'

I glanced at the hall clock. 'My mom's picking me up in an hour. I've got somewhere to go.'

Kate patted my arm and made meaningful eye contact. 'Have to exorcise?'

My chest clenched, and for a moment, it felt like I was having a heart attack. 'Ah.' I gasped in pain. My vision started to darken. My head swam. My knees buckled.

Kate's grip tightened, holding me up. 'Ange, what's the matter?'

Abraim's arm came around me from the other side.

'Hey, are you okay?'

'Don't let me hit the floor if I faint,' I muttered to him. He held me tight against his chest while I caught my breath, concentrated on holding on to myself. The pain vanished as suddenly as it had struck. My eyes refocused on the worried faces of Ali and Kate.

'Whoa, that was weird. Sorry, guys. I just got a muscle cramp and couldn't catch my breath.' Sort of.

The boys threw me alarmed and sympathetic looks, and Kate dived into her purse for an ibuprofen. That was fine. I let the misunderstanding go. A chest cramp would be much harder to talk my way out of, and anyway, it had stopped.

My friend cluster insisted on driving me straight home, and Abraim pressed my hand quietly in the backseat. His dark eyes told me he still had questions for me but wouldn't bring them up in front of his brother. Before I got out of the car, he pulled me tight and kissed me on the lips, the first time he'd done that in front of anyone else. 'Call me later,' he insisted. 'When you're back from the gym. I need to be sure you really are okay.'

★ ★ ★

Mom took her usual seat in Lynn's waiting room and picked up a magazine she had read cover to cover several times already. For God's sake, the woman worked in a library. She could have brought a new book to pass the time. Then again, she probably couldn't concentrate anyway, sitting out there wondering what went on in the room. Lynn was sworn to secrecy, and I wasn't volunteering details, even though most of Mom's salary went to paying for my therapy.

'I have a plan,' I announced to Lynn. I plopped down on the couch. 'All you have to do is get me started.'

We'd done so much hypnosis and guided imagery that it was ridiculously easy for me to lose the office and slip into my head, into the special place where I'd met my alters. Lonely One must be nearby, and I suspected the one logical place to look for her.

I took myself back to the cabin porch, the sunny blue and yellow porch, which looked undisturbed. But the door, the door that only Angel could use, was cracked an inch. I'd never seen it left open before.

Cobwebs spun across the opening wavered in the morning breeze. My hand reached up and pulled the doorknob. The door swung outward with a creak and a crash against the cabin. There was motion inside. A shaft of sunlight pierced the interior darkness, lighting up a hunched figure in the middle of the space. A rhythmic sound reached my ears — rocking, rocking. Runners on a hardwood floor.

I stepped into the gloom. A low oil lamp burned on the floor in the corner, casting a long, flickering shadow on the far wall.

'Who are you?' I asked, my voice hardly above a whisper.

Her head unbent. Our eyes met, at last. So this

was the Lonely One, my mad rocker. Tears stained her cheeks. Her face was my face, twin of the one that greeted me in the morning, but yellowed by the weak flame.

She held a bundle in her arms and raised it toward me. Did she want me to have it? I moved a step forward, took the soft bundle. A blanket. An empty blue-and-white-checked blanket. Strangely familiar. It collapsed in my hands and fell to the floor.

'Who are you?' she sobbed in an echo of my voice. 'Where's my Angel?'

'He's gone. He won't be coming back anymore.'

'NO!' She wept and reached for the empty blanket.

'I'm sorry,' I said. 'He was too violent, too uncontrolled. He couldn't stay.'

'But who will find my baby?' she whispered. 'Where is my baby?' She rolled the blanket into the sausage shape of an infant and cuddled it to her shoulder.

Oh God. That blanket.

She pressed her face against it, devastated with loss. 'I sent the Angel to find my sweet baby.'

Oh merciful God. It wasn't possible.

'The man took him from my arms.'

'Angie, Angie.' Lynn shook my shoulder. 'Can you hear me?' Her voice pulled me back into myself. I fought her, pulling away into the dark again.

'Impossible!' I screamed. Sammy's blanket.

'Angie, what's happening? Come back.' Lynn's command faded away.

Lonely One grabbed my arm with unexpected strength, and a brutal spasm bent me double in agony. Deep, knife-like pain in the gut stole my breath. I twisted and screamed, finding myself on the bed. The bed was slicked with blood, and the tearing pain in my belly went on and on. I gasped for a sip of air. Nothing in my life had ever hurt like this. In front of me, head bowed, white-knuckled hands clenched on my knees, the man said, 'Push now. Push hard, my love.' And I pushed and pushed and screamed and felt the pressure shift.

And then a slippery and squalling newborn was in my arms, and the pain fled, and the bliss as I saw the little red face was immeasurable.

'Ah. A boy,' the man said. 'Feed him.' He pushed the tiny mouth toward my swollen, aching breasts.

And I rocked and rocked, and cuddled him in his blanket, and fed him and loved him until the day the man said, 'This just isn't working out. You have no more time for me.' And he ripped the bundle out of my arms. My heart shattered like dropped porcelain.

Lonely One released me. The connection broke. The cascade ended. Shock waves pulsed through my skull. The imprint of her grip bruised my arm. I staggered back from the dim room into the doorway.

Lonely One rose to follow me. 'I have to come out,' she said. 'To find him.'

'No. You can't,' I gasped. 'No more.'

I slammed the door closed. I knew what to do. Anything was possible here. Boards and nails lay

280

waiting right where I needed them. A hammer appeared.

Lynn called, 'Angie. Angela. Now.'

'No. Not yet,' I yelled at her. I whacked and whacked at the nails, sealing the door shut with boards. It turned the cabin forlorn and derelict. Gray again. Forbidding. That was fine. I was done with it. As long as Lonely One stayed trapped in there, no one needed to know.

Except me. Because now I knew her secret pain, the ache that made her rock all night with empty arms. And I knew where her baby was. I just had no idea what to do about it.

18

DETENTION

'What just happened, Angie?' Lynn's agitation was obvious. Bright spots of red stood out on her cheeks.

I reemerged, back pressed to the wall, arms flung out to the sides, my legs shaking beneath me. Fresh bruises showed on my hands. They ached. I held them up wordlessly, the question written across my face.

'You were pounding the paneling. In a pattern. You refused to wake up for me until you finished the pattern.' She patted her chest above her heart. 'Had me a little nervous there, my dear. Are you okay?'

I nodded. Okay now. Lonely One was locked up for as long as I wanted her to be.

For God's sake! I had a week of exams to get through. Her timing couldn't be worse. And her secret . . . I shoved my thoughts away from that as hard as I could. My heart twisted in pain, my stomach with nausea. It had to be a false memory. Please let it be.

Lynn was waiting, watching.

I had to make up an explanation. Something plausible. 'I — I was trying to break in, through a window. To the inside of the cabin.' Which was a weird excuse, I thought, as I realized there weren't any windows in my mental cabin.

'Did you succeed? Did you find what you were looking for?' Lynn asked.

I shook my head.

'That's a pity,' she said. 'Maybe Wednesday?'

Please no. I needed more time. Time to not deal with this, then time to deal with it. 'Uh, no. I really need all my time this week to study for exams. I've got to do well enough to move up.'

Lynn gave me a more relaxed smile. I'd sold her. I must be one fabulous actress.

'Okay. That's a fine goal. Moving up.' She made a corny little salute toward the ceiling. 'But please, call me if you need to. I'll be thinking of you.'

⋆　⋆　⋆

I slept like the proverbial dead that night. No midnight rocking, no invasions in my dreams, no more cascading flashbacks. It was such a relief. Now I appreciated how much Lonely One had been draining me, like a vampire in the night.

The sun filtered through my lace curtains, casting a soft shadow of panes across my quilt. I pulled my nightshirt over my head and dropped it on the floor. My hands slid down the smooth skin of my flat, tight belly, up to my small breasts. Impossible to imagine this body had ever done what Mom's was doing now. Impossible to believe what Lonely One wanted me to believe was real.

All I wanted was to be a normal high school student again, so that's where I put all my

283

newfound energy. One by one, I aced my exams. Ibuprofen took the edge off my stabbing headaches; warm washcloths helped fade the bruises on my hands and left arm. But having the distraction and a goal to absorb me was the best medicine.

Then the distraction was gone. Exams were done. School was out for two and a half weeks, and I had nothing left to structure my time. I'd already finished my Christmas shopping — books for Mom to read in the waiting room, two ties for Dad in upbeat colors to help his mood, a crystal bud vase for Lynn, earrings for Kate, and a silk scarf for Grandma. She might not ever wear it, but I wanted to go on record as still wanting my grandma.

I had to ask Kate's advice about a present for Abraim. 'Black lace bra,' was her suggestion. 'Not his size — yours,' she added, in case I didn't get her drift.

As casually as possible, I said, 'Already did that. Formal night, you know.'

'What! Formal night? First date?' Her eyes were wide. 'I underestimated you, girl,' she said. 'And him.'

I laughed and confessed to the part about how he'd zipped me back up as fast as he could. 'I think I'll order him a Harvard sweatshirt for luck.'

So Friday morning, my brain alarm woke me at six, even though I could have slept till noon. I lay there wondering what exactly to do with myself, right up to the moment a car rumbled into the driveway. I looked down through my window to see Detective Brogan's green SUV. My heart lurched, dropping a beat. Why was he here at this crazy hour?

The doorbell rang. Downstairs, heavy feet crossed the entryway to get it.

I waited, foolishly hoping it wouldn't involve me, but Dad's voice from the foot of the stairs summoned me. 'Angela? Angel, come on downstairs, please.'

Why here? Why now? Was there news, another break in the case?

I dragged on the crumpled pair of jeans from yesterday and zipped a green hoodie over the T-shirt I'd been sleeping in. And then I realized what it must be. A body. DNA evidence. A positive identification. And maybe a cause of death, and maybe my prints on the killing weapon.

Oh, Angel. What did you do? What did you do for us?

Acid gushed up from my stomach. I dashed into the bathroom, spat the sourness out of my mouth, and wiped my sleeve across my face. I struggled to put on a cheerful face as I tiptoed down the stairs. My empty stomach twisted itself in knots. Things were about to get much more complicated, just when they'd been getting simpler.

The entryway was empty.

'In here, hon,' Mom yelled from the kitchen. Her voice was unexpectedly normal, possibly a little relieved.

'Oh. Just a sec,' I called. I slipped into the downstairs bathroom off the entry, closed the door, ate a glob of toothpaste, and flushed. I came out, drying my hands on my jeans. My legs fizzed with nervous adrenaline. I shivered inside the hoodie.

Brogan and Mom sat close together at the kitchen table, two cups of coffee between them. Dad's cup was full and steaming, untouched in front of him.

'Hi, Angie,' the detective said in the friendliest way. 'I've been filling your folks in. We're real close to closing the investigation. Just a couple of loose ends to tie up.'

'R-really?' I tried to clamp down the tremble in my voice.

'Isn't that great?' Mom asked.

If she was happy, I was happy. 'Yeah. Really great,' I said with as real a smile as I could fake on top of my sick stomach, I couldn't feel relieved. Not yet.

Mom gave me her seat as she rose to take her coffee cup to the sink. That put me awfully close to Brogan, but he wasn't giving off dangerous vibes. His eyes were a soft green-blue, reflecting the moss color of his flannel shirt. And no hunting sparks in the depths.

I had nothing to do with my shaky hands. I hid them under the table, on my lap, pinching my knees, trying to keep the tension off my face. 'So . . . '

He rocked back with his hands behind his head. 'In a nutshell: We combed the area. We found only a single grave containing a single body, which was definitely that of your abductor, not, fortunately, another victim.'

286

'Isn't that wonderful?' Mom said, a huge grin across her face.

'Absolutely,' I said, because it was expected of me. Aside from finding it just a little disconcerting to have my mom cheering for someone's death, I still felt uneasy.

'But how — ' Dad began.

'I'll get to that,' Brogan said. 'The coroner estimated time of death as about eight weeks before we found him, which is consistent with the time of your escape, Angie.'

I listened carefully for any hint of suspicion or threat.

Dad cleared his throat. 'But Phil, that was more than a month ago, then, when you found him. Why didn't you tell us?'

'Ah.' Brogan rocked forward. 'We had to run forensic tests, cause of death, DNA, all that. Try to ID him. We found Angela's prints on the handle of a shovel behind the house.'

My mind immediately flew to an image of Angel smashing a skull with a shovel. That didn't seem right, though. Not his style.

But Brogan was still speaking. To me. 'I'm guessing that you must have discovered him dead and dug the shallow grave we discovered. How you dragged him that far is anyone's guess. Or why you bothered.'

Trust Girl Scout to do the decent thing, I thought. 'How — how'd he die?' I asked in a steady voice, my eyes dead center on Brogan's.

'No sign of violence or injury. He was in his sleepwear. It looks like cardiac arrest. In his sleep.'

'Oh,' I said, and looked at my hands in my lap.

'Bastard,' Dad swore. 'Too easy.'

'Well, he's certainly beyond the reach of human justice,' Brogan said, emphasizing *human*. 'However, his death makes things a lot easier to wrap up. That shiv we found was clean — only Angie's prints — no penetrating wounds on the deceased, anyway.' He shrugged.

'And apparently no one else was involved. No extraneous DNA,' he explained. 'So there won't be any awkward questions for you down the road. No one's going to think a little thing like you could . . . well, anyway, that part of the investigation is closed. Cause of death ruled natural causes.'

'Well, okay,' I replied. 'That's good to know.' I took in a huge breath, silently through my nose. My shoulders relaxed. I wasn't going to contradict the official report. No way. I still wondered, though. Brogan had never seen Angel in action. How hard would it be to hold a pillow over a sleeping man's face long enough to . . . But there wasn't any point in bringing that up, or even allowing my imagination to go there.

'We've got a positive ID as well,' Brogan said. 'On prints. Recently, he came out of Arizona, where he'd been living and working in a bank for ten years. No conviction record there, but he'd been pulled in for repeatedly loitering too near a middle school. Clean driver's license and an apartment he always paid for on time. His name was Brett Samuelson.' He waited for my reaction, for confirmation, maybe.

'I never knew his name,' I said simply. 'None

of my alters did. He was very careful to keep everyone away from his briefcase and wallet.'

'I've shown his photo around, tried to track his movements locally. We've found the grocery where he shopped, the office where he worked — '

I couldn't help myself. 'And I bet they said, 'He was always such a quiet, polite man,' like they always do.'

Brogan quirked a smile. 'Actually, yes. They did. Anyway, I wanted to prepare you for what I hope will be the last media onslaught. We're going to run his photo in the Sunday paper, asking for any more leads or helpful information. The article won't mention you by name, but I think with a case as high profile as yours, people may put two and two together. I'm sorry I can't predict what the local news station will do with it, beyond trying to get the most mileage possible.'

Dad jumped in, a sour look on his face. 'If it bleeds, it leads, right?'

'I'm afraid so,' Brogan replied.

'Any way of avoiding putting Angie through all this?' Dad's voice held a squeaky, pleading note.

I took pity on him. 'Dad. I've handled worse. I'll be okay.'

'Atta girl,' Brogan said. 'Do you want to put up in a hotel for a few days so they can't stake out your front lawn?'

Mom laughed wickedly. 'I'll set up the lawn sprinklers. Let's see them try.'

She would, too. I could see her turning the hoses on all their expensive video equipment.

'So is that it?' I asked.

To my surprise, Brogan shrugged a little uncomfortably. 'Almost. Are you busy today, Angie?'

'I've got babysitting tonight. The Harrises have another Christmas party. Why?'

'I was just wondering if you'd be willing to drive up to the cabin with me, go over the site. See if there's anything you left behind that you'd like or . . . or just get some sort of closure for yourself.'

Mom rose to her feet. 'Phil, I don't think — '

'Margie, you and Mitch are welcome to come along too.'

Dad looked sick to his stomach at the very idea. And I realized I didn't want to fill Mom's head with mental images of the cabin, especially the bedroom.

My voice came out just a little too loud. 'No, not them.' At Mom's stricken face, I got control of my tone, serious and steady. 'You both have to go to work. And anyway, this is something I have to do by myself.'

Her cheeks sagged. 'Oh, hon. Are you really prepared for — '

'It's okay, Mom.' I wrapped an arm around her waist and leaned against her. 'I think it might actually be a good idea.'

Closure. Girl Scout had spent her whole life in that house. I owed it to her to pay my last respects, in some weird way. 'As long as I'm home by four to get ready.'

And let's face it. I was a little curious. Which might not have been the best reason to go.

* * *

The silence on the drive up the Crest Highway lasted all the way up the mountains, with Brogan absorbed in his own thoughts. He drove with one huge hand draped over the top of the wheel, bent at the wrist.

I watched the scenery, low chaparral on both sides of the car as far as I could see. The blackened ground, still scarred from the last big fire, had erupted into that bright green of new growth, fertilized by the ashes. Manzanita bushes, naturally fireproof, still twisted like a black-and-chestnut-red sculpture garden. Trees that still stood were spread wide apart, enough for the understory to take hold again.

'What happened?' I asked.

Brogan grunted. 'Arson. Some fool hiker got lost and set a signal fire for the Forestry Service to find him.'

'Did they?'

'Sure. What was left. After they put out over fifty thousand flaming acres.'

'Idiot,' I commented.

The road wound up and up. At higher altitudes, the untouched pines were close and dry, a fire waiting to happen. Deep in here, an off-grid cabin could easily hide.

Brogan pulled off the main highway, taking a narrow dirt road that led into a dense forested area. The smell of pine penetrated the car. A minute later, a smaller lane branched off, rutted and rocky. The SUV lurched along until Brogan unexpectedly stopped in the middle of nowhere.

The way was completely blocked by trees. He opened his door and came around to let me out.

He gestured to the dense stand of trees. 'You can understand why we never found this place. See how the ground is too dry to hold noticeable tracks?'

I looked behind the wheels of his car and saw what he meant.

'This is where Samuelson parked his car every night. We found it abandoned.'

'How come I never heard it?' I asked. 'Is the cabin far?'

'Not that far,' he answered. 'But the trees absorb sound, and his car was all-electric to begin with. Very quiet. It must have seemed like magic, the way he came and went.'

'Yeah. Black magic,' I agreed.

We walked straight into the trees, and I noticed how a path had been crushed from repeated use by the investigators, or by the man himself. I'd never seen this path before, or the 'parking spot.' Girl Scout had come out another way to get down to the road. I remembered hours of walking between trees before I came to the miles and miles of winding asphalt — cars that gave me strange looks but didn't slow — sun and wind battering me equally. An epic journey.

Now the cabin came into view, and through the memories of Girl Scout, I recognized the well pump that tapped into an underground spring. The water had been cold and minerally, but clear and clean. I discovered I missed the taste.

'Where was the grave?' I asked.

Brogan pointed a ways off, and I spied a blue tarp peeking through the trees. 'A long way for a girl to move a body all alone,' he said in a somber tone. 'I'm so sorry.'

I didn't have a reply. What was he looking for here? Forgiveness? From me?

As we approached the cabin, I tested my emotions. Nothing stood out — not terror, not happiness — just a numb sense that this was how things always were.

I suddenly had the impression that Brogan had stopped walking. I turned to see him, hands on his hips, staring up at the trees.

'I have a daughter,' he said. 'Two of them. The oldest is just the age you were when Samuelson grabbed you.' His voice trembled, and I realized with horror that his eyes were wet. 'Angie, there's one more thing we discovered when we investigated him. I wanted to tell you before your parents. I'm just not entirely sure how to start.'

'At the very beginning?' I suggested lightly.

'Maybe.' He thumbed his eyes. 'Let's go inside.'

Crime-scene ribbon was staked around the cabin, and a padlock had been screwed into the door. Brogan pulled a key from his shirt pocket and unlatched the padlock, which he left dangling from the hook.

Everything was just the way Girl Scout remembered it, except far dustier, I noted with concern. I brushed the thought away. I wasn't the housekeeper anymore. The iron stove, the small kitchen table, the chipped chamber pot in the corner, the pantry, the woodpile — running low. Stop, I told myself. I looked with dread toward the bedroom door — my dread or the dread I inherited from Girl Scout? I can face this, I reminded myself. I am a survivor.

I stood on the threshold, one I'd never crossed, and stepped through. The room looked ordinary. Faded comforter, sheets rumpled. Books on a shelf nailed to the wall. Oil lamps on another shelf.

I felt Brogan's eyes on me. I turned. 'What?'

He sucked in a deep breath. 'I don't know how else to tell you this, kid. About eight months ago, Samuelson gave up an infant to County Children and Family Services.'

My head throbbed behind my eyes. I raised my hands to my temples and pressed.

Brogan misunderstood. He patted my back. 'Given the timing and the age of the infant, it's likely . . . it's quite likely . . . '

'He's mine.' I squeezed my eyes shut against the pain. It didn't help.

Brogan's arm tightened on my shoulder, offering support.

'I can't believe he used his real name on the adoption papers,' I said. 'That must be why the Harrises named him Sam.'

Brogan's eyebrows practically popped off his head. 'You know? Knew?'

I shrugged. 'I half remembered, half figured it out. You haven't told the Harrises, have you?'

'Not yet,' he said. 'Obviously, though, to regain custody we'll have to tell them, and you'll have to take a maternity test, all those legal hoops.'

'Don't,' I said bluntly.

'Don't?'

'Don't tell them. Don't tell my parents. Don't tell anyone.'

'Angie . . . '

'Please. Not yet. I haven't decided what to do. I don't know what the best thing is for Sam. Or me. Or my parents. I only know what's best for the Harrises.'

'Complicated.' Brogan scratched his cheek. He watched me carefully.

I spoke into his waiting silence. 'The Harrises are wonderful parents. They adore Sammy. He adores them. I don't want to taint his precious life with any hint of . . . of where he came from. Can you imagine? Can you imagine what that would do to a kid?'

Brogan sighed. He ran a hand across the top of his short cut, scratched his eyebrow. 'Yes. Unfortunately, I can. But are you sure, Angie? Not even your parents? They could help you with this decision.'

'They're still raw and grieving for their lost little girl. I can't layer another thing on top. I think Dad would totally crack. He's barely holding it together now.'

'How long do you need? The longer the child stays with them, the harder — '

'I know. Look, I think I already know the answer. I just have to convince . . . myself.'

Silence fell like the dust motes we'd stirred up with our breath and movement through the room.

'Okay,' he said. 'Are we done here? See anything you want to take away?'

I glanced around the two-room cabin, familiar and strange. 'Nothing,' I answered. 'Let's get out of here. The light's going.'

I followed Brogan through the kitchen. 'Oh, wait. There is one thing. I'll be right out.' I went back into the bedroom for a battered copy of *Song of Myself* propped on a shelf. No wonder I loved it in school. Girl Scout had read it over and over here.

As I reached for the worn paperback, a shattering pain exploded in my head, as if something had smashed me from behind. My skull echoed with the impact. Blind with agony, I fell to the bed. A terrible cracking and wrenching noise came from a distance. Then a slam. I staggered up, lurching toward the front door. Through squinted eyes, I found my way, heaved on the door handle. Pushed on the door. It was jammed. Or locked.

'Brogan? Detective Brogan,' I yelled. 'Help me! I'm stuck.'

I tugged and tugged on the door, hammered with my fists. Useless. It wouldn't budge. A window. I could break a window. Get his attention that way.

No windows? Where were the damned windows?

In the bedroom? I rushed back toward the bedroom and slammed into a wall. My head spun. Pinpoint stars danced at the edges of my vision, then winked out, leaving me in the gray gloom. I reached around frantically. The stove was gone, the table was gone, the pantry — gone.

Walls pushed in, closer and tighter. In the shadows, I made out the silhouette of a rocking chair, just a chair in the middle of a dark, dusty floor dimly outlined by an oil lamp sitting in the corner. And I knew where I was.

I heard my own voice from far outside of myself. 'All set, Detective. Thanks for waiting. Let's go.'

19

CONFLAGRATION

How? How had she broken out?

As my voice faded into the distance, chatting with Detective Brogan, I knew Lonely One was running the show. Would he be able to tell the difference? Would she give herself away?

I paced her room in near panic. The walls felt tight. I found it hard to breathe, which was stupid. I didn't need to breathe. She was breathing for us.

I pinched myself experimentally. Yes, it hurt. Of course it did, because I expected it to hurt. So I kept breathing, because I expected myself to breathe.

Six steps across, six steps back. Again. I avoided the chair. No way was I going to sit down there and wait passively for Lonely One to come back for me. What if she left me here for three more years? Oh God. What if she left me here . . . forever?

I imagined all the terrible things she could be planning now — stealing Sammy and running away, dropping out of school, saying unforgivable things to Mom and Dad, ditching Lynn — the only person who might realize what had happened. If I could imagine them, surely she'd thought of them too.

My footsteps took on the rhythm of heartbeats

or ticks of the clock, and I realized I'd lost any sense of time. Time had no meaning in here. It could be minutes, hours, even days since she'd switched places and locked me in.

I rattled the door again, banged and yelled till my imaginary voice was hoarse. No response. I stared at my hands, trying to will an ax to appear so I could chop my way out. It didn't work. Maybe my mental conjuring only worked when I was the one in charge.

My heart squeezed bitterness. How could she do this to me?

And then I had the terrible thought — I'd done it to her first, hadn't I?

Stupid. Stupid to think I could keep such a powerful part of me locked away once she'd tasted freedom, once she'd seen Sammy, once Brogan had confirmed that the sturdy toddler was her stolen baby.

I added another element to my pacing. One more step and I could crash hard into the wall at either side. The jolting kept me mad, gave me energy. I needed energy. The chair looked awfully tempting.

I could sink into it, and rock, and it would feel like no time passing. Nothing would ever change in this twilight dark room. I could rock, and mourn my life, and wait. I would become the lonely one. And she would become the Angie.

I took a step toward the chair. That wouldn't be so awful, would it? Just to rest for a moment?

It was so quiet in here, except for the imaginary sound of my footsteps, my unnecessary breathing. The air was still. The flame in the oil lamp was steady and low, unflickering.

It burned there like a metaphor for my Self, my consciousness. Alive but unchanging, unmoving.

I left the path I was wearing across the room and went to the corner, picked up the lamp. It was warm, as I expected it to be. A warm metaphor. Light in the darkness, heat in the cold, a tiny flame of hope. The human brain is so weird, finding symbols and meaning in everything. Here I was, trapped in a metaphor of a walled-off compartment in my brain, holding a metaphor of something that gave me a shred of hope. Why? Why hope?

A spark of inspiration, like the spark of a match, came to me.

I threw the lamp to the wood floor. It crashed into pieces, oil spilling everywhere, catching, lighting all around. I would burn my way out.

Flames rose up the walls, as I knew they would.

The dry pine siding caught like kindling.

Flames danced across the floor, as I expected them to.

Golden-red tongues flicked everywhere, hot and hungry.

I felt their heat, soaked in their campfire light, waiting for the walls to char and crumble.

But the walls held.

The fire crept closer to the center of the room. With a whoosh, the rocker itself went up in flames, consumed to ash in moments. A wall of fire danced, circled me now. The heat intensified.

I moved to step through, but a blast of hot

smoke pushed me back. My sleeve caught fire. Just a metaphor, I told myself, but no — the cloth burned and fell away, then my skin was on fire, painful, black, blistering. I screamed and tried to thump it out against my body.

Stop, drop, roll. The safety mantra ran through my head. Useless! The floor was burning.

Flame licked up the legs of my jeans. The smell of burning cloth and hair and flesh was overwhelming. The pain was unbearable. This must be the hell Yuncle warned us about.

'Lonely One,' I screamed. 'Unlock me! Save me!'

I ran through the flames to the door. Black pegs I hardly recognized as arms banged against it weakly. 'Please! Hear me!'

Oh God. This is it. The air, too thick, too smoky to breathe. I closed my eyes to pray.

The door gave way. It swung open, and there she was. Lonely One, a wide and terrified look in her eyes. A large blanket bundle in her arms. She thrust it at me.

'Take him,' she screamed. 'I can't do it. I don't know how.'

I reached for the bundle. It was heavy and crying. 'Annee, Annee,' it sobbed.

With an electric jolt, my heart hammered again in my chest. I felt it. I heard it. A blast of real heat struck me across the face. My true body solidified around me. I clutched Sam tight with real hands.

Smoke billowed through the doorway.

'Hurry! Leave me!' Lonely One pushed past me toward the inferno in the cabin of our mind, groping through the smoke for her rocking chair.

I dragged her back by one arm, pulled against her protests with all my strength. 'You can't go back in. It's all gone.'

Ceiling beams crumbled as I spoke. Sparks shot up from the ruined timbers. Lonely One struggled in my grip, willing herself to be destroyed with her refuge, her prison.

But I couldn't let her. 'Come with me. Sam needs you. And I need you. Now.'

With a cry of fear, she fell into me, pushing me through the doorway and into full control, full consciousness. I blindly reached behind me for her hand, but she was gone.

The world spun crazily, and the burning cabin dissolved, and the room was Sammy's, and the hallway outside was a mass of flame.

Lonely One's memories tumbled, gushed into my head. She was with Sammy, reading. She was entranced, captivated by his sweetness. The smell of wood smoke all around was so familiar, she didn't realize what was happening until the vaulted ceiling in the living room came down on the flaming Christmas tree with a shattering crash. That thunderous *crack* finally alerted her. She opened the bedroom door into a fiery hell. The house, the Harrises' house, was burning, roaring, falling around us.

Sammy twisted in my arms. We had to get out. Six feet from his door was the bathroom, my only hope if we were going to make it out alive. Sirens sounded from outside the house, far down the street. We couldn't wait for them.

'Be brave, little guy,' I whispered in his ear.

Tucking him back inside the blanket, wrapping one arm across my eyes and nose, I took a last gasp of air from the bedroom and sprinted through the flames to the closed bathroom door. The handle scorched my fingers. I slammed us inside and turned on the shower full blast. In seconds we were drenched from head to foot with icy-cold water. Sam howled with shock.

I pulled two bath towels under the stream, soaked them, and wrapped Sam into a wet cocoon. A hand towel wrapped my nose and mouth. His blanket draped my head and upper body like a shroud. Outside the door, something crashed. Good God. The whole roof was coming down.

I hated to leave the wet, tiled sanctuary, but we had to or else be crushed under flaming beams. Sam struggled and squirmed in his casing. I squeezed him tight and muttered soothing nonsense words through the towels, my face pressed against the hard bulge of his head. 'We're going for it,' I said. 'Now!'

Searing the other hand, I wrenched open the door. I couldn't see past the hall, but no matter. I knew the only way out was through the hall and out the front door. If the living room had gone already, so had the kitchen and garage.

The rest was a blur, running, feeling, burning, protecting Sam's cocoon with my body as best I could, until tile was under my feet, the huge scalding brass handle of the front door in my hand, and then running out into the front and stopping, dropping, rolling the two of us on the front lawn.

A fireman swore loudly, and a heavy smothering blanket dropped on us, along with several bodies.

'They're out,' I heard. With my last ounce of coherent thought, I dragged the smothering towels off Sammy's face.

He glared at me, drew a huge breath, and hollered his annoyance. 'No, Annee! No baff.'

Thank God.

The burning pain I'd been holding off swamped every nerve ending in my scorched skin. And then I really was out.

20

DECISION

My eyes cracked open. I peeked from side to side. Lots of white, lots of equipment. I was in a hospital again.

I raised a hand to rub the grit out of my eyelashes and nearly bonked myself with the giant Q-tip my arm had become. Both arms. Bandaged to the elbows, hands swaddled in gauze. Seeing them, they suddenly itched like crazy. I banged them together and immediately realized what a stupid idea that was as a wave of pain rippled up the length of my arms.

A nurse appeared out of nowhere and held them gently apart. 'Don't do that, honey. There's healing going on in there.'

'Where am I?' I asked, blinking away the tears.

'You're in the burn unit at UCLA Medical Center. It's Saturday morning. And I'm Marie, your nurse for the next twelve hours.'

Twelve hours? 'How — how badly am I hurt?' Stupid question. I felt like a giant bandage.

'Your hands got the worst of it. Third-degree burns. Your legs escaped with second degree. No skin grafts needed.' She gave me one of those encouraging tight-lipped nurse smiles. 'You'll live to play the piano again.'

'Guitar,' I corrected. I shifted uncomfortably. She adjusted my pillow and smoothed my hair under my head. 'Given the rest of you, I'm not sure how you escaped with all your beautiful hair unsinged.'

'I ran out of the fire with a wet blan — oh my God.' It hit me like a two-by-four in the face. 'Sammy. My . . . my child, where is he? Is he okay?' I stopped breathing while I waited for her answer.

Marie's face twisted in confusion. 'Your . . . ? They said you were the babysitter.'

'I was. I am,' I quickly corrected. I wracked my mind, literally. Lonely One? Where are you? Why did I say *my child?*

'The little boy was perfect. Untouched. Somehow you got him out of that inferno before the bedroom wing collapsed, and you took all the damage.' She patted my shoulder. 'You're a very brave girl, from what I understand. A hero. The parents have been to see you while you slept. As have your own, of course.'

Of course. 'Can I see them now? Mine, I mean?'

'I believe they'll all be back up here in a few minutes. They all went off for coffee together. It's been a long, long night for them.'

I closed my eyes, already exhausted from the short conversation. Marie smoothed the sheet under my chin and stroked my hair one more time. 'That's it,' she said. 'Rest and recover.'

But with my eyes closed, I couldn't sleep, could only wander the halls of my brain. I found them deserted. Where I had created the girls' cabin, there was only a pile of imagined ash. So

306

where had Lonely One gone when I pulled her out after me?

'I need you. Now,' I had ordered her. Was it possible? Had she merged into me in the blink of an eye? In the unbearable heat of the moment? Perhaps. Yes.

I gave myself permission to remember, and then — I did. I remembered everything: the gentle swell of my belly, already large when I first emerged as a person; the sickness that came and went; the man's kinder, softer side, making it all the more unexpected when he tore my heart out by stealing the baby, the one we named Sam, after his father, he said; the hours spent rocking and crying alone and forgotten after Girl Scout and Little Wife came back; the bright Angel who came and gave me hope that I'd see my baby again; the nights spent peeking at a sleeping child, who looked and smelled familiar and just might be the one; the detective's words that gave me the strength to burst from my detention cell and make my way back to Sam.

Yes. That was it. We were — I was — together. Complete.

And together we'd done it. My strength and her mother love joined against the fire.

Burnt, aching, swathed in gauze, I finally felt complete.

Tears tracked down my cheek. A tiny *tap-tap* caught my attention, and I blinked to see the Harrises at the ICU window. Sammy was on Mrs. Harris's hip. He gave her a wet, open-mouth kiss on the cheek. She waved his little fist in a hi-bye motion at me. Her face heavy with sleeplessness and gratitude, she blew me a kiss and rubbed her cheek on Sammy's fair hair. Dr. Harris clenched his hands together up beside his right ear, telling me I was a champion in his book. The love was so thick, you could spread it on a bagel.

I sighed with a deep kind of joy and waved my Popsicle arms at them. Dr. Harris saluted me once, then wrapped an arm around his wife and child to head to a hotel for a soft bed.

Mom and Dad came in then for the hug-and-cry session.

★   ★   ★

They let me go home that evening with all my wound care instructions, home to my own bed. The painkillers did their best, but I still spent much of the night awake. There were other wounds that gauze and antibiotics couldn't touch.

Before Lonely One had tossed all her memories and emotions into the mental mixing bowl, I'd already fallen hopelessly in love with Sam. Now I knew firsthand the magic bond they had shared for such a short time. Then I had been fighting with her — now I was fighting with myself in the dark hours of the night.

Should I tell Mom and Dad? Bring Sam home? Raise him with my new brother/sister? There was a certain logic in that. But how could I do that to the Harrises? And what was best for Sam? To believe forever that his mother had died or to know that she had been relentlessly molested by a crazy man until he was conceived?

I stumbled on the stairs, distracted by the dilemma spinning my brain around.

In a moment, Mom was in front of me, arms out, as if she could catch me now when it was far too late to make a difference. Her stomach looked huge. Time was speeding along.

'Your dad's still in the kitchen, watching the morning news. He took the day off work, in case . . . in case you need anything.'

'Um. Okay.' I wasn't exactly sure what kind of thing he was thinking of.

'I made you French toast,' she said hesitantly. 'Feel up to eating some?'

I wasn't typically much of a breakfast eater, but after twenty-four hours in the hospital, I was ravenous. 'Sure, Mom. I'll have a slice or eight.' I slipped in next to Dad at the kitchen table — next to, so I wouldn't have to make eye contact and I wouldn't block his view of the TV. 'Someone will have to feed me, though.'

Mom sat across the table, forking small pieces of French toast at me. She was sweet but unbelievably awkward.

'You're out of practice, Mom,' I teased her. 'Better figure it out before Junior arrives.'

'More like June,' she quipped back. 'Apparently you're having a sister.'

Mom had no way of knowing that the sudden look of horror on my face had nothing to do with her announcement. Behind her head, the entire TV screen had filled with a photo of the man.

'Oh my God,' I gasped.

'Hey, what's the matter with a sister?' Mom demanded.

Dad's fork dropped with a *clang*. His face went pale. 'Damned TV news. That didn't take long.' His eyes darted to the rolled-up Sunday paper, still in its plastic sleeve.

Mom whirled and caught her breath at the face on the screen.

A face I now knew better than my own, the only face that parts of me had seen for three years. So ordinary, except for the narrow dark eyes that looked just a little off, a bit skewed from normal. Sandy-brown hair lightly flecked with gray. A weak chin. Very small ears.

The voice-over did not identify him by name, just asked for any information about his movements and whereabouts in the past five years. He was described only as a person found deceased in the Angeles National Forest — no mention of me or his record.

I was frozen in place, fascinated and appalled at the same time.

Mom slammed off the TV with a bang.

'Oh, my poor Angel,' Dad said, voice cracking. 'I'm sorry you had to see that.'

What a stupid comment. What the heck was he thinking? 'Dad. I lived that.'

His face turned bright red, like he'd given up breathing.

'You couldn't have stopped them anyway,' I said. 'It's news. A body in the park.'

His fists balled up fiercely. He raised them toward the darkened TV screen, like he could reach through it to the man, to the news studio.

'I would have tried my damnedest. I swear I would. I would have done anything to prevent it.' He drew a shuddery breath. 'Damned TV news.'

I knew he meant much more than that. He meant the man, and the fruitless search. He meant Bill, and all those years we could never get back. He meant my long-lost innocent childhood.

'Dad. You didn't know. It's. Not. Your. Fault.'

He didn't say anything, but a tear fell off the tip of his nose and splashed into the puddle of syrup on his plate.

I thumped his shoulders with my bandaged arms. 'Look at me, Dad.' His tear-streaked face was a misery. 'It's done. He's dead. We're alive.'

Dad tore his eyes away from mine.

'Look at me,' I insisted. 'Am I crying? Am I feeling sorry for myself?'

He only made a choking sound.

I shook him lightly. 'You do not have the right to feel worse than I do. So get over yourself and start being here for me and Mom.'

His eyes widened.

A step sounded behind me, and I felt Mom's hands on my shoulders. Her taut belly brushed the back of my head. 'And the baby,' I added. 'She does not need a morose, depressed, self-absorbed father. She needs a daddy. Get it?'

Mom squeezed her appreciation into me with silent fingers.

Dad pulled a handkerchief out of his robe pocket and blew his nose. He nodded.

'So you have the day off. Now go do something fun,' I said. 'Mom, take him

Christmas shopping. I couldn't help noticing that no one's put anything under the tree except me. Ahem.'

Mom smiled. 'You come along too, hon.'

'Not till I get my gauze mittens off,' I said. 'I don't want to spend the whole day explaining.'

I felt like the parent for a moment. Dad stood up and gave me a long, squeezy hug. He whispered, 'Angel. I'm sorry. So sorry.'

'I know that, Daddy,' I said in his ear while he squoze. 'By the way, if you need any ideas, I'm getting my ears pierced, and I wouldn't mind pearls.'

★　★　★

They had been gone for only an hour when the doorbell rang.

I jumped up and realized I'd have a heck of a time opening the door. Through the spy hole, I saw Brogan standing awkwardly on the front mat. His face wore an odd, nervous expression.

'Come in,' I yelled.

The door cracked, and he poked his head in with hesitation. 'Angie?' He looked back and forth from my hand-pods to the smoking rubble across the cul-de-sac, actually at a loss for words.

'It wasn't arson,' I said. 'I'm innocent.'

He shook his head. 'Sorry. Yes. Yeah, I know. I've just spoken to the Harrises. At their hotel. Are your parents around?'

'Nope. They're shopping.' Spoke to the Harrises? Why? Suspicion dawned.

'Maybe I should come back later.' He shifted

312

his weight from foot to foot.

'I think you'd better come in,' I said. 'I think this is a talk we need to have privately.'

He studied my face and apparently came to a decision. 'Okay. Yeah. Okay. Thanks.'

He sat down on the edge of the sofa, his elbows on his knees. I took a chair and leaned back on purpose.

'As I said, I've, uh, just come from the Harrises,' he said. 'They recognized Brett Samuelson on the television. Apparently from the adoption signing.'

Oh, no. 'Do they know it had anything to do with me?' I asked. 'Did they figure it out?'

Brogan shook his head. 'No. I told them it was a homicide follow-up. They felt quite sorry for him.' He raised his eyebrows.

'Let them stay that way,' I said. 'Close the files.'

'Yeah?' He cleared his throat. 'Sam's sure a cute kid.'

'Good genes on one side of the family, at least,' I said lightly.

Brogan gulped, searching for a response.

I rested my bandaged arms on his knees. 'He belongs with them. Close the case files. Please.'

He closed his eyes for a moment. His chest fell with a quiet huff of air. 'I see why you're the survivor, kiddo,' he murmured. 'Tough as nails, softhearted as — '

'Besides,' I interrupted. 'As long as we're all living here, which I anticipate will be a long time, I'll get to see him grow up. I'll help them decorate his new room. I'll teach him to read. I

313

can help him with his homework when he goes to school. So it'll be okay. He'll be fine. Better, even.'

My voice caught, but I swallowed it down. 'I saw him take his first steps, you know.'

Brogan did the totally unexpected. Stood up and hugged me, for a long time. When he let go, I saw the tears in his eyes. I suppose there were some in mine, too.

'Okay, kid. I'll respect your wishes. But I'm putting a note with the Harrises' story and a copy of the adoption papers inside the file before I seal it, in case you change your mind later.'

'Okay. Fair enough,' I said. 'And you were never here, right?'

'I was never here. It's been an honor meeting you, Angie,' he said. He dropped a kiss on the top of my hair. 'I wish you all the best.'

Brogan drove away slowly. Pines swayed madly in the wind that promised a warm December afternoon.

I watched from the front window, at peace with my decision and my final secret. Too much was at stake. Too many lives would topple if all the truth were known.

Some secrets are meant to be kept close to the heart. Forever.

AFTERWORD

Angie's story may raise questions or concerns for some readers. If you would like to learn more about trauma and dissociation on behalf of yourself, a friend, or a family member, here is an excellent place to start:

The Sidran Institute
Traumatic Stress Education and Advocacy
www.sidran.org

The Sidran Institute provides general information as well as referrals to people who can help.

We do hope that you have enjoyed reading this large print book.

Did you know that all of our titles are available for purchase?

We publish a wide range of high quality large print books including:
Romances, Mysteries, Classics
General Fiction
Non Fiction and Westerns

Special interest titles available in large print are:
The Little Oxford Dictionary
Music Book
Song Book
Hymn Book
Service Book

Also available from us courtesy of Oxford University Press:
Young Readers' Dictionary
(large print edition)
Young Readers' Thesaurus
(large print edition)

For further information or a free brochure, please contact us at:
Ulverscroft Large Print Books Ltd.,
The Green, Bradgate Road, Anstey,
Leicester, LE7 7FU, England.
Tel: (00 44) 0116 236 4325
Fax: (00 44) 0116 234 0205

THE LEOPARD

Jo Nesbø

In the depths of winter, a killer stalks the city streets. The crime scenes offer no clues and the police are running out of options. There is only one man who can help, and he doesn't want to be found . . . Deeply traumatised by the Snowman investigation, Inspector Harry Hole has lost himself in the squalor of Hong Kong's opium dens. But with his father ill in hospital, Harry reluctantly agrees to return to Oslo. He has no intention of working on the case, but then a third victim is found. The victims appear completely unconnected to one another, but Harry soon makes a discovery: the women all spent the night in an isolated mountain hostel. And someone is picking off the guests one by one . . .

THE INTERCEPT

Dick Wolf

When six people bravely foil the hijacking of a commercial jet en route to New York City, 'The Six' become instant celebrities. But New York Police investigator Jeremy Fisk believes this is more than a simple open-and-shut terrorism case. Fisk and his team spring into action, but as each promising new lead fizzles to nothing they realise that their opponents are smarter and more dangerous than anyone they've faced before . . .